Praise for Susan Moody's first
Cassandra Swann Bridge Mystery,

Death Takes a Hand . . .

"The marriage of Moody, bridge, and murder is just this
side of
—*The Drood*

"An eminently
—*Mos*

"Strong, eng
—*Mystery Scene*

"Moody enlivens her traditional English cozy with a
welcome new heroine . . . Adeptly mining laughs from the
milieu, Moody leads her likable sleuth to a solution."
—*Publishers Weekly*

"Cassie Swann . . . faces real-life difficulties with a
wonderfully ironic sense of humor."
—*Booklist*

"A well-played game of amateur sleuthing . . . thoroughly
enjoyable."
—*Wilson Library Bulletin*

"Enter Susan Moody's new sleuth in spades: Cassie Swann,
biology teacher turned bridge professional. Classic openers
to some quite stunning finessing. Swann's way is my way."
—*Sunday Times* (London)

"An impressive and enjoyable debut . . . A lively protagonist."
—*Books*

♠   ♥   ♣   ♦

ABOUT THE AUTHOR

SUSAN MOODY, a former chair of the British Crime Writers Asso-
ciation, is the author of the Penny Wanawake detective
series and the bestselling suspense novels *Mosaic*, *Hush-a-Bye*, and
House of Moons. She lives in England, where she was
recently elected to the prestigious Detection Club.

MORE MYSTERIES FROM THE
BERKLEY PUBLISHING GROUP ...

GRAND SLAM

SUSAN MOODY

A Cassandra Swann Bridge Mystery

BERKLEY PRIME CRIME, NEW YORK

GRAND SLAM

A Berkley Prime Crime Book / published by arrangement with Otto Penzler Books, a division of Simon & Schuster Inc.

PRINTING HISTORY
Originally published in Great Britain by Headline Books Publishing
Otto Penzler Books edition published 1995
Berkley Prime Crime edition / March 1996

The Putnam Berkley World Wide Web site address is
http://www.berkley.com

ISBN: 0-425-15229-4

Berkley Prime Crime Books are published
by The Berkley Publishing Group,
200 Madison Avenue, New York, New York 10016.
The name BERKLEY PRIME CRIME and the BERKLEY PRIME
CRIME design are trademarks belonging to
Berkley Publishing Corporation.

PRINTED IN THE UNITED STATES OF AMERICA

10 9 8 7 6 5 4 3 2 1

For Geo. Wm. Harding

ACKNOWLEDGMENT

With many thanks to the ladies of Pegrillou:

Julianna Lees
Elizabeth Simor
Betty Mackay

The aspect of prison life Cassie found it most difficult to come to terms with was the smell. It hung about the landings, a complex amalgam of slept-in bedding, tomato sauce and shower-stalls, overlaid with disinfectant and the kind of exudation peculiar to old brick walls which have been hidden for years beneath layers of thick grey paint.

Her Majesty's Prison, Bellington, where she was currently inhaling this subtle perfume, had been built, more in sorrow than in anger, towards the end of the nineteenth century, and had originally been intended to house one hundred and forty members of the criminal classes. As the local House of Correction, it had deliberately been situated more or less in the centre of the town, both as a reassurance to the virtuous and a reminder to the sinful. Despite that, or perhaps because of it, the place smelled. Not surprising, really. Among other unenlightened omissions, no communal dining-hall had been included in the architect's plans, and the inmates now, as then, were forced to queue at a hatch for tin trays, load them up with food and return with them to their cells where they squatted uncomfortably on the edge of their bunks, balancing the tray on their knees. With three to a cell intended for one, there was no room for tables or chairs. Once they had eaten, they placed the trays on the floor outside their cell. It was one of the more puzzling things about the nick that whatever the day's proferred menu might have been—a choice of two different main courses ranging from meat to fish or something vegetarian— the remains on the plates always seemed to be spaghetti bolognese.

Cassie breathed shallowly as she walked down the polished grey linoleum of the prison landing behind the Duty Officer. Eyeing the jostling hips encased in navy-blue serge, she surreptitiously pinched her own. She sighed. She probably wouldn't make it into a list of Fattest Blobs in the EEC, but, on the other hand, she was equally unlikely to figure in a list of Europe's Thinnest Women. In fairness to herself, she was hardly to blame if people asked her out to dinner and then took her to restaurants renowned for their cuisine. God wouldn't have created chefs, she reasoned, if He hadn't intended us to enjoy the delicacies they set before us. That being so, who could have refused the simply amazing puds at Lichfield Manor, or a second helping of the *feuilleton de canard* at Le Beau Séjour? Certainly not Cassie. Though, if truth be told, it wasn't so much the second helping as the first, which had been enormous. That was the only snag about the Beau Séjour: André, the chef, was a personal friend of Robin Plunket, her godfather, since they both owned houses near the same little town in France. André liked to see women eat, he told her on the all-too-rare occasions that she visited the Beau Séjour, and last time had come out of his kitchen several times especially to see her do so, tut-tutting with Gallic ferocity when she tried half-heartedly to protest at the size of the portion, seizing a knife and cutting a larger one, waving his arms about, generally behaving with temperament.

Someone called her name from the doorway of a cell and she smiled in as friendly a way as she could manage, simultaneously jerking her head at the officer in front of her to indicate that much as she would like to, she couldn't stop for a chat. Not that she wished to. That particular prisoner suffered from a psychosis-induced stammer and had, in addition, recently discovered God. Not the God responsible for the Escoffiers and the Pierre Marco Whites of this world but another Being altogether, One who had an urgent message of denunciation and salvation which He had apparently empowered His humble servant—currently doing bird of three years for aggravated burglary, reduced on appeal to two years and three months—to write down on tablets of recycled paper and then read out to anyone who could be induced to pause as they hurried past with averted eyes. The fact that the servant in question was illiterate and therefore incapable of writing down so much as the first letter of the alphabet did not seem to bother either God or the servant. But it did make for uncomfortable conversation.

Cassie knew all about the indignity of imprisonment, about loss of liberty, overcrowding, society's need to see justice being done. She knew that of any group of a hundred prisoners, ninety-nine of them were completely innocent and should never have been there in the first place. *Wouldn't* have been there if it hadn't been for that bastard judge or the fact that their sodding stupid brief couldn't plead his way out of a paper bag.

There was a shuffle and bustle behind her and she turned quickly. A rabble of men had gathered under the eye of the Class Officer and now waited, as she did, for the Duty Officer to unlock the heavy iron gate which led to Education, the wing reserved for daytime and evening classes. There was something pleasing about the notion that nothing more than a few iron bars separated the current criminal element in society from all the Byzantine riches of science, literature, philosophy and art; that they had only to pass through to the other side and Education would be theirs for the taking, something many of them were skilled at. The only problem was that, more often than not, Education in prison terms meant squares of black velvet with lurid flowers or naked women painted on them which the men could send home to their wives and girlfriends. But Cassie was being unfair. There was also the artwork fashioned from nails hammered into boards and cats-cradled with string, the making of soft toys with googly eyes, guitar tuition, cookery sessions, GCSE coaching in French or English. Even, as of the past four months, Bridge.

"How's it going, Teach?" One of the inmates put a hand on her shoulder and quickly withdrew it before the Education Officer noticed. She flinched and turned, stifling the impulse to drop to the floor and roll rapidly out of range before any lasting damage could be inflicted. Being in prison did that to you.

"Hello, Steve." She smiled in a manner intended to convey a certain amount of friendliness but considerably more distance at the man in prison blues who stood much too close behind her. After a count of two, she moved away from him. He was stocky, no taller than she was, but broad of chest and shoulder, shaven of head. His eyes were large and grey, and unnaturally bright. Between thumb and forefinger he held a thin hand-rolled cigarette containing heaven knew what illegal substances.

"All right, then?" Steve inserted the cigarette between his lips and moved it in and out of his mouth in a deliberate manner. His eyes held hers.

Cassie forced herself not to look away. "Just fine, thank you," she said coolly. "How about you?"

"You know how it goes in here," Steve said, shrugging. "Miss a lot of things, know what I mean?" Again he pulled the cigarette back and forth in a parody of sexual congress, at the same time thrusting his pelvis forward. Only a blind nun could have failed to pick up the innuendo.

The barred gate opened. The crowd of men surged forward, while the Class Officer good-naturedly urged them to proceed in an orderly fashion. Cassie felt Steve push behind her, brushing up against her back, one hand passing so lightly over her buttocks that she could have imagined it. Except she had not. On the outside, she might have confronted him, at the very least would have brought her foot down hard on his instep. In here, a certain amount of respect had to be maintained between inmates and staff, so she did nothing, aware that any complaint would result in consequences which Steve would resent and for which she would feel deeply guilty. A cut in tobacco allowance, loss of privileges, perhaps even removal to another prison. Plus the constant fear that if she did anything, Steve might remember when he had completed his sentence and come back to wreak his revenge.

The papers were full of men who revenged themselves on women: on fiancées who had broken it off, wives having affairs, grandmothers who wouldn't hand over their weekly pension, mothers who switched television channels from the football to News at Ten. In addition to which, Cassie was fully conscious of the fact that men in prison were not always stable, particularly men like Steve.

"Four Spades, bid and made." Steve picked up the spare pack of cards and passed it to his left, as he had been taught, at the same time looking at Cassie for approval.

"Wonderful," Cassie said. "Well played."

Kip Naughton stared morosely at the cards. "Bit of a nancy game, if you ask me. Too much luck involved. Give me a game of skill any day."

"Like what? Snakes and Ladders?" asked Sebastian Haslam-Jones, the bent barrister. His tone was agreeable, his accent of Oxbridge. Any minute now, thought Cassie, he would add a Latin tag, give the room a bit of class.

"Leave it out, Kip," agreed one of the younger men. "My four-year-old kid could beat the pants off you at Snakes and Ladders any day. One hand tied behind her back. Honest, miss." He turned his handsome black face to Cassie and smiled broadly. It was difficult to believe he had been involved in a particularly vicious post-office robbery, in which the Asian postmaster had died while his two nephews were still recovering in hospital.

"Poker, I meant," Kip said with dignity. "That's a game of skill, innit?"

"Poker? What the hell would a nonce like you know about bleeding poker?" Steve said, and for a moment the words hung in silence. It was not only Cassie who was wary of the overflowing rage that powered all of Steve's responses. Whatever the flog 'em and hang 'em brigade thought, life inside was no easy option and could be maintained with even a modicum of civilised behaviour only if everyone—cons *and* screws—accepted that they were forced for the interim to exist as a self-sustaining social group. Loose cannons like Steve were always recognised for what they were: dangerous.

"Anyway," Cassie said quickly, "you played that hand like a pro, Steve." She hoped she had not sounded too warm, too much as if her approval was for the man rather than his ability to play bridge. Since coming to teach at the prison, she found herself constantly treading tightropes. She looked round the table. "Let's analyse both the bidding and the playing, shall we?"

"Pro?" The bent barrister raised well-bred eyebrows.

"You calling me a bleeding prossie, or what, Cass?" Steve took out a packet of Rizlas and a round tin of tobacco, and started preparing another cigarette.

"Of course not," Cassie wished very much he would not use her first name.

"Watch your language," Kip said. "Ladies present."

Steve gazed at Cassie with his immutable stare. After too long a pause, he said, "Sorry, miss."

When she had first come to the prison as a teacher, Cassie had felt an overpowering sense of indignation. The regime was barbaric, the men treated worse than animals, the conditions a denial of human dignity. After four months, her feelings had undergone a reluctant change. Contact with inmates like Steve had considerably shifted her perceptions of good and evil, right and wrong. He was young, vicious, angry. And completely without a conscience, any ability to recognise the needs of other people. A sociopath, the Chaplain had told her once, like so many of the poor souls locked up in here. Cassie questioned just how much of a poor soul Steve was. He was serving too short a sentence for persistent attacks on women. His last victim, a twenty-year-old who had foolishly accepted his offer of a drink in her local pub one Saturday night, had subsequently spent five months with her jaw wired up; her knife-slashed face had needed more than a hundred stitches just to keep it from falling off the bones beneath.

"The point is," Cassie said, "that Steve took time before he started bidding to analyse his cards, working out the losers, seeing where the finesses could be made, listening to the information his partner gave him and adding it to his own. Only then did he—"

"'S wot I mean," Kip said. He sniffed. "Luck, innit? I mean, if he hadn't had the cards in the first place, he wouldn't have had nothing to analyse, would he?"

"As I've told you before, bridge is about making the most of what you have, but at the same time not bidding for contracts you can't possibly make. Unless, of course, they're sacrifice bids. Let's recap on those: if you remember, I discussed them with you in last week's class."

As she made her points, Cassie could not help wishing that of her two most able pupils, Steve was not one. But he was. He had all the necessary skills of logic, visualisation and memory. Where he fell down was on perhaps the most vital need of all: unselfishness, the ability to work with his partner as a team. Steve knew as much about teamwork as a tiger knew about vegetarianism.

She wondered vaguely where her other two regulars were. Though "regular" was only a relative term. In a prison like this, with men coming and going, being transferred to other prisons, having their appeals heard, their sentences confirmed or altered in some way, she rarely had the same men for more than a couple of weeks. She knew, however, that John Burslake should have been here this evening, as well as Jim Leslie, one of the trusties who over the years had become institutionalised and for whom freedom would have been a far worse punishment than any prison sentence.

Having set the first group playing another hand, she went over to her second four, who had given up any pretence of bridge and were unabashedly enjoying a smoke and a moan. Frank Hartley, in for not only illegally possessing a sawn-off shotgun but for, in addition, pointing it with menace at the man who had run into the back of his beat-up Sierra, was having his appeal heard the following day. Frank's air of injured innocence was one with which Cassie had become familiar over the past four months; ninety-five per cent of Bellington's inmates wore it eighty per cent of the time.

He gestured largely with his cigarette. "I mean, it wasn't

even my shotgun, was it? Belonged to me brother-in-law, for starters. How was I to know he'd shoved it into the boot of me car?"

"Why'd he do that, mate?" asked a weedy little man with a bald head fringed in the remains of the red hair from which his nickname of Ginger or, more commonly, Ginge, derived.

"Me sister," said Frank wearily. "She's always on at him to get it out of the house. Says it's dangerous with the kids there and all."

The four men tutted, though whether at the general intransigence of sisters or the danger potential of shotguns it was hard to tell.

"Gentlemen, if you wouldn't mind . . ." Cassie said.

"And then this ponce rams into the back of me car," Frank said. He smiled pleasantly at Cassie. "Mind if I finish me fag, miss? Don't want to get the cards messed up, do we?"

"You seem to have done quite a bit of messing already," Cassie said. She brushed at the ash which lay liberally over the table beneath him, then handed one of the packs of cards to Ginge. "You deal," she said.

Ginge began to do so. He was a back-handed man who found it difficult to lay the cards out with any ease.

"Then this faggot only bangs into the back of me, dunny?" Frank said, blowing a cloud of smoke into Ginger's face. " 'Ere, Ginge, wot you up to?"

"Woss wrong?" Ginge asked mildly.

"What's wrong? What's friggin' wrong?"

"Language," corrected the man they called Eddie Taylor, though Cassie knew his name was in fact Stuart Kingsley.

"What's wrong, me old mate," Frank said, leaning heavily across the table, "is, unless I've gone sodding blind in the last five minutes, there are only four of us playing, aren't there?"

"So?" Ginge continued stumblingly to lay down the cards.

"So why're you dealing for five?"

"Gawd," said Ginge. "Never was much good at figures."

"Not like me, then," Frank said. Taylor sniggered appreciatively.

Cassie, who had been watching the first table, sighed.

"You'd better start again," she said, and Ginge picked up the cards with clumsy hands.

"Anyway, so there's this bum-bandit up your backside," said Taylor. He spoke without any obvious irony. "What was he, drunk or summink?"

"Search me. Saw this mate of mine, didn't I, just coming out of the betting-shop, remembered a bit of unfinished business and pulled up a bit sharpish, didn't want to miss him. Owed me money, know what I mean?"

"And this cream puff don't stop in time?"

"That's right. Must have been following too closely," Frank said. He assumed a look of outraged virtue. "In the heat of the moment, I pulls out this gun of me brother-in-law's, don't I?"

"Probably done the same myself," Taylor said.

"I wouldn't," said the fourth member of the foursome. He was a hulking young Rasta, his hair coiffed in thick black dreadlocks which drooped from his head like Spanish moss.

"Who asked you, Malcolm X?" Frank said without force.

"You too violent, man. Want to cool out, calm down. What you wantin' with guns, man?" The Jamaican shook his head so that his hair flew out in a manner which reminded Cassie of the limerick about the old man with a beard full of livestock. The dreadlocks looked as if they had not seen brush or comb, let alone water, for at least six years, and could have contained almost anything, including the missing heir to the Russian throne.

"Maybe I was a bit out of order," conceded Frank. "But when I saw the mess he'd made of me rear bumper . . ." He drew on his cigarette again. "I mean, who's going to pay for it? That's what I wanted to know."

"That's why you got insurance, man," said the Rasta.

"I don't bother with no insurance," Frank said. "And it turns out this tart didn't either. So naturally I—"

"Can we get on?" Cassie said loudly, Ginge by now having produced four groups of cards. She organised her docile but incompetent pupils into something approaching order, then repeated what she had told them about bidding, in particular the use of strategic doubling, both last week, and the week before. Also the week before that.

"Is that clear?" she said finally, looking round at them. They nodded. "Ginger, it's you to open the bidding."

After due reflection, Ginge said, "No bid." He breathed heavily, clutching the cards so tightly that they formed a semi-circular tube in his hand.

"No bid," said Taylor.

Frank drew air in noisily through his nose. He pursed his lips, set his head on one side, squinted slightly. He looked up at the ceiling, tapped the cards with a nicotine-stained finger and frowned. Marlon Brando couldn't have hammed it up better. Cassie wanted to breathe deeply herself but said nothing, reminding herself that he had probably watched the card game to end all card games in *A Big Hand for the Little Lady*, which had been shown on the prison television the night before. Finally, Frank said portentously, "No bid."

Rastaman frowned down at his cards, then up at Cassie. "Double?" he said hopefully.

Frank threw his cards down on the table with dramatic disgust. "For fuck's sake," he said.

"Language," said Eddie Taylor.

"Look, I don't mind doing me bird—well, I *do* mind, of course—but not if I get nicked fair and square," Frank said. "But does that mean I have to spend the best years of me life with a pissing loonie? I mean, what've I done? I ask you: is it fair?"

"You sayin' I got no brains, man?" Rastaman slammed his cards down on the table and thrust out his chin. "That what you sayin'? Somethin' like that?"

"Go and smoke some ganja, snowdrop," Frank said.

The patrolling Class Officer peered through the square of glass set into the classroom door. He raised his eyebrows enquiringly and Cassie waved, hoping she gave an impression of quiet confidence not only to him but to her pupils. Instead of going away, he unlocked the door and ushered in Burslake and Leslie.

"Been in the gym," he explained.

"Right." Cassie smiled at the two newcomers. Gently she explained to the Jamaican that it was not possible to double a no bid call, dealt with Frank's histrionics, gathered up the cards yet again and gave them to Taylor.

"Why don't you deal the next round?" she said. Surreptitiously she looked at her watch. It wasn't even half-time, and already she was exhausted.

The four men gathered up their new cards and arranged them. Taylor said eventually, "No bid."

"Five Diamonds," said Ginge.

"Five bleeding Diamonds?" exclaimed Frank, who was his partner, emitting an Etna-like eruption of indignant smoke and ash. He spoke through a series of terminal coughs. "That's only bleeding game, innit? How'd you know what I've got in me hand? Might have a slam in bleeding Spades for all you know."

"And have you?" said Cassie

"As it happens—"

"Thought you said we was to mention our minor five card suit first," Ginger said aggrievedly. "Isn't that what you said, miss?"

"Not all five cards at once, you plonker," said Taylor.

At the other table, Steve leaned towards her over the back of his chair. "Here, Teach," he said. "Can I be excused?"

"What for?" said Cassie, before she had time to stop herself and immediately regretting it.

"Got this urge," said Steve, standing up and putting a suggestive hand over the flies of his prison-issue jeans. "Know what I mean?"

It was going to be a long evening.

"Nah, it's hopeless." John Burslake stubbed out his cigarette in the round lid of his tobacco tin and began rolling another. "I'll be sent down and those sods'll get away with it." He was sitting with Cassie and Leslie at a table in the far corner of the classroom, waiting for an opportunity to cut in on one of the two playing tables.

"You can't be certain," Cassie said.

"I can. It's the way things are, isn't it? One law for the rich and another for the poor." He gave an angry chuckle and

Cassie saw the pulse twitching along his jaw. "And yet another for the bankrupt, like me."

There was nothing Cassie could say. John was awaiting trial on charges of trafficking in drugs, as well as fraud and deception; in view of the fact that ten years earlier, aged eighteen, he had trashed a neighbour's car over a parking dispute, he had not been granted bail, even though it was customary in cases of this kind. She was unclear about the exact details, but knew that as a consequence of whatever exactly he had done, his building business had gone into liquidation, his house had had to be sold in order to pay off some of his debts, and his wife had taken their two children back to her mother's.

"What exactly did you . . . ?" It was not a question you were supposed to ask, though the men often volunteered the information, nor had she done so before.

"Someone wanted to build this leisure centre, didn't they?" Burslake said. "Asked me to tender for some of the work. I was only a one-man operation, didn't have huge overheads, so I was able to offer competitive prices. It was a dream come true when they accepted my tender." He laughed his mirthless laugh. "Nightmare, more like."

"Yes?"

"Then one of the blokes putting up the money tips me off about building materials available from eastern Europe: cheap consignments of timber, plasterboard, concrete blocks, that sort of thing. So I went to the bank, took out a loan. The bank was perfectly happy, in view of my previous business record."

"Not your fault, mate," muttered Leslie. Cassie nodded encouragingly, hoping it helped for Burslake to talk about it.

"Worked a treat for about six months. I'd negotiate with these Bulgarians or whatever they was, they'd ship the stuff to the nearest suitable port—Hamburg, Bremen, Amsterdam, places like that—and I'd organise the onward shipment from there. Perhaps it was a bit dodgy, but they got paid in hard currency, I got my cheap materials, everyone was happy—including the VATman, who didn't know sweet FA about any of it. And then . . ."

"And I take the last trick," Frank said loudly. He swept the cards on his table into a pile and raised both his arms in a racing driver's gesture of victory.

"Hang about," said Ginger. "That last trick was mine."

"Excuse me, mate, but I took it with my ten of Hearts," said Frank. "Your partner led a two, right?"

"That's right," said Rastaman.

"My partner discards a Club. Four, wasn't it, Eddie?" Taylor nodded. "You plays your eight of Hearts, and I plays my ten, which I know is good."

"That was *my* ten," said Ginger.

"Leave it out, Ginge, I've been holding on to that ten, hoping to make it."

"Well," Cassie said, "we can't prove it one way or the other, can we, Frank? Not now that you've so conveniently gathered up the cards." She knew he was lying by the way his eyes had taken on a shiny innocent stare. He knew that she knew. He knew, too, that both his partner and Ginger's also knew. Only Ginge, the one who had held the winning card, was unsure. "You'd better help Ginge with his next hand, and we'll let Leslie cut in."

Once she had settled the four, she sat down next to Burslake again. "Tell me what happened," she said.

"Not much to tell. Turns out the Drug Squad had infiltrated the ring."

"Which ring?"

"This fucking drugs ring I didn't even know I was part of. All those consignments I was picking up—turns out they was loaded with the stuff. It was coming in from the Far East via some corridor or something, and when I passed it on to the construction site, all those bastards had to do was pick it up. Next thing I know, the Druggies get hold of this bloke's address book, bug half the phone numbers in it, including mine, hear me talking to someone in Amsterdam about a load of chipboard I was supposed to pick up, and nail me once we get it back to England. There was more heroin in there than sawdust. What could I say? They didn't believe a word, and I can't say I blame them."

"And you couldn't tell them who was really responsible?"

"I didn't know, did I? They picked up a couple of distributors the other side, plus one of the blokes who'd got me into it. But they weren't the real bosses, the organisers, the ones who set the whole thing up. They'll never get them." He leaned forward to drop ash carefully into the lid of his round tobacco tin. His fingers shook. "Told you the wife's filed for divorce, did I?"

"I'm so sorry."

"Yeah." He nodded violently two or three times and chewed the inside of his lower lip. "So'm I."

"Perhaps when you've finished your—"

"What really narks me, what really gets up my nose," Burslake said violently, "is that I had absolutely nothing to do with any of this. I'm not going to pretend I'm Michael the Archangel, but those buggers really set me up. Looking back now, I can see I was stupid but, at the time, I really believed there was someone willing to back me, someone who thought that we could all make a lot of money. *They* did, all right. I just ended up in here. And I never had the faintest idea what they were up to."

Cassie had heard it all before, the protestations of innocence, of ignorance. In Burslake's case, it had a genuine ring. "Can't they be made answerable in some way?"

"Course not. They're too smart for that. Covered their tracks all along the way. If I'd had any sense, I'd have realised there was something not quite kosher about it. But I didn't. Except once. Something funny about an invoice they sent me and I couldn't get no one to return my call. Went down there in the end, to Swindon, where their office was supposed to be, but it wasn't even in the name of the company I'd been dealing with. So they go on driving their Aston bloody Martins and swan off to their tax-free bloody havens in the Bahamas or wherever they go while I end up with my life in ruins. Me and all the other little guys they roped in. Because, sure as eggs, I wasn't the only sucker. God!" He slammed a hand down on the table, causing the other men to look up from their cards.

"Won't your lawyer be able to say all this when you go to court?"

"Course he could. But I'm not going to tell him, am I?"

"Why on earth not?"

"Do me a favour," Burslake said wearily. "This is the third nick I've been in. They keep ghosting me, for my own safety. Half the time I'm in solitary, keeping away from those sods."

Cassie was horrified. "How do you mean?"

"Threats and that. I wouldn't dare say anything, would I? Not if I want to live. The big boys on the outside make sure of that. So I do my bird, keep my head down and my nose clean and hope to God I come out the other end still in one piece."

"That's dreadful."

"Tell me about it. With any luck, I'll get three or four years. With time off, and the time I've already spent inside, I'm looking at twenty months or so. I'll survive. I'll have to, won't I?"

"I wish there was something I could—"

Burslake said, with conversational savagery, "Plays bridge, one of them." He wasn't listening to Cassie's murmured interpolations, which were all she could think of, given the circumstances. "One of the big boys. I heard him talking while I was down there in Swindon, poked my head round the office door and there he was. Suit which couldn't have cost less than five hundred smackers. One of those poncey watches without any figures, blue faces and just a diamond at twelve o'clock. He wasn't too happy when he saw my ugly mug, I can tell you. "Who the bloody 'ell are you?" he said. Just had time to say I was John Burslake, and who was *he*, when this call come through on one of those mobile phones they all ponce about with these days. 'Five hundred pounds a hundred? Sounds expensive—hope we don't go down too badly,' he says, laughing his fucking head off." Burslake made a bitter sound through his nose. "That's why I signed on for this class. Had some stupid idea that when I got out of here, I could take him on at one of these fancy Mayfair casino-type places. Ram his fucking grand slams and his Blackwood Conventions right down his fucking throat. But I don't expect they'd let someone like me over the doorstep, would they? Especially not now."

"Have you spoken to anyone here?" Cassie said. Over the past four months she had watched Burslake slip from merely being angry about the situation he found himself in to being totally obsessed about what he saw as the wrong done to him, bitterness alternating with apathetic despair.

"What bleeding good would that do?"

"It might help to talk to someone who knew more about things than I do."

"Nothing's going to help me," Burslake said.

Later, Cassie had a word with the Chaplain. "I know," the man said. "I've already spoken to one of the Deputy Governors about it. It's difficult to know what we can do for him. Quite apart from his psychological state, he seems to rub the other inmates up the wrong way—he's been attacked three or four times, both here and in other prisons he's been in. There's been some discussion about putting him into the hospital wing, where someone can keep an eye on him." He shrugged, a caring but busy man. "At least he's got you. Maybe it's because you're a woman: according to his profile, you're the only one he's talked to about things."

"I feel desperately sorry for him."

"So do I. At least he has some friends waiting for him outside. His former employer took the trouble to ring me at home to ask about him. Said he'd known him for years and he was sure there was some mistake. He also said that Burslake's trouble was, he bottled things up inside. So I was glad to tell him that the poor man had at least one sympathetic ear." The Chaplain smiled at Cassie. "We'd like to get him into the hospital wing but you know how it is: the system moves very slowly and not always to great effect."

"I just hope it won't move too slowly for Burslake," Cassie said, and didn't mind one bit that she sounded sharp and censorious.

2

Cassie drove home with the windows open. Summer was already in the air and the darkness was warm, the winter bite gone. She could smell the prison odour on her skin, pervasive as cologne, and looked forward to a bath, a drink and a book, not necessarily in that order. In fact, definitely *not* in that order. The drink would be first, brown and stiff and reminiscent of peat bogs. With a faint shudder, she thought of what Steve would reply if she made such a remark to him.

The hedges rose on either side of the road. Through her car windows, she could hear the hoot of a questing owl. Lamps illuminated houses whose outlines she could no longer see as night settled over the countryside. The scene was one of peace and rural tranquility, yet she could not rid herself of a sense of fear. Steve frightened her. There were no two ways about it. He had come to HM Prison Bellington to complete the last few weeks of his sentence, and had already been allowed out on home leave for the occasional weekend. She was not so naïve that she couldn't sense his interest in her. Her name was in the telephone directory. Once he left prison he was perfectly capable of finding out where she lived. The thought was chilling. She lived alone; the cottage was isolated, the nearest neighbour across a ploughed field in one direction and three hundred yards down the lane in the other. She remembered Steve's most recent victim, thought of the scars that a hundred stitches would leave on her face, imagined the blade of the Stanley knife as it sliced through her flesh. Easy prey. The phrase came into her mind and stayed there.

Easy prey.

Turning off the A487 on to the road signposted to Market Broughton, she came into Frith—six flint-and-brick cottages, the Three Bells, the village shop, a church, a row of handsome houses. Then on towards a sprawl of post-Sixties council estate, a recreation ground, some ugly modern shoeboxes, the Moreteyne Arms. Although they were obscured by the darkness, she knew they were there. She could hear raucous shouts, yob calling unto yob, the sound of glass being smashed, the creak of swings. Despite its triangular village green and some obscure connection with Jane Austen, Frith did not appear on the coach-party itineraries, partly because of its less obscure connections with Operation Hiawatha, when the Customs and Excise people had the previous year uncovered a massive crack factory operating from what the villagers had understood was a barn in the process of conversion to three holiday lettings.

Beyond Frith, the road dipped downhill for a couple of miles, meandering between hedges towards Market Broughton. Cassie turned off at Moreteyne Wood, a three-hundred-acre stand of deciduous trees planted in the middle of the last century by Sir Digby Moreteyne. Somewhere in the middle of them stood Moreteyne Hall, once Sir Digby's family home, and now a Special School for delinquent lads.

Several of the inmates of HMP Bellington were graduates of this establishment and, remembering this, Cassie wondered whether she would perhaps have done better to stay in the teaching profession after all. Five years ago—nearly six—she had still been a biology teacher in a girls' school, and while the memory of those adolescent sulks, the constant reproach of those anorexic bosoms, the dreariness of the staff-room, the dreariness of the *staff*, could even now fill her with a terminal depression, she did momentarily ask herself if she had made the right decision to get out of teaching and into something more meaningful, something she actually enjoyed doing. At the time, she had seen the move from biology mistress to full-time bridge professional as a step forward into the desirable states of independence and fulfilment. Now she wondered whether she had not simply exchanged the shades of the prison-house for the prison-house itself.

As she turned into Back Lane, the unmade-up dead-end where she lived, a car beeped lightly behind her. In the mirror, she could see the head and shoulders of her new neighbour. She put her arm out of the side window and waved. She knew almost nothing about her except that her name was Kathryn Kurtz, she was on sabbatical from a university in one of the more obscure states in North America—Nebraska or Minnesota, was it?—and had taken Ivy Cottage, the last house in the lane, for nine months, to finish a piece of research and maybe write a book. Kathryn had told her all this on the only occasion they had encountered each other, at which time Cassie had said she would invite her round for a drink, dinner even, introduce her to some of the local people. Although she had fully intended to, so far she had done none of this; seeing the American woman again, she felt ungracious and inhospitable.

She parked in front of the shed which was attached to the side of her cottage, and got out. The scent of lilac filled the air; each year she found it miraculous that although the lilac blooms would not be out for another two weeks, the clusters of tiny green budlets could still exhale their future fragrance. A white shadow slid across the grass and oozed round her legs like spilled milk. It was not her cat, but it frequently dropped in to visit; she leaned down and smoothed a hand along the undulations of its spine.

Straightening up, she walked towards the kitchen door and felt the adrenalin caused by the strain of two hours in the prison begin to leak away.

Within seconds it came surging back. There had been four plant pots on the kitchen windowsill when she left that evening, two containing healthy pink African violets, two containing healthy white ones. There were still four pots, but now two of them contained only relics, lifeless remains, while the other two held plants which, while still clinging to life, nonetheless looked as though they had pretty well reached the end of their tether.

What the hell had she done this time? Under-watered? Over-fed? A combination of both? Or was there some other cause for this premature decease? Did the remnants of plague still linger between the stones of the walls of Honeysuckle Cottage? It was, after all, over four hundred years old. But it couldn't be that. Plants had been dying to left and right, not to mention directly in front of her, long before Robin had suggested that she move out of the flat she shared with her cousins and into his weekend place.

"It'll just stand empty if you don't," he'd said, five years ago. "Another winter in this hideous climate will simply finish me off, which is why I'm removing myself to France. Nanny always said I would never make old bones and I'm beginning to think the old bag was right."

"Depends on how you define old," Cassie had said, rather pertly, as Robin was quick to point out. "I mean, if you'd been knocked down by a trolley-bus at the age of three, you'd still have made old bones. You were *born* old."

"True," Robin said. "Meanwhile, I'd like to think of the house in safe hands. I wouldn't want it to fall into a decline. Quite apart from anything else, there's the historic interest."

Cassie put her hands over her ears.

Robin raised his voice. "As I may have mentioned before, Fanny Burney is supposed to have been deflowered by Keats right at the top of the stairs."

"Last time you told me about it, you said it was Mary Wollstonecraft and Lord Byron."

"Did I?"

"Frankly, I think you made the whole thing up."

"*Moi?*"

"It's what Nanny would have called trying to make yourself interesting."

"My dear, that's *never* been a problem. Anyway, I'd have you know there are literary historians, not to mention biographers, who would give their right arms to have access to the attic here. Why, only last week I had a call from Michael Holroyd, looking for something to follow his *oeuvre* on Shaw."

"I hadn't realised he only had one arm."

Robin sighed. "I wish you weren't quite so facetious, Cassandra. It's certainly not a trait you inherited from me."

"Hardly surprising, given that you were in Mexico at the time of my conception. Not to mention my gestation and eventual parturition," said Cassie. "Even supposing you could have brought yourself to sleep with my mother."

"I was deeply in love with Sarah," Robin said stiffly. "And always will be. It's why I was asked to stand as your godfather."

"A pity she had a fatal flaw, really, wasn't it?"

"There were no flaws on Sarah."

"But I think you'll agree she was a woman."

"Don't mock, Cassandra. The wounds have not yet healed."

"Anyway . . . I'd be delighted to take over as keeper of a small but significant part of England's literary heritage."

"And get away from those fearsome twins, no doubt."

"That particularly."

Cassie remembered this conversation as she picked up the two dead plants and took them outside. The path towards the compost heap was worn to a deep groove; this funerary journey was one she had undertaken many many times since coming to live here. Was it that she set up an allergy in any houseplants which were brought in? She simply couldn't understand why they died so completely, or so swiftly, the moment they were taken into her care. The fact that they did so had been a precipitating factor in her decision to leave the teaching of biology to people with more understanding of vegetative needs.

That, and the thought of escaping from the tendril clutch of her minute twin cousins, Primula and Hyacinth. They were an obnoxious pair who, since pubescence, had bought their knickers in toyshops and still wore dresses from the Girls' Department of the bigger London stores, thus not only escaping payment of the VAT levied on women's clothes but at the same time effortlessly emphasising their superiority over Cassie. Rose, their elder sister, was two sizes larger. If there was anything bitter in Cassie, anything which occasionally verged towards the mean-spirited, it was directly attributable to an adolescence spent with this trio. At least her dead parents had not lumbered her with a name out of some Victorian wedding bouquet; at times, during her troubled youth, it had seemed little enough to be thankful for.

"*You're* the freaks," she had frequently wanted to shout, kicking aside the A-cup pieces of froth in which the twins encased their non-existent boobs. "I'm *normal*."

More or less. If not normal, then at least no different from the majority of adult women in the British Isles. Nonetheless, since the death of her mother, when Cassie was six years old, her experience of other women had largely been shaped by her three cousins and their mother, Aunt Polly. Or, rather, not largely at all. Quite the stringbean opposite.

Oh well. Those traumas were long past. Fast approaching her thirty-third birthday, Cassie was confident that by now she was able to handle them, though at the same time acknowledging that they had scarred her to the point that she was almost incapable of looking into a mirror and liking what she saw.

Inside the house, the telephone began to ring. Knowing who it would be, she hurried towards the sound, but ran painfully into the wheelbarrow left out earlier that day and swore vigorously. A branch swung across her cheek and caught in her hair so that for a moment she swung William-Rufus-like. At the same time, she trod in something squishy and undoubtedly unpleasant which insinuated itself between the open toes of her new and expensive summer sandals as she tried to untangle her hair from the tree. Damn and blast it.

Even as she unhooked herself and wiped her feet on the grass verge of her little lawn, she was asking herself exactly why she should have chosen to wear the shoes to go to the prison. It couldn't possibly be because she knew they flattered her legs, could it? She couldn't be guilty of desiring to titillate, while at the same time shrinking from the attention thus aroused, could she? From the first moment she had walked down the polished landing to the Education Wing, she had known that for a woman working within the system, there was a very thin line between the wish to look as if she had taken some trouble over her appearance, and deliberate arousal. It seemed important that she show some respect and not turn up dressed like a slob, as though men serving prison sentences were not worth bothering about. It was precisely because most of their lives no one had bothered about them that they were now inside. On the other hand . . .

But there was always another hand, if you wanted one. Sometimes, she got sick of being so damned evenhanded. Sometimes she wanted to be bigoted, to let her prejudices show.

She reached the back door just as the telephone stopped ringing.

It rang again at nine the next morning. "Royston Chilcott here. I tried to get hold of you last night, as arranged, but there was no answer."

Cassie did not feel up to explaining that that was because she was suspended by her hair from a tree. It lacked the note of efficiency she liked to project whenever she was working in a professional capacity. Especially with someone like Chilcott: rich, powerful, Cass-friendly and a potential source of further income. On the other hand, she lied only when absolutely necessary.

"Sorry about that. I was—uh—held up," she said. It was no more than the literal truth.

Chilcott's faintly antipodean voice—or was it cockney? Although he had hired her as his partner on several previous occasions, she could not determine which—was insinuating. "Kept you late, did he? I'd have done the same."

It didn't seem worth setting him right on that one. Besides, like a high-class call-girl—which in a way, she was—she preferred to maintain discretion about her other clients, even when the other client was a lilac tree. Or perhaps especially. "I'll meet you at the Savoy, shall I?" she said. "As usual?"

"Why not come a little earlier? We can have a drink or two before we go on to the club."

"All right."

"What's the matter, Cassie? You don't sound like yourself. Has something happened?"

"I guess I'm just depressed by the essential unfairness of life," said Cassie. John Burslake's story did not differ much from others she had been told during her time at the prison, including the essential factor of his innocence. Nor did she see him as somehow set above the others, someone more worthy to be believed, someone more unfairly treated. Society itself was unfair to these men. They were given no standards, taught nothing, abused by parents, employers, each other. The system ignored them until they finally took it on and then champed down with little or no interest in the precipitating factors, none whatsoever in seeing that they were given a chance to change their lives.

"Don't tell me," Chilcott said kindly. "Yesterday was one of your evenings in the prison, wasn't it?"

"How can you tell?"

"Because, even in our limited acquaintance, I've noticed how depressed you always are afterwards."

"It's that obvious, is it?"

"Did it ever occur to you that you don't have to do it? Nobody's *making* you teach bridge to society's misfits."

"That's exactly what gets me down. Not all of them are misfits. For instance, there's this poor man in there—I told you about him before . . ." She stopped. "Oh, what's the point in talking about it?"

"Talk. It won't make much difference to him, but it might help *you*."

Cassie explained the facts she had. "The worst thing is that Burslake—"

"Burslake's your bloke, is he?"

"Yes . . . He's really tried to make a go of things," she finished. "And if it wasn't for the men who got him into it, he would still be running his business, going home to his wife and kids, planning for the future."

"I doubt if he's as much of a deserving character as you're making out," Chilcott said bluntly. "On the other hand, he probably deserves better than he's getting. It's just bloody hard on those who get caught up in these scams. The really guilty ones always get away. Comes down to money in the end."

"As always."

"If you can pay your way out of a situation, you're always going to be OK. Believe me, I know all about it."

"It just makes me kind of mad," said Cassie. "So much so that I seriously think I might just try to find these people and tell them what I think of them. Or alert the Press. Or one of those watchdog programmes on Radio 4."

"Do you know who they are, then?"

"No."

"You can't go round accusing people without proof."

"You're right." Cassie could feel her indignation cooling. "But I bet I could identify one of them, if I had to."

"Get real, Cassie. How?"

"Well . . ." By a watch? By the fact that he played bridge? Of course Chilcott was right. "Perhaps not," she finished lamely.

"You could ask your friend John next time you go in," Chilcott said. "Get something concrete—if he's got something concrete to tell you, and not just a load of whinges."

"That's an idea."

"It'd be a damn sight more helpful to him. Especially if he feels he can't tell his lawyer the truth."

"I don't suppose I'd do anything about it, anyway." Cassie lifted her shoulders and let them drop defeatedly. "What bloody good would it do?"

"Want my advice, girl? Pour yourself a drink—"

Cassie laughed. "I already did."

"Have another. Take a couple of aspirin and lie in a hot bath. The Chilcott cure for the blues. Never fails."

"Thanks, Mr. Chilcott."

"Roy, please." Cassie heard the clink of bottle against glass. Sounded like Chilcott was trying his own recipe against depression. "I'll see you tonight, then."

"I'll be there."

3

"Sorry about the change of plan." Royston Chilcott leaned towards Cassie and put a hand on her knee. He chuckled. Under his hand the material of her evening dress rustled pruriently.

The car turned a corner, and she took the opportunity to shift along the leather seat towards the door. "Tell me again where we're going tonight," she said.

"Halkam Court, somewhere near Stow-on-the-Wold."

"That's not too far from where I live." Perhaps, if they had a good evening, she could persuade Chilcott to drop her off at the cottage.

"I'm sorry about dragging you all the way up to London, in that case. But this bloke Lloyd Wickham's supposed to be some real hot-shot in the City. Could do me a lot of good, so when Sir Peter Aubrey rang up and asked how I'd feel about playing at Wickham's place instead of Mayfair, as usual, I jumped at the chance." Chilcott's balding head gleamed briefly as he turned his head to stare out of the window at the Edward-Hopper-type starkness of suburban London after the shops have closed.

Cassie reflected that baldness was one of those manly traits which to some extent evened up the score and helped women to reconcile themselves to their lot. "Lloyd sounds more like an American name than an English one—where's he from?" she asked.

"I didn't ask. I want to do business with the guy, not research his family tree."

"Did you check him out?"

"I don't see that that's any of your business, young lady." The tone was jocular, the meaning clear. Cassie sensed anger tugging at an unseen leashes and realised she had overstepped some boundary of which she had not until now been aware. Just like the wheelbarrow last night, it was difficult to avoid obstacles if you did not realise they were there.

"Sorry." Bad move, she thought. Feather-light, a premonition of trouble brushed against the sensors in her brain. If they were going to play expensive bridge, surely it would make good sense for Chilcott to have previously assessed their opponents' ability to honour any debts incurred. Still, it was not, as he said, any of her business.

"As it happens," Chilcott said, perhaps worrying that he had been more abrupt than necessary, "for once, I didn't. Peter Aubrey recommended him, and his word was good enough for me."

As, no doubt, was his title. Amazing what wonders could be wrought with a simple Sir in front of your name. Doors opened, rough places plained—though probably not the crooked made straight as well. There are limits.

"Did he mind that we won't be playing at his club?" Cassie asked.

"I doubt it. As long as he gets his cut, I don't suppose he gives a damn where we play."

"Will we know anyone there?"

"I doubt it."

As they pushed onward, out of the city towards rural isolation, Cassie wished that she was in quite a lot of other places than this chauffeur-driven Rolls, heading towards an unknown destination to play bridge with people about whom she knew nothing except that they were bound to be seriously rich. In her limited experience, that was seldom a character recommendation. For a reckless moment, she was almost ready, were the choice to be offered, to return to the cramped little flat she used to share with her cousins. Horrified, she felt a thin creep of nostalgia for the sight of Primula standing in front of the full-length mirror in skimpy knickers, pinching her bones and exclaiming at her weight. Or Hyacinth clutching a hot-water bottle to her belly and moaning about stomach cramps. If there was one thing Cassie could do without, especially after a day teaching biology to adolescent girls, it was women who made a fuss about their periods.

The moment passed as swiftly as it had come, leaving behind the cheesy aftertaste of a nightmare. As it happened, neither of the twins still lived in the flat. Both of them were long married now, Primula to Derek the Headmaster, and Hyacinth to Eric the Estate Agent. It had been a double wedding, the twins cute as mice in identical wedding dresses, Rose and Cassie acting as bridesmaids. Cassie, acutely aware that lilac chenille became her less well than most, was not at her best, having been at the champagne (very inferior indeed) before the wedding party set out. In the photographs she loomed obliquely, head and shoulders above the rest, causing considerable irritation to Aunt Polly and the twins. Especially when the contact prints arrived.

"What on earth do you think you look like?" Aunt Polly had said.

"The Leaning Tower of Pisa," said Cassie.

"Snow White and the fourteen dwarfs?" suggested Eric.

"That's not funny," snapped Primula.

"Isn't it?" Unlike Derek, Eric was not yet fully trained.

"She's so unsymmetrical," wailed Hyacinth. "Look at her, towering over us like a condemned block of flats."

"Just after they've detonated the demolition charges," snickered Eric. He grinned secretly at Cassie.

"I still cannot fully comprehend why, in all these photographs, our dear Cassandra is inclined to one side," said Uncle Sam, holding the contact sheets close to his spectacles.

"Because at the time, our dear Cassandra was as drunk as a skunk," said Primula.

"Primula, my dear . . ."

"Surely not on that champagne," Eric said.

"It's your own fault." Cassie had little sympathy with anyone who chose lilac chenille for her bridesmaids' dresses and then insisted on Cassie being a bridesmaid. "Anyway, I can't help being taller than you."

"*And* you're in practically every single picture," bitched Primula. She had been drinking sherry with an air of unaccustomed depravity, and spots of colour burned in her cheeks.

Cassie was not going to explain that that was probably because the photographer had propositioned her in the church porch as they waited for the brides to appear, saying that he was deed keen on bi-i-ig women—his hands encased the air—and would she be interested in some private sessions sometimes, he had a good outlet for special pictures, did she know what he meant?

"Anyway, as far as I'm concerned, she's ruined The Most Wonderful Day of My Life," said Hyacinth.

"Exactly," Primula endorsed. "Who's going to want their friends to see photographs like these?"

"Certainly not me," said Cassie. Lilac chenille, indeed.

Seen from the perspective of a leather-seated, walnut-panelled Rolls-Royce, this scene had assumed a heart-warmingly comic air which had definitely been missing at the time. She reminded herself that Chilcott was paying her a good deal of money to partner him this evening: enough to cover last quarter's enormous heating bill *and* to keep her solvent for a good part of the next month.

"This Wickham person: have we played with him anywhere before?" she asked. "I don't recall the name."

"No. He's some friend of Aubrey's, as far as I remember. He was going to join us in Mayfair this evening and then something came up—I'm not sure what—and he asked if we could play at his place instead. Aubrey rang round the other people who were coming tonight, and they apparently jumped at the chance to play at a place like Halkam Court." Chilcott rubbed his hands together. "Wickham's something in the City and as rich as Onassis, according to Sir Peter. Could do me a lot of good, business-wise, if I play my cards right."

Which was precisely what Cassie had been hired to help him do. "Are we playing well tonight, or badly?" she asked.

"Come on, Cassie. What do you think?"

"Depends on whether you want him to take you for a sucker, or to expose the sharklike ferocity lurking beneath your mild exterior."

Chilcott laughed, the chins under his jaw trembling like quicksand. "Sharklike ferocity: I like that." He reached into the breast pocket of his dinner jacket and, bringing out a chased silver cigar case, tapped out an unwrapped cigar. "Mind if I light up?" Before she could respond, he had bitten the end off, opened the window and spat it out into the damp night.

In front of them, the chauffeur's neck quivered.

Chilcott pressed down again on the electronic button and the window closed smoothly. "To answer your question, tonight I want to take them to the cleaners. All right?"

"All right."

Or semi all right. Chilcott was an impatient man. Which was probably fine in the cut and thrust of the financial world in which he operated, but not to be recommended for bridge-playing. Not over the long term. Slow and steady bidding was the only way, learning your partner's hand, not making deductions based on insufficient evidence. You might produce a considerable splash or two by forcing to game every single time, but, equally, you could make spectacular losses. When you considered the stakes these people played for, the cautious approach was always going to be best. She'd told him that before, on other occasions when he had hired her to play with him. Once when only an ill-considered discard by the opposition had saved them from going down doubled and vulnerable, the other time when her own skilful play had narrowly retrieved them from an almost unwinnable contract he had recklessly bid them into.

On previous sessions, she had learned two things about

Roy Chilcott. One, that he did not take kindly to instruction from her. Two, that although he was an extremely good bridge-player, he would never be top class. He did not have the ability to wait. In addition, she suspected him of being the kind of man who, however charming he appears on the surface, dislikes women. So far, she had not had the opportunity to confirm this hypothesis. He had first contacted her only three or four months back and, in that time, they had played together no more than half a dozen times. She hoped their relationship would continue: not only was it lucrative, but he was easy to talk to, and seemed to take a personal, if paternalistic, interest in her and her various activities. He had even hinted that he might be prepared to invest money in setting up her bridge sundries business, if the idea ever got off the ground.

His cigar smoke filled the car and Cassie lowered the window again. He would see this as criticism, but too bad. They were deep in the countryside now: no lights, a meadowy smell, trees outlined against a sky which had the sheen of a black pearl. It looked as though there might be a storm later. She could smell rain on the fresh air coming in through the window. It was a chilly evening, despite summer's near approach. She shivered, wishing she'd worn something less flimsy than her evening stole. She had debated wearing Gran's old fur but, in view of the long car-ride, had decided against it. Structurally, there was nothing wrong with the coat, which Gran had cared for with the same devoted attention she lavished on the weakest member of a kitten-litter. The trouble was, it smelled. And not just of mothballs. Some seventy years ago, immediately prior to Gran's proud purchase of it, there had clearly been a major hiccup in the curing process. In the warmth of a closed car, the insidious stench of decayed stoat-pelts or whatever the coat was made of would have wound its way round the two of them and later, clung to the folds of her dress. It was not a scent conducive to either friendliness or good order. Cassie knew that political correctitude demanded that she throw it away, but Gran had loved it and she could not bring herself to do so. The coat was almost all that was left to remind her of the old days in the Holloway Road. Of her fa-

ther. Of Gran herself. Aunt Polly had, in fact, dropped the coat
in the dustbin ten minutes after Cassie, aged thirteen, had arrived to live at the Vicarage wearing it, but Cassie had immediately cast herself to the ground and given vent to a series of
howls and bellows until Uncle Sam had persuaded his wife to
retrieve it.

A pair of gateposts appeared ahead, and the chauffeur
turned in between them. They drove past what, in the fading
light, seemed to be acres of tree-studded lawns which
stretched on either side of a gravelled drive and gave off a
scent of new-mown hay. A large country house waited for
them at its far end.

"Did you say something about dinner?" Cassie asked.

"I can't remember."

"I hope not. I don't like the combination of serious bridge
and dining. It means you end up doing neither particularly
well."

"Now that I think about it, I believe there was mention of
smoked salmon," said Chilcott.

"I can live with that." Fairly comfortably. One of smoked
salmon's many virtues was that it contained only forty calories
per ounce. And although Cassie did not like playing bridge on
a full stomach, it was none the less important to establish that
one was not going to starve. She had learned the hard way that
not everyone considered it necessary to eat regular meals in
order to sustain life.

They drew up in front of a flight of shallow steps leading
up to a door set back under a column-supported upper
storey. There was a number of other cars already there,
mostly upmarket: BMWs, a Bentley, a Mercedes, an Audi.
And, somewhat incongruously, a shiny black VW with mirrored windows. While they were getting out of the Rolls, the
door of the house opened and yellow light slipped out into
the darkness around a hefty silhouette. As they mounted the
steps, Chilcott's hand under Cassie's elbow, isolated needles
of rain tapped at their faces and, somewhere behind the
trees, thunder yawned.

Above them the silhouette spoke. "Mr. Chilcott. Miss
Swann. Good evening."

Cassie had never seen a butler before. Not in the flesh. And this exemplar possessed a lot of that, though it was not so much substantial as solid. Stepping into the circular hall, she saw that far from being the plumped-out senior citizen of popular imagination, Lloyd Wickham's butler could be no more than twenty-five, if that. He wore his hair long and golden. His limbs strained indecorously at the cloth of his black coat and striped trousers. There was a gold ring in his left ear-lobe. This was a man whose body suggested that any minute now he would be donning a posing pouch and attempting to snatch the Mr. Universe title from the current holder. Cassie had an incongruous vision of him pumping iron during his off-duty hours, posing like an oiled Discus Thrower in front of long mirrors, flexing his pecs in order to bring the veins writhing to the surface of his muscles.

Chilcott at her side, she followed the butler down the hall towards tall double doors from behind which came the sound of moneyed laughter. She could not help noticing that a miniature pigtail nestled just above his collar. He flung open the doors and announced their names, and Cassie walked forward to meet the people who awaited them. Most of them were men, dinner-jacketed and stiff-shirted. A few were women. Two almost identical ones were talking with each other; two others stood together near a blazing log fire, one with the boneless posture and fuck-you stare of a top professional model, the other with the swansong looks of an ageing siren. Both had eyes like hostile diamonds.

Behind her, Chilcott stepped forward. "Hope we're not late," he said, joviality to the fore.

"Actually, you are." A tall well-cut man whom Cassie took to be their host, Lloyd Wickham, came over. He was thinnish and elegant, his grey hair combed straight back to form clubman's curls at the nape of his neck. His tan whispered of health clubs.

Chilcott seemed confused. "I thought you said eight o'clock."

"Seven-thirty, old boy. But don't worry about it."

"I was sure you said eight. I must have misheard. Sorry about that." Chilcott laughed, but there was annoyance beneath. "May I introduce my partner for this evening: Miss Cassandra Swann."

Wickham shook her hand. "Delighted." His eyes passed over the space she occupied but did not take her in. "Drink?"

"Whisky, please." Cassie spoke firmly. Gave him her don't-you-tread-on-me look. She guessed that Wickham was playing games, the rules honed to perfection by sojourns at both public school and university. Ritual games of intimidation and humiliation which he had been practising all of his life on people like himself. She would bet that Chilcott had intentionally been told the wrong time at which to arrive, in an attempt to nobble the opposition before it had even reached the bridge table. Chilcott, not being a person like himself, would not recognise the rules. She began to assess and calculate. If she was right, was the fact that their host had resorted to such tactics a good sign or a bad? Did it mean that his bridge was not as good at it ought to be, or merely that this was going to be one of those knives-at-the-ready, no-holds-barred evenings? She hoped her partner was up to it. "A small one," she added.

Wickham handed her a glass. "What about you?" he said to Chilcott.

Cassie could see Chilcott weighing up the options. To ask for mineral water might imply that he was dreading the evening ahead and needed to keep all his wits about him. To accept alcohol might equally be seen as an indication that he felt in the need of Dutch courage. She willed him to go for the booze: even if Wickham deliberately made it a stiff one, Chilcott did not have to drink the whole thing, and a small intake of alcohol might loosen him up.

Knowing what was expected of her, she walked towards the women, choosing to join the couple standing by the fire. "I'm Cassandra Swann," she said.

"I know," said the elder.

"Oh?"

"I play regularly with Hilda Comberley," explained the Sunset Boulevardier, "and I've know Mercy Laughton forever. We were at school together, you know."

"Ah." Cassie could feel a blush forming. Mercy Laughton.

Mother of Giles. Who, despite suffering from terminal irritation, was extremely good at kissing and other related things. Who had already proposed marriage once and showed every sign of doing so again. And again.

She realised she had not been paying attention when she heard the lissom blonde saying, "—either Hilda Comberley or Mercy Laughton. But I do know Giles." She moved her big mouth about and raised eyebrows curved like the sickle moon.

"*Still*, dear?" asked the older woman.

"Only in a manner of speaking, Mother. As you may possibly have forgotten, I've been *very* happily married to Winston for the past eight years."

"Winston? Remind me which one that was," Mother said. "The ferrety one with thin lips, or the lippy one with the thin ferrets?"

"*Très* droll, Mother. And we're talking about mink, not ferrets, as you're perfectly well aware."

"Mink?" Cassie said, hoping to defuse what seemed to be a potentially explosive situation.

Melissa barely glanced at her. "A mink farm," she said briefly. "Providing us with a very nice income, too." With a sudden vicious spurt, Melissa added, "A damn sight nicer than Daddy ever made at the same age."

"That wouldn't be difficult," agreed Mother. She raised a much-lifted jawline and snuffed at the air, a tigress scenting game.

"And nor does Winston have to send his wife out to sell herself to the highest bidder in order to make ends meet, the way Daddy did."

"Darling Melissa: I usually *was* the highest bidder. How else do you think we managed to pay the fees for that useless school he insisted on sending you to, except through my skill at bridge?"

"I thought Grandfather paid."

"Grandfather *helped*," said Mother.

"Just as well you drove poor Daddy into an early grave," said Melissa.

"I do so agree. Ricardo was so much richer than your father.

And Humphrey was not only richer than either of them, but better-looking too."

"Do you two partner each other?" asked Cassie, hoping they did not. She'd met double acts like theirs at the bridge table before. She felt rather sorry for Melissa: it was clear that Mother had a head-start on her as far as malicious repartee was concerned, and was always likely to win any oral confrontation.

"Unfortunately, yes," said Mother. "Since Melissa has a disturbing tendency to confuse her Hearts with her Spades."

"That's unusual." Cassie looked from one to the other. There was obviously more to the remark than bridge: perhaps she had blundered into some kind of familial conflict here. Trying not to think too hard about what episode in Melissa's past—or present?—Mother could be referring to, she hurried on. "Do you know Mr. Chilcott—my partner? Have you played with him before?"

"I can't speak for Melissa—she lives a life far removed from my own staid existence—but *I* certainly haven't." Mother raised spectacles which hung around her neck on a pearl-studded gold chain and peered through them at the men, who all stood around the drinks tray, being blokey, laughing heartily and without humour at a remark one of them had just made, while they sized each other up. A pretty girl of seventeen or so was walking around with a plate of canapés, while the butler hovered here and there, filling glasses when asked. Not many people took advantage of his presence: they were about to play serious bridge and no one wanted their thought processes impaired by alcohol.

"Is your partner Australian?" asked Melissa. Her mouth was enormous, impastoed in dark red lipstick which had been applied without regard for the natural lip-lines.

"I'm not entirely sure." Cassie glanced over at Chilcott, who seemed to be more at ease than he had been at first.

"Isn't he your husband?"

"Not at all. We're—we're colleagues," said Cassie. "And friends, of course." She had forgotten to check with Chilcott whether their strictly commercial relationship was to be disclosed this evening or not.

"Poor Melissa," said Mother. "She has this quaint notion that the minute you meet a thoroughly unsuitable man, you should marry him."

"Poor Mother," said Melissa. "These days, the minute she meets a man, suitable or otherwise, he runs a mile."

"At least I don't have to poach someone else's husband," Mother said, grinning like a shark and leaning on the verb in a manner which caused Melissa to flush. "Unlike some I could mention."

"Meaning?" Melissa's face suddenly hardened.

"Meaning that *I* didn't have to break up someone else's marriage before I could find someone who'd marry me."

"Well, at least now I've got him, he's able to fulfil his husbandly duties," Melissa said. "Which was rather more than your Ricardo was able to do. And I had my doubts about Humphrey."

"Humphrey was a man in every sense of the word," Mother said loudly. Over-loudly, in Cassie's opinion. She was beginning to feel distinctly uncomfortable. She had never gone in much for swapping sexual statistics with the girls, and had no intention of starting now with a pair of total strangers. Though to be fair, neither of them seemed to be aware that she was present.

"Going back to Winston," Melissa went on. "Was it you who pushed Portia Wickham into joining that demonstration?"

Mother laid a Tenerife-browned hand laden with diamonds on her bosom. "Me? Why would you think that?"

"Because neither Winston nor I has ever met her. So why should she suddenly take it into her head to start hijacking our delivery vans?"

"Perhaps she just reached boiling point," Mother said, again with an emphasis which escaped Cassie, though it seemed to make Melissa pretty mad, judging by the way her eyes narrowed.

"Mother, whatever you may think, I'm not ashamed of what Winston does," she said through her teeth.

"Of course not, my darling," Mother said.

The two women smiled at each other in a way which made

Cassie, standing between them, feel that she had just stepped into an Iron Maiden and the door was closing fast.

It was hard to tell whether they were joking. Probably not: the smell of unhealed wounds lingered behind the words. Would she and her mother have ended up like this, exchanging loaded sentences in front of total strangers, if Sarah had not died? She resolved that next time they met, she would try not to chafe at the veiled criticisms of Aunt Polly, the mother-substitute foisted unasked on her when Gran, too, had died. She might even try being nice to Hyacinth.

Being nice to Primula was another question entirely.

The big room was warm, heated by discreetly concealed radiators, as well as log fires burning at either end. The walls were white and panelled, hung with dark portraits in need of cleaning. Curtains of ruby velvet hung heavily across the windows and elaborate floral compositions indicated the fact that, at some point, Mrs. Lloyd Wickham had almost certainly completed a Constance Spry flower-arranging course.

Wickham stepped forward. "Right, everybody," he said. "Now that we're all here, shall we go in and sit down?"

On a small tide of approval, they followed him down the rug-scattered parquet flooring towards wide doors which led into a library where bridge tables had been set up. Floor to ceiling bookshelves lined the walls except above the fireplace, where a portrait of a woman hung. In one corner stood a set of library steps; in another, a lectern holding a volume which, although she was too far away to be sure, seemed to Cassie to be an illuminated Book of Hours. There was an array of booze on a table, accompanied by munchy things. Cassie seldom turned her back on temptation. She walked over and ate several large crisps with considerable satisfaction. Ready salted; the only acceptable kind.

Wickham addressed his guests. "House rules," he said. "We draw for opponents, the two highest playing each other and so on down the tables. Introduce yourselves to each other when you meet at the tables. We play five hundred pounds a point. Game bridge, naturally, not duplicate." He looked round at his audience. "Everybody happy about that? No one wants to back out?" His gaze lingered on Chilcott in a manner calculated to offend.

Whatever Chilcott wanted—business contacts, social acceptance, the adrenalin rush of big-money gambling—he wanted it badly. Playing for those stakes, anyone going significantly down stood to lose a sum which if not exactly a small fortune was somewhere fairly close to it. Although the prospect probably added an acid edge to the game, it was too rarefied a pleasure for Cassie, even though her arrangement with Chilcott specifically excluded her from responsibility for any debts incurred. All these people were loaded; they smelled of money the way a damp cellar smells of mould. Not that this worried her in any way. She had played bridge with the seriously rich before, at the discreet salon run by Peter Aubrey from his house in Mayfair. But never for stakes this high. Five hundred a point was *ser*ious money.

"Vulnerability as in duplicate," Wickham continued. "Dealer, dealer, everybody, nobody. Chicago rules, keep your own totals, play four hands, pay your debts at the end of every four hands, the losers moving down one table, winners staying put." He indicated the boyish butler, who had followed them into the library. "Jamie, or—uh—Tamsin . . ." he smiled at the pretty girl who stood demurely beside Jamie, ". . . will be on hand throughout the evening's play. You can either ask them to bring you something from the sideboard, or help yourself. Smoked salmon sandwiches will be freely available; anything else you'll have to ask for. Any questions?"

There were not. The atmosphere in the room had sharpened as though sprayed with a thin coating of vinegar. People avoided looking at each other as they moved towards the green-baized card tables set up in the centre of the room. There was an individual retraction of personality: the switch into automatic mode, the mental clearing away of extraneous detail, as each of them shifted down to a different part of themselves and locked into their storehouses of memory, logic, skill and daring. On an evening like this, with people like this, the satisfaction of winning was going to be enhanced by knowing that the losers would be considerably out of pocket. Cassie reminded herself that she was playing cold, that none of this was personal; whether they won or lost, she was simply there as a hired hand, paid to use her skills.

4

Chilcott and Cassie played first at Table Three. Their opponents were two men, both of them younger than the other men in the room, one called Jeremy Marling, the other named Jacko. Jacko had a mid-Atlantic accent, a lot of overlong curly hair, a plum-coloured dinner jacket and very dirty fingernails. The rimless lenses of his glasses were square and at least a quarter of an inch thick. Marling wore his hair smoothed straight back across his head. City-slicker style. His eyes were hotly blue, the colour emphasised by a healthy outdoor tan. Before they started playing, he complained about the seafood restaurant where he and Andrew Pascoe—he indicated one of the married couples—had eaten lunch, saying the *moules marinières* had been far from fresh; Jacko countered with an anecdote about a place in New Orleans where the entire staff had turned green and slumped to the floor because of something they'd eaten, to be found there by the first clientèle arriving for the evening sittings.

Cassie could have done without either piece of information. She and Chilcott ended the round with a reasonable profit, which their opponents merely shrugged over before ignoring them and settling down to discuss exactly where they had gone wrong. They won marginally against one of the married couples, and lost marginally against the other. Against Melissa and Mother, they won handsomely. Melissa, pulling a crocodile-covered chequebook from her matching bag, said passionately, "Have you finally gone senile, Mother? Surely by now you know I never *ever* say four Clubs unless I'm asking for Aces."

To which Mother responded "Not senile, dear. You were merely witnessing the kind of lapse of attention only to be expected from someone whose brain has been *scrambled . . .*" A pause, while she looked triumphantly at her daughter, ". . . after so many years of making mental adjustments."

No contest, Cassie wanted to say; leave it. But Melissa fell for it, as she had probably been doing since she first learned to talk. "Mental adjustments? What's that supposed to mean?"

"Darling, we all know you have a heart of gold," Mother said warmly. She paused. Melissa waited. Mother went on, "And a brain the size of a hen's-dropping." Again the strange emphasis. "A bridge-player you're not and never have been, although I taught you myself. Over the years I've had to partner you, I've learned to compensate for the fact." She looked round at them pathetically. "I'm no longer young: sometimes, I suppose, I drop my guard for a moment."

Melissa signed her cheque with a Mont Blanc pen and tore it out of the book. "Please, Mother," she said, "you'll have us all in tears." She handed the cheque to Chilcott. "By the way: did I say that Mr. Abbot from the Rosedale Nursing Home was coming by tomorrow morning? He wants to talk about you moving in."

"And did I mention that I thought I'd take Betty with me to Egypt instead of you?" said Mother.

"You wouldn't!" Melissa stared at her parent furiously. "You *couldn't*! You know I always—"

Chilcott cleared this throat. "Thanks, ladies," he said. "Enjoyed the round."

He and Cassie moved away, leaving the two women to continue the bickering which had probably been a lifelong occupation.

"Phew," Chilcott muttered under his breath. "What a prize pair of bitches."

"It's obviously a relationship built on deep mutual respect," said Cassie.

"Are you kidding?"

"Yes."

Chilcott walked over to the big oak sideboard and poured two glasses of champagne. "If that was my mother, I'd have sent her to the dog-food factory years ago."

"If that was my daughter, I'd have taken a taxi to get there," said Cassie.

There was something uncomfortable about this room, she thought. Admittedly it wasn't one of those snug places which tempted you to let your hair down and swap dirty jokes with the rest of the gang. But the discomfort lay less in the furnishings and accoutrements, which were impeccable, than in the people. Who were they? What did they stand for, if anything? Had they gathered together in this room for the thrill of playing for high stakes, or simply in the hope of making more money to add to the large amounts they so clearly possessed already? They were well dressed, well spoken, well behaved. Yet there was about them an air of ruthlessness more suited to a gathering of Mafia godfathers than to an English country house.

"You're looking at decadence in its purest form," a voice said quietly behind her.

She turned to find Jamie, the butler, wrapping the neck of a champagne bottle in a white napkin. "Sorry?" she said.

"Come the revolution, this lot'll be the first to go." Jamie nodded at the tables.

"The days when revolution was likely died with the advent of the video," said Cassie.

"Don't you believe it. It's happening all round us," said the butler. "The rise of the unemployed working class. The yob society. Haven't you noticed the way they're taking over? Don't you read the papers? The Royal Family's already threshing about on the canvas, mortally wounded. The aristocracy are tottering. Even the middle classes are under threat."

Outside the curtained windows there was a sudden rumble of thunder, and rain spurted against the panes. "Lord," gasped Cassie. "For a moment there, I thought I heard the tumbrils."

"I'm serious," said Jamie. "Attacks on the middle classes are increasing all the time. If you sound posh, or look as if you've got a job or go to the wrong school—which used, of course, to be the *right* school—you're a target for any yob who wants to take a swing at you with a baseball bat or a pair of Doc Martens."

"Are you writing a thesis on the English class system, or what?"

Jamie shrugged. "Just a participating observer of the social scene."

"You don't exactly sound as if you grew up in a cardboard box yourself," said Cassie.

"I can if I need to."

"Useful."

"Necessary." Jamie gave her a challenging grin. "Perhaps you weren't aware that I belong to the most vulnerable section of British society: the young single male."

"There's not a lot you can do about that."

"Except get older, and become a member of the second most vulnerable group: the frail elderly. Believe me, I know."

Before Cassie could ask how a stripling of twenty-five could know any such thing, Tamsin came over. She wore a low-cut black dress with a very short skirt and, over it, a little white muslin apron. It was the stuff male fantasies are woven from; Cassie almost expected her to pull out a feather duster and bend saucily over a chair to reveal that she had forgotten to put on her knickers.

"Jamie," she said, putting one small hand on the butler's sleeve and giving him a look from beneath her eyelashes which she must have spent hours practising.

"Yes, Tamsin?" Jamie said, surreptitiously removing the hand and striving to sound efficient and butlerlike.

"The man over there wants Irish whiskey, not Scotch. Have we got any?"

"In my pantry," Jamie said. "I'd better go and look."

"Shall I come too?"

"That won't be necessary." The flush which grew out of Jamie's collar made it clear to Cassie that, even if not tonight, Tamsin quite often did accompany Jamie to his pantry. This close, Tamsin seemed vaguely familiar to Cassie, but before she could ask how this might be, one of those still playing out the second round called Tamsin over and she moved away to bend over the man with deliberate solicitude. Cassie wandered towards the bookshelves. Melissa and her mother were still arguing over their chequebooks in fierce undertones, poking fountain pens at each other with all the ferocity of duelling rivals. The two married couples were discussing their hands amicably together. The third table was grimly finishing what was clearly a tense game. Lloyd Wickham sat impassively staring at the three cards left in his hand, giving nothing away. His partner, a solid man with rimless glasses and greying hair who looked like—and perhaps even was—an international banker, waited behind the Dummy hand, while their opponents—Jeremy Marling and Jacko—both held their cards below the table and avoided eye contact. Bridge as a business tool, Cassie thought. Show your weakness or, for that matter, your strengths at the card table and you showed the same strengths or weaknesses in the boardroom. Perhaps that was why games like these were set up in the first place, as a kind of psychological testing.

Her eye was caught by a tall volume in a glossy cover which featured grapes and vine leaves on the spine. *Wickham on Wine*—that must be why the name seemed vaguely familiar when Chilcott had first mentioned it earlier that evening. Robin, her godfather, who could now afford to take his wine-drinking seriously, had the same book in his house in France. She took it down from the shelf and turned to the back flap. There was no author photograph, but the blurb drooled over Darcy Wickham and his deep knowledge of oenology, the enthusiasm he brought to his subject, his eloquent prose and the evident joy he took in passing on the vast amount of information he had amassed in a lifetime of research. In other words, Cassie thought, the man's a drunk.

She wondered what his relation to Lloyd was. Father, brother, uncle? Not that it mattered. Darcy and Lloyd: marginally better than Hyacinth and Primula. Why were men never given the names of plants? Apart from Lupin Pooter and the Joseph Cotten character in *The Third Man*—Holly Martin— who else was there? Though, come to think of it, hadn't Hyacinth originally been male, a beautiful youth beloved by one of the more powerful gods, and struck down, if she remembered correctly, by the Olympian equivalent of the frisbee? She replaced *Wickham on Wine* on the shelf and walked over to stand by the fire.

Above her hung the portrait of a woman in a black evening gown which revealed a small acreage of bare flesh. This was clearly a woman who had never learned to say no, a woman whose face and figure demonstrated a willingness to sit down at groaning boards, quaff foaming beakers, romp energetically with a multiplicity of lovers, separately or all at once. Looking up at the curving mouth, the generous boobs and swelling hips, the mischievous eyes, Cassie was instantly engaged. This was a woman she would like to know. A woman with the same appetites and attitudes, even the same amplitudes, as herself. There was a small plaque affixed to the dull gold curlicues of the frame, and she leaned forward.

Portia, Lady Wickham, Cassie read, *by Archibald Stevens, RA, 1993*.

So it was recently executed. But just a moment: she turned to look at the bridge-players still sitting at the card table. If this was Lady Wickham, surely their host must be in some way related to her. Which probably meant, did it not, that—

"She's a fine figure of a woman," someone said. One of the husbands of the two married couples. He had a brandy balloon in his hand. "I don't believe we were properly introduced, but I'm Andrew Pascoe. My wife and I drove down from Town with Jeremy Marling."

"Cassandra Swann."

He nodded at the portrait. "It's a good likeness. Do you

know her?" At Cassie's headshake, he added, "She's a Texan."

"Why isn't she here tonight?"

"Partly because she doesn't play bridge. Partly because, as I understand it, she's attending a charity concert at Kenwood or somewhere similar."

"You know the family well?"

He smiled slightly. "I used to know Portia particularly well." His smile broadened. "Despite its being extraordinarily difficult at times, we've managed to remain more or less friends. More or less most of the time. Which is considerably better than some have managed." He looked at the level of brandy in his glass, and then back at Cassie. "This is purely medicinal. Something I ate at lunchtime seems to have disagreed with me."

"Mr. Marling mentioned mussels," Cassie said sympathetically. "Is Lady Wickham at the concert because she likes music, or because she likes—"

"Charities? She certainly does a great deal of voluntary work." His emphasis on the word "voluntary" gave it a curious significance. Before she could start to analyse exactly in what area that significance lay, Pascoe looked across at Chilcott and slightly lowered his voice. "How did you do?"

"Sorry?"

"Win? Lose? Break even?"

"So far we've done all right." It was not Cassie's place to bandy figures about unless she was sure Chilcott wouldn't mind.

At his table, Wickham said loudly, "And the last trick is ours." He threw down his final card and blew out a satisfied rush of air. "God! For a minute there, I thought they were going to get us down."

"Not me, old chap," the banker-type said. "I had complete faith in you from the beginning."

"With a Dummy hand like that, you could scarcely go wrong," one of their opponents said enviously. He felt in his breast pocket. "So, Wickham, what's the damage?"

♠   ♥   ♣   ♦

There was a general milling about in front of the sideboard before they took up their position for the final round of the evening. Cassie and Chilcott had increased their winnings; Jeremy Marling and Jacko were well down. They were either poor players or unlucky ones. Outside, the weather had clearly worsened: the flames in the fire-grate billowed every now and then as wind rushed down the chimney, and the sound of rain drumming on the stone flags outside the windows added an extra dimension of siege and danger to the already febrific atmosphere.

"Roderick Symington." The banker—if that was what he was—nodded at Cassie as they sat down.

"Cassandra Swann."

"Should I know you?" Symington looked over his rimless half-moons at her with the air of a man who has discovered a sure-fire cure for facial blemishes and is wondering whether to recommend she try it.

"Not unless you want to," Cassie said. Her godfather would have called her response pert, but it was the kind of question to which it was difficult to formulate a polite answer without abandoning one's personal integrity. Not sure how much of this she had, Cassie liked, where possible, to hold on to the little she was certain of.

"You run a tight ship, Lloyd," Chilcott said in a matey fashion which caused the curls above Wickham's collar to clench.

Symington stared at him rudely. "I beg your pardon." He removed his glasses and held them by one ear-piece. "*What* did you say?"

Chilcott raised his eyebrows. "I merely said that Lloyd here runs a tight ship."

"Who's Lloyd?"

Chilcott turned from one to the other. "Isn't that—? Aren't you—?"

"It's Lord, actually," said Wickham. "Otherwise known as Darcy."

"Not *Lloyd*," said Symington with disgust, tonguing the word as though it were an inadvertent fleck of gooseshit.

Chilcott laughed self-consciously. "Sorry about that. Must have misheard Aubrey when he first spoke of you."

"Peter Aubrey," said the banker, articulating with clarity, "was at school with us. Won an Elocution Prize in the Remove, didn't he, Darcy?"

"Absolutely," said Wickham.

"Never mind," Chilcott said, laughing again. A red tide of embarrassment and humiliation was flooding the bulldog flesh beneath his jaw. "An easy mistake to make."

"Is it?" Raising his eyebrows, Symington turned to Cassie. "Shall we draw for deal?"

If this were Lord and not Lloyd Wickham, then the lady above the fireplace was his wife, and the book on the library shelves almost certainly his work. Watching as the cards were dealt by the banker, Cassie again wondered to what extent the mistake had been deliberately engineered in order to make Roy Chilcott feel foolish. As anyone would who had mistaken one word for the other. Who might, furthermore, be deemed to have addressed his host by title rather than name by those not paying full attention.

Chilcott's angry flush did not die down at once. In the first game, he made a couple of elementary mistakes which Cassie, luckily, was able to counteract. In the second game, his response to Cassie's opening bid was so slow that she feared at first he would pass. The third game was won by their opponents, though only just. It was on the fourth hand that disaster struck.

Having dealt the hand, Chilcott opened. "Two Spades," he said.

On his left, Wickham passed.

Cassie, who had only one Spade in her hand, showed her other suit and bid three Hearts.* Symington passed.

Chilcott, bidding in the second round, said, "Three Spades."

It was a stronger bid than four Spades, since it left the door open for a slam. Cassie, having no real choice, knowing she had to say something, rebid her Hearts.

"Four No Trumps," said Chilcott.

This was the Blackwood Convention, asking for Aces. Obediently, Cassie replied with five Diamonds, showing that she had a single Ace.

*See p. 52

"Six Spades," said Chilcott. He was holding his cards too tightly, both elbows on the table and the cards close to his face. There was sweat on his forehead.

Cassie looked again at her cards. With a singleton Spade, could she risk leaving him to play six Spades? He obviously had a lot of them, but on the other hand if she bid up her own suit, he still had the choice of leaving her in Hearts or going back to his own suit. "Seven Hearts," she said.

Over the top of his cards, Chilcott glared at her triumphantly. "Seven Spades," he said.

Wickham leaned back in his chair. "Double," he said, his voice expressionless.

"Redouble," said Chilcott.

What was the matter with Chilcott? Cassie hoped the flicker of anxiety she felt did not show. Doubled and redoubled? And a slam bid in a suit of which she had only a single card? Before she laid down her hand, she reviewed the bidding once more and was satisfied that she had bid impeccably.

Wickham opened play, leading the ♦Queen. Which probably indicated that it was the top of a sequence in an unbid suit. Chilcott took the trick with his ♦King. Needing to get to the table in order to make a ♠ finesse, he played his ♥2 and took it with the ♥A in Dummy's hand. Playing the ♠5, he tried for the finesse, but as soon as he laid down his ♠Queen, Cassie knew they would go down. Sure enough, Wickham covered the ♠Queen with the ♠King.

Wickham and Symington exchanged looks. No one said anything. Wickham glanced at the long string of Hearts in Dummy's hand, and, because his partner had played a ♥Jack in the last trick, led a small Heart himself, obviously in the hope that this signalled a void and Symington could now trump it. This Symington duly did, and Chilcott was now down two tricks. Cassie sensed the build-up of rage in him as Symington returned his partner's original lead and put down a Diamond, which Chilcott took with his ♦Ace. The rest of the tricks were his.

Two tricks down.

Cassie didn't even try to compute what this meant in terms

of losses, but she was sure that it would not be the money which bothered Chilcott.

As the last trick was played, Symington said, "Bad luck, Chilcott." The regret in his voice was perfunctory, masking glee.

"Should have stayed in Hearts, old boy," Wickham said. "Your partner was right. Made it clear she didn't have any support for your Spades."

"Why the *hell*," Chilcott said to Cassie, "didn't you take me out into No Trumps?"

"Because there were two unbid suits," said Cassie. "We obviously didn't have a fit."

"Anyway, why blame your partner?" said Wickham. "She'd already made it clear that she didn't like your suit."

"Quite," said the banker. It was up to you to bid No Trumps." He stared judiciously down at the cards.

"I'd have doubled that too," Wickham said.

"I think we could have made the contract if we'd stayed in Hearts,"** Cassie said, as non-confrontationally as possible. "Because of my singleton Spade."

"She's right," said Symington.

"You just got the wrong contract," said Wickham.

With a palpable effort, Chilcott forced himself to smile. "Which means I owe you some money," he said pleasantly. "So. How do I make it out? I've never written out a cheque to the nobility before."

A cold wind tore at the fringes of Cassie's silk shawl as she ran down the steps to the waiting Rolls. Rain fell dully from the darkness above their heads, hitting the ground with the plodding long-term sound of weather which does not intend to change in the foreseeable future. She was glad to lean back against the leather upholstery, kick off her shoes and close her eyes. The car was warm. At the end of the long drive, they passed between the gateposts and out on to the road; in a minute, when they'd got going, she would ask whether it might be possible for her to be dropped off at the cottage, explain that it would not be more than ten miles out of the way. They had gone about a mile and a half when Chilcott leaned forward and tapped the driver on the shoulder.

★

Chilcott

♠: A Q J 10 8 6 4

♥: 4 2

♦: A K

♣: A K

Symington

♠: 9 3 2

♥: J

♦: 9 7 6 5

♣: Q 10 9 4 2

Wickham

♠: K 7

♥: 6 5

♦: Q J 10 2

♣: J 8 7 5 3

Cassie

♠: 5

♥: A K Q 10 9 8 7 3

♦: 8 4 3

♣: 6

★★ To make 7♥, whatever Symington led, Cassie had an Ace to cover it. Having taken the first trick, she would play out her ♥ Trumps, dropping the singleton ♠5 so that when the ♠K appeared, she would be able to trump it.

With Trumps palyed out, she could then play the ♦A and ♦K, and ♣K (and/or ♣A), leaving only two ♦ in her hand. These would fall on good Spades from the table, leaving her with a clear run of Trumps.

"OK," he said. "Stop right here."

"Here, sir?" The driver sounded astonished. "But aren't you—"

"That's what I said: here," said Chilcott. He turned to Cassie. "And you, you fucking slut, can get out."

"What?" She was still smiling, expecting some ordinary remark. The sudden violence of his tone, hurled at her from the semi-darkness of the car, made her literally fall back against the seat.

"I said, get out."

"But it's raining."

"But it's raining," mimicked Chilcott in a high savage voice. "I don't give a dam if it's shitting Chinese noodles. Get out."

He was serious. Cassie scrambled for her bag while the driver tried to protest.

"But, sir, you can't—"

"Listen, sonny Jim, I'm paying for this fucking car, right?"

The driver said nothing, staring rigidly ahead.

"And I get to say who rides in it and who doesn't, right?"

Again the driver did not reply. Chilcott squeezed the man's shoulder. "Am I right, son? Or am I wrong?" He squeezed again, and this time the man twisted away.

"You're . . . you're right."

"*Sir.*"

"Sir."

"And I want this fucking useless cow out of here before she breathes any more of the air I'm paying your company for, or sits on the fucking seats which're costing me almost as much as she's lost me this evening, all right?"

Cassie, over by the door, attempted a protest. The metamorphosis of Chilcott's manner had been so sudden that she was still not entirely sure whether he was making some clumsy attempt at humour. "You can't seriously blame me for that last hand," she said. "We were in the wrong—"

"Shove it, slut," Chilcott said, and this time his voice was cold enough for her to realise without any difficulty at all that he was indeed serious, that he had every intention of dumping her out on a deserted country road in the middle of a stormy night without adequate clothing.

"You won't get away with this," she said. And knew, even as she uttered this theatrical piece of bravado, as her hand groped behind her for the door handle, that he would. Who would stop him? There was only the driver, and however humanitarian his instincts, he had his own livelihood to consider.

"I've had whores who cost less than you," Chilcott said, his voice now barely more than a mutter. "I've had *cars* which cost less than you. When I pay for something, I expect service, do you understand that? Do you? When I buy something expensive, I expect it to give good service. You call yourself professional—well, Miss Cassandra Swann, there's only one profession you're likely to be any good at and that's scrubbing floors in a fucking brothel."

"You're being quite rid—"

"Don't you tell me what I'm being, whore," Chilcott said. The tone of his voice suggested that only the presence of the driver prevented him from striking her, perhaps even beating her senseless.

"Mr. Chilcott," she began. "I really think—"

He slammed his hand down on the seat beside him with a noise like a starting-pistol. "Just get the fuck out of here," he shouted. "Get out! And don't think I shan't pass the word around about you and your so-called professionalism. Call yourself a bridge-player? Christ! I wouldn't hire you to play Snap with my pet monkey."

He reached into his dinner jacket and pulled out a wad of notes clamped together in a gold Dunhill holder. "Here," he said. "Just so you can't say I didn't"—he spoke the final phrase in a savage parody of Lord Wickham's cultured tones—"do the right thing, old girl." He peeled off some notes and, screwing them up, tossed them at Cassie. "Now. Get out."

Cassie got. It was pointless arguing about it. Standing in the middle of the black wet road, she watched the taillights of the Rolls grow smaller and fainter until finally they disappeared around some unseen bend.

♠ ♥ ♣ ♦

"No," said Cassie urgently. "Don't tell anyone I'm here. Just call a taxi, a hire car, whatever." She did not want Wickham and his cronies to see her in this state.

"But you're soaked." Jamie watched her anxiously, obviously wondering what it was best to do with her. "You ought to get those clothes off."

"And risk being found cavorting around Lord Wickham's hall in my underwear?"

"You wouldn't be the first."

"Just please call the cab," Cassie said. She sat down on an upright mahogany hall chair which stood to one side of the front door.

"I'll be back in a minute," Jamie said.

"Fine."Cassie leaned her head against the wall behind her and closed her eyes. God, she was tired. And *wet*! Although it was almost an hour since she and Chilcott had driven away from Halkam Court, voices could still be heard coming through the half-open door of the drawing-room, and snatches of conversation.

"—*obvious* I was asking for Aces . . ."

"—not an entirely disastrous evening . . ."

"—hospitality tent at Wimbledon this year?"

And, closer at hand, as though they stood just inside the door, the voices of Wickham and another man she could not identify.

"—prepared to believe a man is sound until proved otherwise."

"Not me, my dear Darcy—or should I call you Lloyd?" There was a guffaw of malicious amusement. "Quite the opposite, in fact. I've always found it good policy to believe a man unsound until proved otherwise. Safer in every way."

"Well, which is your friend Chilcott? Sound or unsound?"

"I'm still trying to find out. Though, after tonight . . ." The two drifted away, while at the same time a bell jangled loudly by Cassie's head. The front door. What was the etiquette here? Did she wait for the butler to do his job, although she herself was only inches away? In the end, given that it was such a dreadful night, she opened the door to let in Roderick Symington.

"Hello, again," he said, without any obvious surprise at seeing her. Rain had soaked into the shoulders of his navy topcoat and darkened his hair. He smiled briefly. "I can see they're still up—I left my briefcase behind, and since I've got an important meeting in the morning . . ." He moved towards the door of the drawing-room, nodding at Jamie who had now appeared from the kitchen quarters. "Don't bother. I can find my own way."

Cassie and Jamie watched as he went into the drawing-room, to a chorus of cries.

"Roddy, old boy!"

"Back for another rubber?"

"You've played with me before, Roddy. What *else* would I mean if I bid four Clubs?"

"Whisky, Roddy?" And Symington's refusal on the grounds that he had to drive back to London.

Jamie said apologetically to Cassie, "There's a bit of a problem."

"Oh?"

"I've tried three different places and either they haven't a car available or they aren't prepared to come out for you at this time of night."

"Not even for ready money?"

"What I suggest is, you come into the kitchen—there's a fire there—and as soon as they've all gone, I'll drive you back myself."

"That's incredibly nice of you, but I wouldn't dream of—"

"You could ask one of them." He jerked his head at the drawing-room door.

"I'd rather not."

"Then I don't see that you have much alternative."

But she did. Following him along a corridor floored with small black-and-white tiles and lined with ancient photographs of cricket teams, past sculleries and storerooms and pantries, into a big country kitchen, Cassie was already reaching into her bag for her address book. "I've just remembered," she said. "I've got a—a friend who doesn't live too far away. I'm sure he wouldn't mind."

She dialled the number from the telephone attached to the wall. After three rings, it was answered. "Yeah?"

"Mr. Quartermain?" She gritted her teeth. "Uh—Charlie?"

"Speakin'."

"It's Cassandra Swann here. I'm in a bit of a—"

"'Ullo, darlin'. What a surprise to hear from you."

"Isn't it, though?"

"What can I do for you, then?"

God. "I'm really sorry to have to bother you at such a late hour, but I wondered if you could possibly . . ." Cassie explained while Quartermain breathed noisily into the receiver. When she'd finished, he said, "Give me twenty minutes and I'll be there," and put down the telephone.

The kitchen was old-fashioned, Aga-ed, full of the kind of domestic paraphernalia which suggests the imminence of mob-caps and mangles. In one corner stood a walking-machine and some Nautilus equipment; in the other, a drum kit and some huge round discs made of blue plastic which Cassie finally identified as the kind of weights which you fix on to either end of a long steel tube and lie down on a padded bench and attempt to raise above your head. She presumed they belonged to Jamie rather than to any kitchen-maids there might be about. She looked around.

"Where's Tamsin?"

"I—I took her home," Jamie said. "I shouldn't really have left, but it's a shitty night and she only lives in Marsh, two or three miles from here. Besides, she gave up an evening of revision—she's got A Levels next term—so Darcy can't really object."

"Are you two—uh—walking out?"

"Definitely not," Jamie said with vehemence.

"She seemed rather keen on you," Cassie said.

"She is a bit. We—uh—got together when I first came here. That was before . . . Here . . ." Jamie handed Cassie a towel for her wet hair. He brought her a cup of tea and a brandy glass half full of armagnac, then sat down in the basket chair on the other side of the open wood-burning stove. "What happened?" he said. "The last I saw of you, you were heading off down the drive in a Rolls."

Again, Cassie explained, adding further detail this time, some of it less than flattering to Chilcott. Given the circumstances, discretion seemed misplaced.

"Interesting," said Jamie, when she had finished. He nodded a couple of times. "But not surprising. Darcy and his mates, particularly Symington, were behaving very badly all evening. No wonder Chilcott was in such a bate."

"It doesn't excuse him slinging me out into a blizzard."

"Of course not." Again Jamie nodded. "My mother will be delighted to hear of this. It'll confirm all her left-wing prejudices about the rich."

"How does your mother get into this?"

Jamie shrugged. "If you'd met her, you'd realise that she gets into everything. A formidable woman, and becoming more so, I fear. If not downright nuts."

"Look," Cassie said. "Either I've been reading the wrong kind of book, or you're a very unusual butler."

"A bit of both, I should think," Jamie said.

"You don't act like a butler ought to act."

"This is how butlers *are* these days. I'll have you know I spent a year at butler school before I came here. Anyway, I know about butlers; we had one at home."

Cassie clutched at her forehead. "I'm getting lost here. Are you telling me that despite your mother's socialist views, you had a butler?"

"The butler was my father's. It's because of him that my mother is so anti the Establishment. She's always banging on about abolishing the House of Lords and stuff like that, when what she really means is she'd like to abolish my father."

"I see."

"The thing is, I couldn't find any kind of congenial job when I came down from Cambridge and I'd always admired the way Saunders—our butler—had things organised. All the fun of living in one of the nicest houses in Scotland, and none of the responsibility—unlike poor old Dad. And it was all arranged that I was going to go round the world with my girlfriend, only at the last moment she was offered a job on a woman's magazine and decided it was too good a chance for her to miss. So I enrolled at this butler school."

"Is butling hard work?"

Jamie shrugged. "All the hard work's done by the house-keeper and the people who come in to clean. I just have to stand around looking pertinent, if you know what I mean. Count the spoons from time to time, check out the contents of the cellar. No problems there, since I did maths at university and also know a lot about wine. And Darcy's awfully good about letting me keep my car in the stables, and giving me time off for things like Henley and Glyndebourne. Not to mention all those tiresome balls one gets invited to in the Season."

"I don't believe this."

"It's true. Butlers are an endangered species, and it pays their employers to treat them well."

"I thought butlers were a species which knew its place. Which, as far as I understood it, definitely doesn't include Glyndebourne. *Or* Henley."

"You're looking at the new face of British democracy here, in case you didn't recognise it." Jamie removed his black jacket and draped it over a clothes-hanger on the back of the kitchen door. "Just as I'm the up-to-date version of the butler, so Darcy is the new breed of entrepreneurial aristocracy. He doesn't want to ponce about in ermine and strawberry leaves, any more than I do, nor waste time making speeches in the Lords about blood sports and fishing quotas."

"I thought that was why we had a second House, so that—"

"He wants to be out there in the real world, making money."

"The real world," Cassie said slowly. How real a world did either Darcy Wickham or his engaging butler occupy? And was it less real than, say, the smelly landings of HMP Belling-ton, or more?

She was too tired to take the question up with Jamie. And too wet. The sleeves of her dress chafed the tender skin of her armpits; her damp skirt clung uncomfortably to her thighs. As for the damage to her self-esteem . . . she'd have to deal with that later. "Jeeves would be spinning in his grave," she said lightly.

"Jeeves isn't dead," said Jamie. "He's just living in some golden Never-never land, eating fish and ironing newspapers while he waits eternally for the summons to knock up one of his hangover cures or rescue Bertie once again from Madeleine Bassett." He looked at his watch. "Uh-oh. Time to prepare Madame's tray." He went over to a door leading into a stone-shelved larder and brought out a large platter containing, among other things, quails' eggs, smoked salmon, asparagus, pieces of chicken breast, pastrami and tiny tomatoes.

"What's that?" Cassie immediately felt ravenous.

"Madame's evening snack."

"Madame being Lady Wickham."

"Portia. That's right. She's been to—uh—to a charity concert in London and she's always starving when she gets back. Says her brain needs constant sustenance or it withers and dies."

"I know exactly what she means. I'm the same."

The butler looked at Cassie. "I think you'd like her. You're the same sort."

"She sounds fun."

"She is," Jamie said fervently. "More than fun. She's absolutely . . . *won*derful."

5

There were builders downstairs, tearing the kitchen apart. Cassie lay in bed, listening to the destruction taking place. She'd been wanting to do over the kitchen for some time but until now had not been able to afford it. As far as she was aware, nothing had changed. So how come . . .

She raised herself on one elbow and listened more intently. Crash! Slam! Builders? It sounded more as though a visually challenged elephant had been let loose among the casseroles and jaunty mugs, the formica-fronted white-wood units and red enamel sink which had been the previous owner's idea of contemporary chic.

"An Aga," Robin had said, when he first saw it. "No genuine country cottage is complete without an Aga."

"Unless it belongs to genuine country cottagers," said Cassie.

"You have to make *some* concessions to the twentieth century, even in a rural hideaway," said Robin, plucking at the cobwebs which wreathed the windows. "My dear, didn't some literary predecessor of mine have his ties made out of these things?"

"You don't mean Robert the Bruce, do you?"

"He was more impressed by the weaver than the web. Anyway, he wasn't literary, as far as I recall." Robin paused gracefully, striking an attitude with outflung arm. "Yes. An Aga, definitely. An old pine dresser *here*. A scrubbed table instead of this hideous plastic-topped relic of the Fifties *here*. Lots of lovely spongeware and hand-thrown pottery about the place. Meadow grasses and cowslips in an old jam-jar on the windowsill—it'll be too *Cider With Rosie* for words."

In the event, Robin had moved off to France before anything more substantial than the removal of the cobwebs had been undertaken. So who had called in the builders?

Clutching her duvet round her, Cassie shuffled to the top of the narrow stairs which twisted up from a cupboard in the sitting-room. "Hello," she called. "Anyone there?"

Stupid question. Someone indubitably *was* there—and memory suddenly sprang back from the empty box in which she had placed it the night before as she crossed the bare planks between bathroom to bedroom and fell into the comforting nest of her electric-blanketed bed. But not before wedging, with considerable difficulty, a chair under the latch.

She hated herself. No question. On the other hand, in the short span of their acquaintance, Charlie Quartermain had consistently refused to take no for an answer and their conversation on the way home from Lloyd—sorry, *Lord*—Wickham's place the previous night had not given her any reason to suspect a recent conversion. He had been kind. Very kind. Over-bloody-whelmingly kind. He had handed her into his discreetly fancy car with the tenderness of a mother cat removing her new-laid kittens from the cardboard box in which they'd been born to the luxury of the airing-cupboard. Lap rugs had been wrapped round her. Brandy poured. Cushions placed behind her back.

Arrived at Cassie's cottage, he had even made an heroic attempt to lift her from car to house, despite every form of discouragement known to woman. After that, what choice did she have except to offer him a bed—not *her* bed, she'd made that forcefully clear—for the night? The only other bed, in fact, which the cottage boasted. In the room next to hers.

Once, around four, she woke and was sure the residue of a tentative rattle at the bedroom door hung in her ears. But nothing more happened and she drifted back to sleep, revelling in the warmth. Ejected from Chilcott's car, she had decided that Halkam Court was nearer than the village, but it had been a long trek back. A long wet *cold* trek. First there'd been the road, each passing car sending a fresh cascade of water over her. Then there'd been the sodden drive to negotiate in inky blackness. She had ruined an almost new pair of shoes. Her evening dress might recover, but there again it might not. The label said Dry Clean Only. It hadn't said anything about it not being suitable for wear in heavy rain. It hadn't needed to. As for her wrap, it had fallen off at some point and by then, with her hair hanging in dripping points around her face, up to the goosepimpled thighs in mud spatters, teeth chattering, arms gritty from the fall she had sustained by tripping over something just inside the gates, she had been too dispirited to go back for it, even though it had been a present from Robin.

Luckily, she had not been too dispirited to keep hold of the crumbled ball of notes Chilcott had flung at her at the moment of ejection from his car. There was enough there to cover any number of evening dresses—at least, at the prices Cassie could afford to pay—and evening sandals to go with them. She could hardly quibble. Well, she could quibble very strenuously, but she wasn't going to.

"Hello," she shouted again. "Mr. Quarterm—Charlie! What the hell are you doing?"

The door at the foot of the staircase was closed and he could obviously not hear her. She dragged downstairs, jerking at the duvet when it snagged on a hidden nail and feeling it tear. On the bottom step, she caught her foot in folds of 24-tog goose-down and burst through the door into her sitting-room, banging her head on the edge of the raised hearth and causing the maidenhair fern which had until then been rallying bravely to expire with shock.

Blast it. She trailed into the kitchen on a waft of inviting smells. Bacon, yes. Fried bread, almost certainly. Mushrooms, tomatoes and—was that really kidneys? The kitchen was in the kind of chaos Cassie could condone in herself but not in others. Quartermain stood at the red enamel sink holding two halves of a mug and doing what Cassie decided to be generous and call singing.

"Oh . . . can't get a man with a gun," he rumbled, setting the crockery tinging. He put the broken mug down on the ridged wooden draining-board. "With a gu-un, with a gu—"

"Charlie!" Cassie said.

He spun round. One hand flew to his massive chest. "Christ," he said. "What're you doing here?"

"I live here."

"I mean why've you come downstairs?"

"It sounded like they were doing a remake of *Calamity Jane* and I wanted to audition for Wild Bill Hickok."

He stared at her, big moon-face uncertain. Then he grinned. "Joke, right?"

"Charles, I'm deadly serious."

For a moment, his snaggle teeth played with his lower lip. Then he grinned, spreading his arms wide. "What do you think?"

"Doris Day did it better."

"I mean, about breakfast."

"In principle, do you mean? I'm all for it."

"Why don't you go back to bed?" Charlie said. "I'll be up in a moment."

"That's why I'm not going back to bed."

"With your breakfast, I mean."

Breakfast. The word had a comforting sound. An insidious let-me-take-care-of-things sound. She ought to resist, she knew that, but what the hell. "All right," she said.

"You can take this up with you, if you like." Charlie beamed as he handed her a newspaper.

"Where did you get this? I don't have one delivered."

"Went out and got it, didn't I? And everything else. You certainly don't keep much in your fridge, do you?"

"That's because I'm on a diet . . ." Cassie began. But there was something too intimate in this, something stealthily domestic, something she had to fight against. It was one of the reasons why she had turned down Giles Laughton's proposals of marriage. Coping with the trivia of daily living was bad enough one on one: scuffed heels, stray hairs, crumbs on the table, dirty knickers. To choose voluntarily to assimilate someone else's trivia as well, made about as much sense as booking into Norman Bates' motel. That—and the fact that she had realised that she was not sure if she really loved Giles. And if you weren't sure, that meant you didn't, right? Anyway, if she were to settle for domesticity, it certainly would not be with Charlie Quartermain. ". . . and I like it that way," she said, employing a considerable amount of hauteur.

She turned, sweepingly. Hauteur was difficult when you were wrapped in a duvet—so was sweeping—but as she clambered back up the narrow, now feather-strewn, stairs she figured she had pulled it off.

In bed again, she watched rain pelting against the windows. The tops of the trees at the end of the garden shook; the sky was dull and cold-coloured. She picked up the paper and read unenthusiastically about war in central Europe, political corruption in Italy, avalanches in Switzerland. In her father's pub there had been framed newspapers from yesteryear on the wall; she was sure she recalled one dated 21 April 1910 which had the exact same headlines. In the sidebars down the right-hand edge of the paper, she read that hunt saboteurs had been taken to hospital after a fracas involving a hunt in Shropshire, that a teenager had been remanded in custody following the rape of three women in Glasgow, that a woman had been found murdered at the home of Lord Wickham in Berkshire, that the DSS was issuing new guidelines following a spate of—

Just a minute. Woman found murdered at the home of Lord Wickham? What woman? She went through the paper again, but that was all the information there was. *What* woman? It was 8:59, according to her bedside clock, and she switched on the radio. After the pips, a female voice spoke in measured tones of the Bosnian crisis, the Italian crisis, the avalanche in Switzerland in which three Britons were now known to have died. She said nothing at all about women being murdered in

Berkshire, though, to be fair, neither did she mention Glasgow or Shropshire.

Once more Cassie got out of bed. From the back of the door she unhooked her towelling dressing-gown, an unflattering garment of cherry-red. She stomped down the stairs again and into the kitchen.

"Charlie," she said.

He was in the middle of pouring boiling water on to tea-leaves. He turned. At the sight of her, his expression softened. "Face like an angel," he said.

"Don't give me that angel crap," Cassie said. "Have you heard the local news this morning?"

"Yeah."

"What did it say?"

"Some crisis in Bos—"

"I'm not interested in avalanches and governmental corruption in Italy," said Cassie impatiently. "Did it mention a murder?"

"Murder?"

"Some woman. At Lord Wickham's place. Where I was last night. Did it mention someone being murdered?"

"As a matter of fact, it did." He turned back to the counter and carefully put the lid on the teapot.

"Did it say who she was?"

"Yeah."

"Who?"

He banged the heel of his palm against his temple. "Can't quite remember."

"Was it a woman called Melissa Something?"

He shook his big head. "Doesn't ring a bell."

"Or—" what the hell was Melissa's mother called? Had she ever known? "—um . . ."

"Hang on," Quartermain said, "Lady Pauline."

"What?"

"That's who it was. Lady Pauline Wickham."

"Not Portia?"

"Perhaps it was. Anyway, they found the poor old girl shot through the head lying in the middle of the drive."

"What time was this?"

"Dunno." He turned to look at her. "They're not able to say at this precise moment whether there was a sexual motive or not."

"How awful. How *awful*." Inexplicably, there was a lump in Cassie's throat and her eyebrows drew together as she tried ferociously not to cry.

"Why're you so upset, Cass? Did you know her or something?"

"No." Cassie shook her head. "Not really. Not at all."

Yet, in a way, she did. Had. She remembered looking up at that portrait in Wickham's library, thinking: there is someone I would like, someone whose wavelength would match my own, someone who obviously shares my feelings about the general bloodiness of things and at the same time, enjoys life to the full. There, in other words, is a kindred spirit.

She tried to do justice to the food Charlie brought up to her, but it didn't taste as good as it ought to have done. Quite apart from the massive cholesterol hit involved in eating a full English breakfast, he insisted on sitting on the edge of her bed, weighing down the mattress and off-puttingly watching every bite. He had put flowers on the tray, and even one on the plate, which touched her.

"I'm sorry," she said finally, putting down her knife and fork. "I can't manage all this. I'm trying to watch my figure and . . ."

"There you go," he said, leering at her.

"How do you mean?"

"I knew we had something in common."

"What?" She wanted to say they had not got a single thing in common, but it seemed a bit cavalier when the man had not only turned out the night before to drive her home but now was also bringing her breakfast in bed.

"I'm trying to watch your figure too," he said.

She cast her eyes to the ceiling and said nothing. Sexual innuendoes, for God's sake. At this hour of the day. She could go down the pub if she wanted that. Or into the nick.

Quartermain got up and took the tray. "It's a pig of a day," he said. "Why don't you stay where you are for a bit?"

"I'm terrifically grateful for all you've done," Cassie said, her consciousness of harbouring mean thoughts making her over-effusive. "Don't worry about the kitchen or anything. I'll do it later."

"That's all right."

"But haven't you got to get to work?" The thought of Quartermain in the cottage was not one which soothed or comforted.

"I'm the boss, remember?" he said. "I work when I want to."

"That's right." She *did* remember. He was a stonemason, a *master* mason, self-employed, a specialist in his field, in demand all over Europe by those concerned about the fabric of the sacred buildings in their charge. Cologne, Canterbury, Chartres, Rheims: places like that. Plus a host of smaller parish churches the length and breadth of England.

He walked to the door, his head almost brushing the low beamed ceiling. He looked at her, his face serious. "As sure as there's a God in heaven," he said, "one day I'll share that bed with you."

"No!" It came out like a shriek of pain. Talk about bloody nightmares . . . She wrestled for a moment with the duvet. "Look, would you *please*—"

"But only when you want me to, Cassie."

He went out of the door and shut it behind him, leaving her to shout, "Don't hang by your thumbs while you're waiting," to the walls. Had he heard? She thought so: she could hear the rumble of his laughter as he crashed down the stairs.

Around ten-thirty, she took a bath, making sure that the door was locked. She lay somnolent in the water, occasionally turning the hot tap with her toe when the temperature cooled. Her head hurt in an unlocalised sort of way, as though a cold lurked somewhere among the synapses, and her joints ached. Getting out of the bath, she wished she could go back to bed and sleep. She threw paracetamol down her throat, praying she would not have to do battle with Quartermain; for a while she thought he had gone, but every now and then she heard him moving about below.

Dressed in jeans and an Aran sweater, she went downstairs. The kitchen was relatively tidy, the tea-towel hung to dry over the edge of the sink. One of her plates lay on the draining board, in several pieces. Quartermain sat at the table with the white cat on his lap, reading the sporting pages of a tabloid newspaper and messily smoking a cigarette. A picture of domestic harmony. Which was perhaps why it enraged her. If Charlie Quartermain wanted domestic harmony, he could find it in someone else's house.

"What the hell do you think you're doing?" she yelled, deliberately breaking the tranquility of the scene.

The white cat leaped off Charlie's knee and slunk out of the back door. Charlie looked up at her and shook his head from side to side. "Gawd," he said. "You look a treat in that sweater."

She marched across the floor and snatched the cigarette from him. "I can't *stand* people smoking in my house," she said. "And you didn't even ask if it was all right."

"Sorry, luv. Didn't want to disturb you in the bath."

"And that *rag* you're reading," raged Cassie.

"What's wrong with it?"

"Quite apart from its illiterate format and cretinous editorial," Cassie said, "it's both sexist and racist."

"I don't buy it for its political views," Charlie said mildly. "I wanted to see yesterday's racing results."

"You do realise, don't you, that every time you buy a paper like that, you're reinforcing stereotypical attitudes towards women?"

"Am I?" Quartermain wheezed asthmatically and then coughed, scattering the ash which had collected in the ashtray beside him.

"Oh *God!*" Cassie knew she was being ridiculous, but could not help herself. "Look, I'm sorry, but I wish you'd just go. I don't feel well."

"Wrong time of the month, is it?"

Cassie leaned over him. She could feel her mouth working like some demented woman in a Ken Russell movie, but that didn't stop her. "If you ever *ever* say that to me again, I swear I will kill you," she said dangerously.

"You'd better go back to bed," he said. He attempted to put a large hand on her forehead but she evaded him. "Maybe you've got a temperature."

"Yes," she said. "I'd like to simply lock the doors and sleep some more." He opened his mouth to say something, but she forestalled him. "You've been so kind," she went on, choking back other more unflattering remarks. "But I really think it's best if you go."

"Whatever you say, darlin'." He lumbered to his feet without argument. "I'll give you a ring, shall I?"

"That would be lovely." Relief at getting rid of him comparatively easily made her fervent.

"Right." At the door, he turned and said: "You don't look too bright, now you mention it. Day in bed'd do you good."

"Yeah."

Back in bed, she opened the post. There was a letter from Robin, saying that his solicitor would be in touch with her shortly, since it appeared that they had at last received planning permission for the conversion of the outbuildings behind Honeysuckle Cottage. He also told her that he planned to be back in England in time for Henley, and would she like to go with him? If so, could he remind her that ladies' skirts had to be below the knee, or the stewards wouldn't let them in, and had she seen his Leander socks anywhere about—he rather thought they might be in the left-hand top drawer of the chest in the spare bedroom?

There was also a thick letter from the solicitor about the planning permission, containing pages of regulations, lists of rules with which the builders would have to comply, information about council grants, forms for her to countersign. She did not, however, feel able to give the papers the attention they needed, although she and her friend Natasha Sinclair had been waiting for months for the Council to allow them to use the outbuildings for commercial purposes. A bridge sundries business, to be precise. The idea had come to them as they partnered each other at a charity bridge tournament and heard one of the other women moaning about the impossibility of finding a decent bridge table.

"Nothing like combining pleasure with business," Natasha

had said when, driving home afterwards, Cassie had mooted the idea. "But we'll need premises of some kind."

"There's those old barns behind the cottage," Cassie said. "They're crying out for conversion."

"The Small Business Award," Natasha said thoughtfully.

"Businesswomen of the Year."

"Tycoons."

"Millionaires."

"Queen!"

"The possibilities are endless," Cassie said. "Let's just see whether we can persuade Robin to go along with it, and then whether we get planning permission."

That had been six months ago. Gaining Robin's approval had been the easiest part of what the two women began to see was a tortuous route towards tycoonery. Since then, they had had to contend with a small mountain of forms and papers, bureaucracy, red tape, council bylaws, health inspectors, safety inspectors, architects. At times, Cassie had been ready to give up, but Natasha had refused to lose faith. Formidable when on the trail of some new bridge-related product, she was already planning their first catalogue, even though they did not, as yet, even have a company name.

Now, at last, the permission to convert had come through. Cassie wished she could raise more enthusiasm.

Later, she listened to "The World at One," but there was no further news. Nor was there any on the bulletins at six or nine. By the time she went to bed that night, she knew very little more about the murder than what Quartermain had originally told her.

Lady Portia Wickham had been found lying beside the gravelled drive leading up to her own house. She had been shot. No weapon had yet been found. The police were saying very little beyond the fact that they were treating it as murder. A clever piece of deduction, that, given that it could hardly have been either suicide or an accident.

Part of Cassie's sense of outrage and shock at this murder of a woman she did not even know was due to the fact that she had been in or near that very same drive at more or less the same time. It might have been her. It might have been *her* corpse lying there with its face pillowed in the yellow mud of the drive, *her* blood seeping from a savage blow to the head, *her* hands which had scrabbled for some kind of hold in the soaking sand before death had finally overcome. One minute sooner, five minutes later, and she might not have escaped the same fate as Lady Wickham. Might even have been the substitute.

Once more she relived the walk up that drive. Had the murderer been there all the time, peering from behind one of the trees as she stumbled through the wet and windy night? She found she was deeply unsettled by the thought that she might have passed within feet of a man with a gun in his hand and murder on his mind. And then the remembrance of tripping over something in the drive kept intruding. My God. It couldn't have been Lady Wickham herself—an outflung arm, a sprawled leg—could it? Wouldn't she have realised? Again and again she went over that cold wet walk along the road, in at the gates, up the drive. She had heard nothing, no car, no screams, no footsteps, no shots. Only the wind in the trees, and the steady pour of the rain.

But perhaps it had happened some other way. Perhaps the murderer had followed Lady Wickham from London. Or perhaps he was her lover. Perhaps he had driven her back home and the two of them had quarrelled. Perhaps, in the heat of the argument, she had jumped out of the car and started walking while her enraged companion had seized a handy gun and shot her dead before driving back to London.

Or could it have been someone who had been there that evening? Someone who had calmly sat in the library playing bridge and then, knowing the time Lady Portia would be returning, had deliberately gone out in search of his prey?

Or perhaps it was . . .

Eventually she slept, but it was an uneasy sleep, from which she kept waking with panic in her heart. At 03:49, she woke again. It was still dark, but she could hear some bird whose timer had gone wrong already trying to herald in the dawn, though without much support from its fellows. She got out of bed and went into the bathroom, where her evening dress was still hanging. Steeling herself, she picked up the folds of the skirt and examined them. Mud, yes. Grit, yes. And something darker. Something which might be—she held the skirt to her face and sniffed at it. Blood was supposed to smell metallic, faintly sweet. This just smelled of earth and the remains of the Calèche with which she had sprayed herself before setting out.

But she knew already that she was going to have to call the police.

6

It was the following morning, and someone was knocking insistently on the front door of the cottage. While it would be an exaggeration to say the rafters shook, they certainly registered the effect. Standing naked on the floor of the bathroom, one foot already in the water, Cassie groaned. Strike one. Why was it that the minute she tried to get into a bath, people decided to call, either on the phone or in person? She had remedied the former problem by installing a cordless phone, but there was little she could do about the latter, short of bathing on the front doorstep.

As she was wrapping herself in a bath-sheet, she inadvertently caught sight of herself in the mirror. Oh, God. Strike two. She went downstairs and opened up.

"Dear, oh dear, oh dear," said the nearer of the two men standing on her doorstep. "Have we called at an inconvenient time, Miss—uh—Swann?"

"Absolutely not," said Cassie. "I never wear anything but towelling next to the skin."

"May we come in?" said the man.

"Is there a choice?"

"None at all."

"In that case . . ." Cassie stepped back and allowed them both to pass into the little sitting-room.

Mantripp and Walsh. Ah yes: she remembered them well. Since she had last seen Detective Inspector Mantripp, he had grown his hair longer and dyed it an unlikely shade of golden-brown. Either that, or he had allowed it to revert to its original colour. Whichever, it looked considerably less like road-kill than it used to. Behind him, Detective Sergeant Walsh winked in a friendly fashion.

"I thought that *real* policemen hardly ever worked together on more than one case," Cassie said. "Any more than they drive red Jaguars."

"Sharp, isn't she, Walsh?" said Mantripp.

"Needlelike, sir."

"What you see when you look at me and the Sergeant here is what I would call coincidence," Mantripp said, as though the word were one of his own devising.

"Serendipity," said Walsh, waggling his eyebrows at her. His eyes were an unusual colour, somewhere between brown and green.

"One of those few occasions you referred to, both of us happening to be on duty at the time the call about Lady Portia Wickham was logged in at the station. You *did* realise that was what we've come about, did you?"

"I suspected it might be," said Cassie. "I was actually just about to ring you."

"Oh, yes?"

The way he said it made Cassie immediately feel guilty of something. Anything. "I was there, you see," she added.

"That fact has been brought to our attention," Mantripp said heavily.

"By Lord Wickham, husband of the deceased," said Walsh. "He gave us the names of those who'd been playing bridge the night of his wife's demise and, of course, I recognised your name immediately."

"So did I," said Mantripp. He stared past her shoulder at the daily newspapers scattered all over the sofa, which Cassie had earlier driven to the village to buy.

The tabloids had dredged up Lady Portia's past: her former escorts, her marriage to one of the more eligible bachelors-about-town of the day, her charity work, a snap of her on holiday generously filling a swimsuit, a more recent picture of her with her husband at a society wedding. She had been the daughter of a Texan millionaire, and heiress to a considerable fortune. Her marriage to Wickham had produced no children. The more sober papers had added little to the portrait of the woman but were more specific about the murder. It appeared she had been shot twice with a Baby Browning .22 automatic. The first bullet had pierced her abdomen, the second had gone through her head, killing her instantly. Both shots had been fired from behind. The body had been left where it fell. No attempt at concealment had been made, nor had any murder weapon been found.

"No doubt in time you would have contacted us," Walsh said.

"Of course I would. I just said so, didn't I?"

Mantripp spoke. "Funny, though, wouldn't you say, Walsh?"

"What's that, sir?"

"The way Miss—uh—Swann seems to make a habit of being on the spot."

"Hardly a habit, sir," said Walsh. Which was exactly what Cassie had been going to point out.

"It was bridge-playing last time, wasn't it? And, if memory serves, bridge-playing is involved this time, too, isn't it?" Mantripp meshed the wrinkles on his forehead about in quizzical fashion.

"Marginally," Walsh said.

"And only," said Cassie, "if you think I'm involved too. Otherwise, it's entirely irrelevant."

"Sounds like bridge is one of those games which ought to carry a government health warning," said the Detective Inspector, clearly with jocular intent.

"Like Russian roulette, do you mean?" asked Cassie.

"Perhaps we could sit down." Walsh stepped forward and cleared away the newspapers into a pile. "Sir?" He smiled at Cassie as he straightened up, and she realised not only that she was still swathed in a bath-sheet, with nothing on underneath, but also that his mouth was beautifully shaped.

"Thank you, Walsh. All we need now is a cup of coffee and perhaps a digestive biscuit or two . . ." Mantripp gazed hopefully at Cassie, who sighed elaborately and made for the kitchen.

". . . and I have a horrible feeling that I might have tripped over her—or, at least, over her arm, or something," Cassie finished. It was more than a mere feeling. She had thought of little else since learning about Lady Wickham's murder: the more she reconstructed that fifty minutes or so between eviction from Chilcott's car and lifting the knocker of Lord Wickham's door, the more convinced she was that she had indeed fallen over the dead woman's body.

"The timing certainly fits in with the PM report," said Walsh.

"She can't have been dead more than half an hour by the time you came across her," said Mantripp. And seeing her expression, added hastily, "in a manner of speaking."

"Certainly narrows down the time, sir," said Walsh.

"That's right. The chap might even have still been hanging about," Mantripp said thoughtfully.

"Wouldn't he have already gone?" said Cassie. "Perhaps in one of those cars which passed me on the road."

"Did you notice anything particular about any of them?" Walsh said.

"Not a thing."

"Nothing at all?"

"It was pouring with rain," said Cassie. "I was freezing to death. One of my shoes fell into the ditch at the side of the road and I spent ages feeling around for it in the dark. Every passing car sent a wave of water over me. I wasn't even registering types of vehicle, let alone individual number-plates."

"Types?"

"I mean, whether it was a—a pantechnicon or a Passat."

Mantripp leaned keenly forward. "Are you saying that a removal van, or something similar, passed you?" He stared meaningfully at Walsh.

"Only that if it had, I wouldn't have noticed."

"What about motorcycles?" asked Walsh. He looked over at his superior. "It's the vehicle of choice for hitmen these days."

"Hitmen?" said Cassie. "You're not suggesting that Lady Wickham was—was assassinated, are you?"

"We're not saying anything at the moment." Mantripp tapped his teeth for a moment. "*Did* a motorbike pass you on the road, Miss—uh—Swann?"

"I'm trying to remember," Cassie said. Now that it had come up, she rather thought one had. It had all been so miserable, stumbling along with the bright lights of oncoming cars blinding her and the wash from their tyres soaking her. But yes, she thought a motorbike had screamed by.

"Two shots, sir?" Walsh said. "A professional wouldn't need more than one."

"Even on a dark night? With the victim wearing dark clothes?"

"He'd have been expecting her, sir. Waiting for her. She doesn't know he's there. One shot, and he's away, with anyone who heard it thinking it's a backfire or something. Two shots, and people might start asking themselves what that noise was, maybe even investigating."

Mantripp was reluctant to let go the idea of a hit, but relinquished it in the end. For a while the three of them discussed other possibilities, but since it was all speculation, in terms of extracting nuggets of information this was clearly not a rich seam.

They went through the evening with her again, and yet again, but she could add nothing. As they stood to leave, Mantripp said, "One other thing. We recovered a sort of scarf thing lying not far from the body."

"More of a wrap," said Walsh. "Oldish, but obviously expensive. French make, black moire lined with green taffeta."

"Yes, well," Mantripp said. "I'm sure Miss Swann doesn't

need detailed fashion notes." He looked at Cassie. "Did you happen to notice it on your walk up to the house?"

"You're making it sound as though I was out for an evening stroll," Cassie said. "I don't think you understand what conditions were like out there."

"Tough, was it?" said Walsh. He clicked open a briefcase and brought out a plastic bag which he passed to Mantripp.

"It was hell," said Cassie. "I mean, we're talking Scott of the Antarctic."

"Lord Wickham says this scarf—or wrap—most definitely did not belong to his wife," said Mantripp. He waved the plastic bag about in front of Cassie. "We're hoping it might be a clue to her killer."

Cassie wondered how. Murderers weren't usually in the habit of wearing evening stoles, were they? Even if they were women.

"Now," Mantripp said. "Think very carefully: have you seen it before? Did you see it on the evening in question?"

Cassie looked. "Yes."

"Was someone wearing it that evening?"

"Yes."

For a moment, Mantripp stared at her with the delight of a man who has caught a moving bus without having to run for it. "Do you remember who?"

"I was."

His face crumpled. "*You* were?"

"Yes. It fell off while I was struggling up the drive, and by then I was so exhausted, and so wet, as well as it being pitch black, that I couldn't be bothered to go back for it."

"You mean it's yours?"

"I'm afraid so."

Mantripp clicked his tongue. "Damn." He frowned at her as though wondering whether he ought to charge her with wasting police time.

Detective Sergeant Walsh picked up her plastic-bagged evening dress which earlier she had brought down for them to examine. He draped it over one arm, like someone who has just been to the dry-cleaners.

"You'll be careful with that, won't you?" Cassie said. "It's the only one I've got."

"Don't worry," said Walsh. "I've got a long one myself." He moved his eyebrows about meaningfully.

"*What* did you say?"

"Or my wife has. *Had*." Walsh patted the plastic wrap. "I'll look after this as though it were my own." He stared deliberately at her.

"I don't find that entirely reassuring," Cassie said. His mouth was disconcertingly attractive. It seemed unseemly, somehow; policemen ought to be physically inconspicuous.

Opening the door and stooping as he went through, Mantripp said, "We'll be in touch as soon as we've carried out forensic tests."

"Good."

Or was it? Watching their car back out into the lane, Cassie knew she really did not wish to learn that the hem of her dress was stained with Portia Wickham's blood.

At midday, a florist's van pulled up outside the gate. A girl got out and delivered an elaborate bouquet of red and pink roses mixed with asparagus fern and gypsophila. There was a card attached.

I behaved abominably the other night, it read. *There was no excuse for it. Put it down to stress and overwork. In the hope that we can play together again some time soon, please try to forgive me.*

It was signed by Royston Chilcott.

Cassie studied the roses. They were undoubtedly beautiful. Her instinct was to chuck them onto the compost heap, but was it their fault that they had been chosen by such a bastard? In the end she compromised by setting the flowers in a vase and tearing the card into several pieces before throwing it into the garbage.

Was she being financially foolish in rejecting Chilcott's overtures? She thought not. Besides, during a lull in play the previous evening, Jeremy Marling had asked whether he could ring her sometime, since his wife did not play bridge and he was often in need of a partner. Marling instead of Chilcott? It seemed a fair exchange.

At five-thirty, she got into her car and backed down the grassy track to the lane. It had been warmer today, the rain had died away during the night, and by mid-afternoon the sun had begun to emerge. Pausing by the hedge which ran in front of the cottage and its small front lawn, she smelled mock-orange, even though it was too early for it to be in bloom. Although she was not a country-lover at heart, rural living undoubtedly had its compensations. Honeysuckle Cottage looked idyllic in the golden light of early evening, the garden peaceful. The thatch above the little porch had deteriorated badly over the winter and if rain flooded the porch, that meant water seeping into the sitting-room under the door. She had booked Mike the Thatcher as long ago as February of last year and she hoped he would manage to get to it before the cold weather returned. She was none too optimistic: thatchers were a busy breed of men, with more calls on their time and skill than they could decently handle, and Mike was in particular demand because of the high quality of his workmanship.

As she passed Moreteyne Woods, she glanced sideways. The tree trunks glowed in the late sunshine, the damp of the previous days meant that moisture rising from the leaf-carpet underfoot had thickened the air so that the bars of light between the trees seemed almost solid. Nonetheless, through them, she thought she saw a figure running, bent over, keeping low to the ground. Was it a deer? Or merely an absconding delinquent lad? And ought she to do anything about it? She glanced at her watch. She decided to leave it. She was supposed to be at the prison in thirteen minutes and had just about enough time to get there for seven o'clock. Besides, boys were always running away from the Hall; nine times out of ten they were found and brought back, often from their Gran's house, seldom from their parents'.

Passing the rubbish-strewn recreation ground in Frith, she slowed down. Beer bottles, fish-and-chip wrappings, enough polystyrene fast-food trays to keep McDonald's happy for a year: somehow litter looked less obtrusive on urban territory than it did here, under the chestnut trees which stood around two sides of the grass, with the blue Cotswold hills fading into darkness beyond. Close to her, three leather-jacketed sub-adolescents, having wound all the swings round and round the support posts so they could not be used by the children until someone unwound them, were now busy kicking to pieces the bench by the bus-stop. Behind them, the long rocking-horse had also been rendered unusable, its tail jacked up so high that its head almost touched the ground. Although she was pressed for time, she braked. Leaving her engine idling, she wound down the window and watched them. Finally one of them said rudely, "What's your problem?"

"My problem," said Cassie, "is that I can't decide whether to let you go on doing that, or whether to get out of my car and beat you forcefully round the head and shoulders."

"Yer," jeered the largest of them. "You and whose army?" He tossed his empty drink can over his shoulder in a manner intended to cause offence.

"On the other hand," Cassie continued. "I could try the voice of reason."

"You what?"

"Something that I suspect is going to be entirely new to you. For instance, you, Jason. Your mum has to go into the hospital every Friday about her leg, doesn't she?"

"So?" said Jason.

"And you, Sean, isn't your sister pregnant again?"

"What's it got to do with you?"

"Nothing at all. I'm just glad it's them and not me who has to stand here waiting for the Bellington bus to arrive, with a bad leg, or trying to control two toddlers, instead of being able to sit down in relative comfort, just because someone's destroyed the bench. Especially as that bus is often late."

They looked at each other.

"Think about it," said Cassie. She drove on.

Two years ago, she had been forced by economic circumstances to take a term's supply teaching at the comprehensive in Bellington. Twelve weeks from hell, in anybody's book. But she had at least gained a working knowledge of most of the local kids from the experience. Even if Jason and Sean and Mikey, their friend, didn't know her, she knew them.

Thursday evenings was debate night at the prison. This meant that a selected group of the men were gathered together under the eye of the Class Officer and allowed to dazzle each other with reasoned argument for or against motions dreamed up by the Education Officer. This House Deplores the Poll Tax had been a favourite for some time. So had This House Would Bring Back Hanging (it always surprised Cassie that this motion was regularly carried), This House Believes in National Service and This House Would Fight for Queen and Country.

Fat chance.

Cassie was sitting in for the Education Officer, who had to attend a symposium in Oxford that evening. Tonight, the subject under discussion was the abolition of the speed limit. Debate was spirited. Most of the men saw their cars as extensions of their dicks. The suggestion that limits should be placed on the use of either was anathema to them. The proposers had already put their case. Now Sebastian Haslam-Jones, the bent barrister, and Kip Naughton were gamely winding up their argument for the retention, even the further lowering, of the current restrictions, to a chorus of groans and whistles from their audience.

"And so, gentlemen—and lady," purred Sebastian. "I know you all share my conviction—"

"Thought you was still on appeal," someone said audibly under his breath.

"—share my conviction that the motor car is, in the familiar words of Virgil—"

"Is he the bloke got the china stall in Portobello Market?"

"the *motor*-car," said Sebastian, unruffled, "is *monstrum horrendum, informe, ingens, cui lumen adeptum*." He spoke with a fearful rolling of both eyes and "r"s, clutching the lapel of his prison-issue jacket as though back in court. "A monster, gentlemen, fearful and hideous, vast and eyeless. A danger to us all, as my distinguished colleague, Kipper Naughton, has so movingly described. And the faster it is allowed to travel, the more dangerous it becomes. I trust, therefore, that you will take the only intelligent course open to you and defeat this motion out of hand."

They didn't, of course. The motion comprehensively won by seventeen votes to four. After that, the men were free to talk among themselves while tea was served from a big urn. Cassie, waiting while Kipper brought her a thick white cup of ginger brew, pondered the conservatism of the average con. They were all for privilege, all in favour of the public school system, all loyal to the Royal Family. Sebastian Haslam-Jones had once explained this to her, saying that most of them made their living out of the first, would send their children to the second if they could afford to, and revered the third because it gave them something to look down on.

"I jest, of course," he had added. "About the third, I mean. The criminal mind is uncurably sentimental, and the Queen, God Bless Her, stands for all the stability most of them have never known, while at the same time representing the most enduring aspects of the country they themselves have done so much to destroy."

"An interesting proposition."

"But specious," Sebastian had said, shaking his head. "Very specious."

Kipper came back and sat down beside her.

"Frank lost his appeal, I presume," Cassie said.

" 'Fraid so. He's been ghosted—they moved him out to Lincoln the very same day," Kip said. He supped noisily from his cup.

"What about John Burslake?"

Kipper looked vaguely round. "Oh yer. He's gone, too. Think he went to Durham."

"Durham." The prison he particularly did not want to be moved to. "He's been sentenced, then?"

"Yeah."

"How long did he get?"

"Dunno, dear."

"I thought you spoke very well tonight," said Cassie. "Was it true?"

"What, about my little girl?"

"Yes."

"Word of a lie," said Kipper. "Straight up. I was standing right there when it happened. Bleeding great Ford or something, came down the road like it was trying to win the Grand National. Didn't stop or nothing. Really cut me up, that did. She was all I had, ever since the wife pissed off with one of me mates."

"The same thing happened to a girl in my class at school," said Cassie. "I was only nine at the time, but I'll never forget it."

"My Tessie was ten." He turned away from her as though to hide any emotion he had not been quick enough to conceal. In the nick, it was best to keep your weak points to yourself, if you could. "Never mind, eh? That Sebastian's really something, isn't he? All them bits of Latin."

"Where was it that your daughter was killed?" said Cassie.

" 'As I'm sure you are all aware, gentlemen,' " said Kip, in a very passable imitation of Haslam-Jones at his most orotund. He stopped. "Pardon?"

"I said, whereabouts was it your daughter was killed."

"Outside her school, like I said."

"Where was the school?"

He looked at her sadly. "Water under the bridge, luv. It doesn't matter now."

"But I want to know."

"If you're really interested, it was in Upper Street."

"Do you mean in Islington?"

" 'Course."

"It wasn't by any chance the William Tyndale School, was it?"

"Yer."

"I don't believe this," Cassie said. "Is Kipper your real name?"

"Yes," he said.

"You mean you were actually christen—" She stopped. These days, it was not safe to assume anything about anybody: for all she knew, Kipper had been raised as a Muslim and would take mortal offence at any suggestion of alternative faiths. "The name Kipper appears on your birth certificate, does it?"

"Matter of fact, I *was* christened. Keen on that sort of thing, my mum was. Cartwright, they called me. Arfur Cartwright."

No point asking why, in that case, he now went by the name Naughton. Cassie drew in a long breath. "Was your little girl called Teresa?"

He reared away from her. "You been looking at my file?"

"You know as well as I do I'm not allowed to do that."

"How come you know about Tessie, then?"

"Because I was at the same school myself. I was there when she was run over. I was in her class. We all went to the funeral."

"Gordon Bennett," said Kipper. "You knew my Tessie?"

"Yes."

"It's a bloody small world, innit? Fancy you knowing my little Tessie." He rubbed a hand over his forehead. "What was your name, then?"

"Same as now. Cassandra Swann."

"With two 'n's?"

"That's right."

"Hang about. Your dad wasn't Harry Swann, was he? Big chap, ran the Boilermakers'?"

"Yes. Did you know him?"

"Did I know Handsome Harry Swann? I'll say I did."

Someone squeezed into the space between them. "Evening, Cass," he said. "You aren't trying to avoid me, are you?"

"Of course not, Steve."

"'Cos I'd take a dim view of that. A very dim view."

"Leave it out, Steve," Kipper said. "Can't you see we was having a private chat?"

"I could indeed. I'd like a private chat myself," said Steve. "Got quite a lot of things to chat to Cass about in private."

Cassie gave him her best touch-me-and-you're-dead stare. Were she to show the slightest indication that she found him in any way threatening, she sensed that she would have surrendered something of herself it was vital to retain. The inimicality of his close-cropped hair and expressionless grey gaze, held deliberately overlong, was only an exterior manifestation of an inner hatred, not just of her in particular but women in general. She wondered, not for the first time, exactly what ugly emotional deprivation had turned him into this social time-bomb. Because, like other staff in the prison, she was convinced that one day Steve and his knife would inflict a wound on a woman which all the stitching in the world would not be able to mend. She knew, too, that until he did, there was nothing at all anyone could do about it.

Kipper's mention of her father set off a train of melancholy thought that lasted all the way back to her cottage. At her age—another eight years and she would be facing forty—she ought to be her own woman, with the traumas of adolescence behind her. Yet she could not help wondering how different a person she would be if she had not suffered her own particular dichotomous upbringing. Thirteen years in the flat above the pub, at first with the mother she could barely remember, then with Dad and Gran until first Dad, then Gran, had died. After that, the culture shock of being removed from the hum of the Holloway Road to the rural peace of Uncle Sam's vicarage. She had not wanted to go. She had thought of running away, of trying to live on the streets, of dropping down from the platform at Highbury tube station just as a train bulleted in. In the end she had no choice but to get into Uncle Sam's car and drive away from London to live with the cousins she scarcely knew. They had been painful years, years she was still trying to survive. Sometimes, only the thought of Gran had pulled her through. The tug of different values, working-class on the one hand, middle-class on the other, was one which even now she had not yet fully resolved.

Her best dress. Why should she think of that now? Gran had taken her up West to buy it and they'd found something in C & A. Gran had loved it. "You look a real treat in that," she said. "A real treat."

When Cassie pulled it out of the plastic carrier bag in which she had packed her few possessions, Aunt Polly had fingered it with a hateful expression on her face which made Cassie want to be able to put her arms round Gran again and cry.

"But it's made of polyester," her aunt had said.

"What's wrong with it?" Cassie had demanded belligerently. "My Gran says you can't tell the difference from silk."

"We say grandmother, Cassandra, not Gran."

"I don't." Cassie stuck out her lower lip.

Aunt Polly ignored that. "And you should remember that ladies don't wear manmade fabrics."

"Why're you wearing them nylons, then?" Cassie had said rudely.

"We're really going to have to work on your grammar," her aunt had said coldly, and left the room. Cassie had defiantly worn the dress on every possible occasion, suitable and unsuitable, even after she had grown out of it. Her aunt did not comment on it again.

She drove home the long way round, past the entrance to Lord Wickham's house. There were cars parked along the grass verges of the road, and groups of men stood smoking in the darkness, chatting together. The Fourth Estate? The police? The gates stood wide open and she thought she could see the dim glow of lights between the trees. Had Lady Portia seen them, too, in the minutes prior to her death? Had she hurried through the rain towards the sanctuary of home, full of pleasurable anticipation? Or had she run, staring over her shoulder, stumbling and gasping, knowing that her killer stalked her? Thinking about it, Cassie wondered why she should have been doing either. Surely, given the weather, she would have either driven—or been driven—right up to the front door, not dropped at the gate. Unless it had happened as she had theorised: the quarrel, the slamming out of the car, the walk through the rain.

But how could her killer have known? If he had been expecting her, he would have waited much nearer the house. Or had he, hearing angry voices, the car door slamming, the screech of tyres as the driver turned and headed back to London, run silently along the grass to meet Portia and done the deed when he reached her? But, given the noise of the wind, it seemed unlikely he would have heard a thing if he'd been by the house.

Cassie wondered what, in the minutes before the bullets smashed into her body, Portia Wickham had been thinking about. Love, money, food, sex? Violent death leaves the victim no time to prepare for life's greatest mystery, no time to adopt a suitably earnest mind-set. To be precipitated into the great beyond with nothing more memorable occupying your thoughts than whether the bath water would still be hot, or wondering if the seafood you'd eaten at lunchtime could be causing the uneasiness in your bowels was surely unsatisfactory. Everyone had the right to reflect, to come to terms with themselves. Few who died by the hand of another were afforded that right.

Certainly not Harry Swann, her father, brought down in front of his pub by the blade which had pierced his heart. There had been some sort of street fight involving an attack on a policewoman; he had stepped out to try and stop it; someone had thrust at him with a knife and that single blow had killed him. The next morning his blood had still been on the pavement, a dried dark line of it leading into the gutter. Blood, and flowers. Lots of flowers, laid there by the locals during the night. She remembered Gran weeping in her bedroom, the harsh sound filling the pub like a bad smell. She remembered her own crippling sense of loss.

Nobody had ever stood trial for his murder; it was far too late now to imagine that anyone ever would. The death of Handsome Harry Swann, who had won the heart of Sarah, the vicar's sister, the judge's daughter, was the result of just another pub brawl, to be shunted into the pending file and forgotten about.

Turning into Back Lane, she drove a hundred yards or so, then pulled off the road on to the grassy track in front of her lean-to shed-cum-garage, and parked. The white cat glimmered on the front doorstep, under the loosening thatch, as she walked around the side of the cottage. The heady scent of incipient summer filled the air. There was no sound except, far away, the faint grind of the last bus from Bellington changing gear as it took the hill from Frith down to Market Broughton.

For a moment she stood there, remembering the bustle of north London on a Friday night, the heat of summer pavements, the litter and noise, the way the dust got into your nose, the orange glow from the sodium lights. It would be easy to cry, to rail, to demand that things be different. But, as Kipper Naughton had said, it was water under the bridge. *Blood* under the bridge. Not just Harry Swann's blood, but Tessie Cartwright's as well. Vividly she remembered staring at the spot on Upper Street, the piece of tarmac where it had happened, forcing herself to imagine Tessie lying there, thinking: *that's where Tessie died*, overcome by the magnitude of death, the oily tarmac taking on a new awesomeness. And the funeral, the white coffin up at the front of the church, unaccustomed adult sobs, the hymns. Standing in the dark of a Cotswold garden, time melted in her mind like a candle as she considered the fact that her path and Kipper's must have crossed long before she had met him in Bellington Prison.

Steve's interruption had prevented her from asking more. It was the first time that anyone had ever spoken of her father's death in front of her, the first time she had met anyone who had known him, other than Uncle Sam and Aunt Polly. And Robin, of course. She was conscious of need growing in her, like an encysted seed suddenly watered. At her next bridge class in the prison, maybe she would have a chance to talk to Kip again.

Inside the cottage, the telephone began to ring and she ran towards the sound it was always so difficult to ignore. Picking up, she heard someone say her name.

"Yes," she said. "It's Cassandra Swann."

"Cassie, it's Lionel Hand." The name was familiar, but out of context she couldn't place it. "The Chaplain at the prison," Hand supplied.

"Of course."

"I'd have told you earlier, only not being there this evening . . ."

"Yes?"

"I thought you should be told, Cassie, since you took such an interest, about John Burslake."

She felt dread, knowing already that she did not want to hear this. "What about him?"

"I'm afraid he—" Hand cleared his throat. "—well, he received a six-year sentence yesterday."

"Six *years*? That's a bit stiff, isn't it?"

"The judge said he wanted to make an example of him, that the drug traffic was eroding the fabric of society, destroying family values—you know how it goes. I'm not sure he didn't have a son who got hooked on heroin at university, which might explain it. They transferred John to Durham this morning."

"So I heard. So what happened?"

"On the way up there, he managed to break free while they were filling up the van at a petrol station. Ran straight on to the motorway and was hit by a TIR lorry. The driver had no chance whatsoever to avoid him." Hand sighed. "A tragic accident. Really tragic."

Strike three. It had been that sort of a day. "It wasn't an accident, it was suicide," Cassie sad flatly. "If not murder." She put down the phone.

"I'm going to buy a house," Giles said.

"Why?" asked Cassie.

"Why the hell do you think? To live in, of course."

"I thought you were perfectly happy with your mother."

"Does perfect happiness exist?" Giles stared gloomily into his pint of Ruddles.

"Possibly." As a matter of fact, Cassie felt pretty happy right then, in the Private Bar of the Old Plough in Market Broughton, with the gas-logs of the fire burning a heatless blue and the sound of darts-players, the click of snooker balls, coming in from the Public Bar. Not to mention the fact that she was with Giles.

"Anyway, you know I'm as miserable as sin living with my mother," Giles said. "Almost as miserable as she is having me there. So," he shifted his gaze to look at her. "How do you feel?"

"What about?"

Giles pulled his glass towards him with such ferocity that a wave of beer slopped over the edge and on to his brown corduroys. "God!" he exploded. "You can't rely on anything these days, not even the bloody beer."

"Force of gravity doesn't change much," Cassie said, moving her knees as beer slid towards her across the table and began to drip on to the floor.

Giles swiped crossly at his trousers and nodded at Cassie's glass. "Can I get you another?"

"I'll buy," she said. Two small dogs with bulbous eyes appeared from behind the bar counter, and after sniffing at the spilled beer, stood beside her seat and stared at her accusingly. They reminded her very much of her cousins Primula and Hyacinth. "It's my turn."

Around them, the locals squared up to their pints, men for the most part, with no more than a sprinkling of women. The men tended towards stolidity, farmer-types with Barbours and squashy tweed hats lying across the chairs beside them. The women were all unnatural blondes and nervously thin. Perched on a bar stool was the statutory Character who comes with the fixtures and fittings of any rural pub, a vast shapeless woman with a red face and the kind of round tortoiseshell specs you only saw these days in old newsreels.

If you were looking for any kind of action other than the lifting of elbows, this was not the place to come. Cassie liked it mainly because it had not been tarted up. There were no collections of ancient ploughshares on the walls, no pictures of anthropomorphic cats pissing against lampposts, no pseud mirrors painted with advertisements for long dead breweries. The loos were labelled WC, none of this Fillies and Colts nonsense; it might make for occasional confusion but at least you knew where you were, even if it was not always where you intended to be.

With a fresh pint in front of him, Giles said, "What do you think, then?"

"About what?"

"About this bloody *house* for Pete's sake."

"It's difficult to have much of an opinion when I haven't seen the place, isn't it?"

Giles stared at her as though she had just thrust a bandaged stump in his face and informed him that she had leprosy. "I didn't say I'd *bought* it," he said finally. "Just that I was *going* to buy it. Obviously I'm not going to choose a house without you."

"Why on earth not?" Cassie's heart sank. She sensed a proposal coming on.

"For Christ's sake, Cass. Can't you bloody see that I'm asking you to marry me?"

She was right. "Actually, no, I can't," she said. "And anyway, you did that the other day. The answer's still the same."

There was a silence during which Giles stared into the gaslogs, sighed deeply, frowned, dragged one hand hard across his forehead, shuddered, and drank most of his pint. He said, "I thought you might have changed your mind."

"Not yet."

He looked hopeful. "But maybe some—"

"If ever," Cassie added quickly. "I told you I need to think about it."

"That means bloody no, doesn't it?"

"Not necessarily."

"Not that I can blame you." One of the dogs stood on his hind legs and put both its front paws on Giles' knee. Gently, he brushed a finger over one of the silky brown ears. "No woman in her right mind wants a man who's still living with his mother at the age of thirty-five." Clumps of red hair stood up on his crown. Cassie thought it looked cute. Very endearing. As, indeed, she found the man himself. But marriage?

"It's just . . . I'm not sure I want to get married again," she said. "Last time, it didn't work out too well. I really need to think about whether I want to get involved again." She didn't though. She knew perfectly well that involvement was the last thing she wanted. What she was less sure about was whether that was because Giles wasn't the right man, or because she herself was frightened of commitment.

There was a burst of cheering from the Public Bar, followed by the kind of bucolic banter which prompts American philologists to produce seminal works on Language and the Working Man.

The door opened and two men came in.

"I'll get them," one of them said. "What'll you have?"

"Whisky," said the second. "Double, please, Peter." They stood at the bar, backs to the room. One of them murmured something and they both laughed.

Cassie watched as they carried their drinks over to a table in the corner and sat down. The one called Peter brought out a pocket calculator and the two bent over it, heads close together, while he tapped in numbers.

She touched Giles on the arm. "Tell me," she said. "Just supposing we *were* married, and then I was killed, would you be in the pub a week later, ordering double whiskies?"

"Christ, no," Giles said violently. "I'd probably have topped myself." He thought about it. "Unless I was trying to drown my sorrows, of course."

"Wouldn't you tend to drown them in the privacy of your own home?"

"I suppose I would."

"Me, too."

Cassie watched the two men. Any sorrow-drowning going on was being kept well hidden. Wickham's body-language did not suggest a man receiving help from his bereavement counsellor. From here, it looked much more as though the two were checking balance sheets. There were all sorts of reasons why Darcy Wickham should be in the Old Plough with a pocket calculator and a man called Peter, instead of at home mourning his wife. Nor were the two activities necessarily mutually exclusive. It was, however, marginally strange, wasn't it? Marginally callous? Maybe she should give Jamie, the butler, a ring and check out the state of the Wickham marriage. Though even if she found that Darcy and Portia hated each other's guts and had done so for years, what would it prove? Wickham certainly could not literally have murdered his wife, since he had still been entertaining his bridge party in the drawing-room at the time Portia must have been struck down. Idly, Cassie wondered who got Portia's money since, according to the newspapers, there were no children of the marriage.

But what would knowing any of this prove? And why should she bother to find out? They were the obvious sort of question and ones to which the police would certainly have wanted to know the answers.

As though she were holding a hand of cards, she assessed the options and possibilities. Suppose the papers were wrong and Portia had not inherited a fortune after all: what else might drive a husband to kill her—or have her killed? Jealousy? Perhaps Portia was having an affair. Expedience? Perhaps Wickham was. Simple loathing? The lust for power? Plain perversion?

The act of murder, Cassie knew from experience, was usually fuelled by basic motivations. The elaborate scenarios so beloved by the writers of Golden Age crime fiction were no more than puzzles to exercise the mind of the reader. Even so, it was not inconceivable that a husband might desire to have his wife removed and had taken steps to have that desire fulfilled. Paid killers were readily available these days, if you believed the papers. Pop into any East End pub and there they were, lined up against the wall for the choosing, two a penny, like a latter-day hiring fair. She'd even read a newspaper article recently about men who set up in business as professional eliminators. Even allowing for journalistic license, a man like Wickham would have no difficulty in finding someone to get rid of his wife for him, while he was otherwise engaged and alibied by any number of respectable citizens.

The thing was, would a man like Wickham really take such a risk? Hiring a freelance murderer would immediately render him susceptible to blackmail, unless he was prepared to take further risks and subsequently kill the killer. From what she remembered of him, she was more than ready to believe him capable of that. There was the fact that he was a bridge-player too, a gambler for high stakes. Undoubtedly he had used a false name, perhaps even disguised himself—but no, what would be the point of that? Once he knew the identity of the victim, even the most cretinous of killers would be able to make the logical step towards the identity of the person who wanted her dead. Unless it was more than a businessman's credibility was worth, to start blackmailing the clients.

But suppose it was murkier than that? Suppose he'd hired someone to hire someone to—but the same arguments would apply, wouldn't they? More chance to get out the cheek-pads and the false eyebrows, admittedly, but in the end the risks were the same. Unless, as already premised, the hirer too was intended for the chop.

"Are you listening, Cass?" Giles said plaintively.

"No. Sorry, I was miles away." Though not all that many, as it happened, since Wickham's place was no more than half an hour's drive from here. Less if the roads were clear.

"I was saying that I've been trying to expand our range a bit," Giles said. He ran a small dairy farm some miles on the other side of Bellington.

"Sounds interesting. How're you going to do that?"

"Cheeses. I've been reading up on some of the local ones which have died out due to all the ludicrous health restrictions they keep bringing in. We're still allowed a small quota of milk which doesn't have to conform—could be fun to try and revive them." His face was flushed with animation. "I've already started in a small way: some of the blue cream cheeses are quite delicious."

While he enthused, Cassie's thoughts returned to Wickham. Did she have the brass neck to drive over to Halkam Court and visit Jamie? There were a great many things she'd love to ask him. Not for any desire to be clever—and God forbid she got into a situation like the one a few months ago where she'd found herself playing the girl detective—or to beat the police at their own game. It was just that she had found herself assessing Wickham in a way they never could. She had been there that evening, and they had not.

Inwardly she groaned. She seemed to remember saying that once before, when all those people had been found dead round the bridge table—or if not round it, alongside it. And look where she had ended up: trussed in tape like a fly, with a maniac spider about to chew her to pieces. If it had not been for the intervention of Charlie Quartermain . . .

Bloody hell. Charlie Quartermain. Someone she would have to do something about. She drank the last of her beer and tried to remember whether or not it was rabies which had a cure worse than the disease itself.

♠ ♥ ♣ ♦

"Held in great respect, your Dad was," Kip Naughton said. He held his mug of tea with both hands, as though cold, although in fact the room was stiflingly hot. The debate this evening had been lively, bordering on the lubricious; the motion—This House Believes in Equal Rights for Women—had been defeated, despite the fact that Steve had been proposing it, and no one wanted to get across Steve if he could help it.

"Was he?" From memory, Cassie dragged one of the few snapshots she had of her father. It was the day they went to Bognor, the summer after Sarah died. Her and him and Gran who'd insisted on wearing a ridiculous hat. He was tanned. Smiling. His thick hair was Brylcreemed close to his head; he wore a white shirt with the sleeves rolled up.

Dad . . .

"Did a lot of good things down our way, your Dad did. Old folks' bingo, seaside trips for the kids, taking the customers to the races, raising money for cripples," said Kip, unaware that since he had gone down for his latest stretch, political correctness had entered contemporary speech. "Never turned down anyone, did Harry Swann."

Did he mean it? Or was he just saying that because, despite his numerous offences against society, he was a kind little man and could see how hungry she was for even the most insignificant detail about the father she could now barely remember?

Kipper lit a thin hand-rolled cigarette. "Yer. Only Harry Swann would have tried to break it up between those two."

"Which two?"

"Them villains fighting outside the Boilermakers' that night. Gawd, I remember it like it was last week. Whole crowd of them, half cut and looking for trouble. Meacher was there, and the Maloney twins, Looney Barnes and Tony Spetz—Spezzioli, his real name was, but we called him Spetz, for short, see?" Delicately Kipper removed a shred of tobacco from his lip.

"I can see that one would."

"A couple of lads had come down from the Seven Sisters Road, and there was two or three more—I can't remember now who they was. It was Tony pulled the blade, of course. Looney didn't know the difference between a knife and a lawnmower, poor sod. He'd have been a goner, if it hadn't been for your Dad stepping in between them and copping it himself instead."

"I thought he tried to protect a policewoman."

"Oh, yer. There was a bluebottle tart about," Kip said vaguely. He turned away, avoiding her eyes. "But it was because of them two fighting that she got into it. Like I said, Tony had the knife—

"Do you mean you knew who was responsible?"

"Everybody did," said Kipper.

"How can you be sure? You didn't see it happen, did you?"

"Not with my very own eyes, no, can't say I did. But I was in the Saloon, that night, having a quick pint with me mates. Helped bring poor Harry—your Dad—inside while they waited for a doctor."

"If people know who was responsible, why didn't they tell the police?"

"Because by then Tony Spetz had pissed off, hadn't he? They never did find him. Me, I reckon he went out to Australia or somewhere like that, changed his name, maybe even went straight. Who knows? One thing's for sure, he would never've dared show his face up our street again, I'll tell you that. We'd have had him if he had. Your dad was a good bloke, one of the best. Make a thousand of Tony Spetz, any day of the week."

"But that's—surely the police could have found him," said Cassie. She found there were tears in her eyes, though whether of rage or delayed grief it was difficult to tell.

Kipper shrugged. He lived in a world she knew little about, a world where the expectations were as unspecific as the surnames, and as interchangeable. "Don't suppose there was much they could do," he said. "Not once the bloke had buggered off."

An arm interposed itself between them like a buttress. Steve's arm, recognisable by the escutcheon-like tattoo picked out by some amateur, just north of the wrist, and the word HATE inked across the back of his hand, one letter to a knuckle. Steve's voice said, "We'll have to get together one of these days, Cass."

"What?" She broke away from her thoughts. Away from the past.

"I'm out of here, Monday."

"Good," she said. And didn't even want to make it sound as if she meant it. The minute they opened the wicket gate in the tall double doors of the prison and let Steve out, danger threatened some woman—all women. It was simply one of the hazards of living in a democracy that although everyone knew he was dangerous, nobody could take any kind of preventive action.

"That's what I think," said Steve.

"Where will you go?" Cassie asked. "You're originally from Leicester, aren't you?"

"Gawd, that's a long time ago," Steve said. As he had before, he pushed himself in between Kipper and Cassie and sat down, and, as before, neither of them dared to protest. "No, I think I'll go up to London. Or maybe stick around this area for a bit. They say it's pretty country. There must be odd jobs going—gardening and such-like. Have you got a garden, Cass?"

"Yes." The tattoo on his arm could have been the family coat of arms, or a regimental crest. If she looked closely, she would probably find it contained some simple message like FUCK THE PIGS.

Steve gave her his hard stare. "Perhaps I'll drop in and mow the lawn, eh?"

"I do all my own gardening," Cassie said. Too late, she wished she had said she had a regular gardener, a live-in gardener, strong of arm and quick to rush to the defence of his employer were she to be threatened by visiting ex-cons. She laughed lightly. "Me and my dog, that is."

"Dog?" said Steve, raising his eyebrows. "What kind of dog would that be?"

"A German Shepherd," said Cassie. She saw it clearly, a large black-tinged animal with yellow eyes and ferocious ears. "Called George."

"George?" Steve said. "Makes a change from Rex, doesn't it?"

"I had a Jack Russell once," said Kipper dreamily. "Called him Mars. Ever such a sweet tooth, he had."

"Fierce, is he?" Steve asked.

"Mars? Long gone, mate. Snuffed it years—"

"George, I meant. Cassie's—uh—German Shepherd." She could see he didn't believe she had a dog at all.

"Only with strangers," she said. "Otherwise he's mild as milk. A terrific watch-dog, though. Barks his head off the minute anyone appears. Only bites if you flinch."

"I expect you need one," Steve said, "living alone and all. Out in the country. Thatched cottage, isn't it?"

She stared at him. How did he know that? How could he have found that out? Fear prickled the skin under her arms and tingled at her wrists. Easy prey—if he chose to come after her. She told herself that, of course, she was fantasising, scaring herself unnecessarily. The first thing a man released from prison wants is to get back to his nearest and dearest.

The only problem was the difficulty of conceiving anyone in this wide world whom Steve regarded as his dearest.

"—how much Ruby knows," Kipper was saying.

Cassie tore herself away from a vision of a blood-steeped bed, her body no longer recognisable as human, butchered to make a psycho's holiday . . . "What did you say, Kip?"

"I said I still don't know just how much old Ruby knows."

"Old Ruby?" It sounded like a C & W classic.

"Tony Spetz's aunt. She brought him up, if that's what you want to call it. Mind you, he was always a wild one. In trouble with the police ever since he was a nipper . . . Gawd, I remember when he—"

"And his aunt's still around?" Cass interrupted because she could see the Class Officer looking at his watch and fingering the bunch of keys which hung from a chain attached to his belt.

"Not just around—or she was, last time I was on the outside—but doing very nicely, thank you." Kipper tapped the side of his nose. "Ask me, she's being looked after, know what I mean?"

"No," Cassie said.

"Means someone's paying her to keep quiet," said Steve.

"Don't know about that." Kipper turned his tin of tobacco round and round between nicotine-stained fingers.

"Keep quiet about what?" asked Cassie. "You don't mean her nephew, do you? Tony—uh—Spetz?"

"I'm not saying nothing like that," said Kipper. "All I know is, she'd doing OK, is Ruby. Last time I was down the local, she was sitting up at the bar like a queen, all tarted up in furs and diamonds, knocking back the gins like her last name was Gordons. In the old days, it used to be a port and lemon and see how long you could make it last."

For a moment, Cassie was dizzied by nostalgia, by the richness of the past. The pub on a Saturday evening, beer smells, smoke, women's perfume, the noise volume climbing higher and higher as the hours passed, shouts of laughter, the subdued click of the shove ha'penny board, the clunk of the beer handles as Dad and Gran pulled an unending stream of pints. In retrospect, her life at the pub had taken on a round-bellied Falstaffian aspect, all the more so because of what came after: the thin white spaces of the vicarage, the greyness of it all, Aunt Polly's despair at the difficulty of maintaining any social pretensions on the inadequate income of a vicar.

"So, what you reckon, Kip?" Steve said. His knee pressed against Cassie's; at the same time he grabbed the underside of her chair so that she was unable to shift away from him. Under the rolled-up sleeves of his striped prison shirt, the muscles bulged. "This Spetz bloke looking after his aunty in return for her keeping mum, or what?"

"Dunno," said Kipper. At the end of the room, the Class Officer started calling out names. A Duty Officer appeared at the door and stood jangling his keys on the chain at his belt, waiting to escort the men back to their various wings.

"Sounds like it to me." Steve turned his unblinking gaze to Cassie. "What do you think, Teach?"

"I don't know enough about it," Cassie said. But she ought to. "Kipper," she said urgently, laying a hand on his striped shirt, even though it was strictly against the rules, "what was the fight about?"

"Fight?" Kipper looked up mournfully as the men began to shuffle out of the room.

"Between—uh—Looney Thing and Tony Spetz?"

"Gawd knows," said Kipper. "Wouldn't have been a woman, because Looney never had one of those, not with his affliction. Couldn't have been dosh, because neither of them ever had two bits to rub together. Good friends, they were."

"Naughton," the Officer called. "Over here."

"Coming, mate." Kipper wrinkled his forehead. "Come to think of it, I never asked myself that before. What the bleedin' 'eck *were* those two fighting about? Beats me."

The Class Officer prepared to move off down the landings towards the main gate. Cassie followed. How could it have taken her so long to wonder what had happened to the man who murdered her father? To wonder whether he had been in the pub that night, or simply passing. Whether Harry Swann had just been unlucky. The wonder was that she should have allowed herself to ignore such questions for so long. Would it not have made more sense to ask? Or had she simply wished to avoid the whole issue of her father's violent death. Even worse: had she once been told? Had she asked, and found the facts too difficult to cope with so that her mind had subsequently blocked it out? Cleopatra, the Queen of Denial . . .

The phone was ringing as she came into the house. Picking it up, she heard an unmistakable asthmatic wheeze. "Ullo, darlin'."

"Who is this?" she said repressively.

"Been down the pub, have you?"

"Certainly not. I've been working," she said. "What can I do for you, Mr. Quartermain?"

"Two things. Three."

"What are they?"

"First, wanted to check that you were OK."

"I'm fine, thank you. And very grateful for all your help." She wished she knew why she felt so antagonistic to Charlie Quartermain; she guessed it was because she sensed that given the slightest chance, he would overwhelm her.

"Second," Charlie said. "Will you be there on Thursday night?"

"Naturally." Thursday was the first night of the summer

term of evening classes. Still, for the moment, Beginners' Bridge. In the autumn, should enough of the Beginners want it to, the class would undergo a sea-change and metamorphose into Intermediate Bridge. She hoped a viable number would. The money was not enormous, but it all helped. And often led on to other things, such as afternoon lessons for local wives. "Why? Will you be there?" Too much to hope for an answer in the negative.

"Will I be—? Course I will, darlin'. Wouldn't miss it for the world."

"What was the third thing?"

There was a pause. Then Quartermain said, in a rush, "Have dinner with me next Saturday."

"I don't really think—"

"Please, Cassie. I've got a particular reason for asking. Won't tell you now because I'm off to a meeting in London, but I will on Thursday, after the class, OK?"

She wanted to say no, it was most definitely not OK. But he had, after all, turned out on a cold wet night to drive her home from Lord Wickham's place: she owed him one. Besides, she was finding it increasingly difficult to think up convincing reasons for refusing his constant invitations; despite his thick skin, he was a kind-hearted man. Good-hearted, even, which was not at all the same thing. Perhaps, if she accepted this one, he would let her off the hook. "All right," she said, "but please don't regard this as a—"

"See you, darlin'." He put down the phone before she could complete the sentence.

"—precedent," she said, into the dead receiver.

The phone rang again almost immediately. "Cassie!"

"Hello, Primula."

"Guess what."

"Derek's got AIDS."

"Don't be ridic—"

"You're opening the batting against the West Indies."

"Have you been drinking, Cassandra?"

"Not yet. But since you mention it, what a good idea." Carrying the cordless phone, Cassie walked across the kitchen to the whisky bottle. "Look, Prim, I'm hopeless at guessing, so why don't you just tell me whatever it is you want to tell me?"

"We're pregnant."

"Both of us?"

"Me, I mean."

Aware of genuine pleasure on her cousin's behalf, Cassie bit back any sharp retort that might have been preparing itself for utterance. "That's marvellous, Prim. I'm really pleased for you."

"Oh, God. So am I. I was beginning to think I'd have to start going in for tests and things. can you imagine it? Derek having to—you know—into a milk bottle?"

"Please," Cassie said. "I haven't had supper yet." Like fingernails, sharp retorts can only be bitten back so far. She opened the whisky bottle and poured some of the contents into a glass.

"What are you doing?" Primula said suspiciously. "I can hear water or something."

"I'm—you know . . ."

"You're not," Primula shrieked. "Cassie, you're not seriously talking to me and at the same time having a—"

"Drink? I most certainly am. I need it."

"But should you? Think of the calories."

"I've done that. And decided the hell with it." Cassie looked compassionately at the remaining pink African violet, then reached out and stroked one of its hairy leaves. The leaf promptly fell off.

Fuck you, too, Cassie thought.

"Anyway, I'm thrilled to pieces," trilled Primula. "We both are."

"Me, too." Cassie really was. She knew how much Primula and Derek longed to have a baby, and though the thought of the two of them actively engaged in the necessary procedure was close to nauseating, Cassie was aware of the heartache Primula had endured as the months—the years—went by and nothing happened. Particularly as Hyacinth and Eric had finally produced their daughter Georgina over a year ago. "That's wonderful. Congratulations to both of you. When's it due?"

"Not until after Christmas."

"That give me time to save up for a christening spoon."

"Derek's father is going to put down a pipe of port," Primula said. "He's got a friend in the wine trade."

"I hope I'll be around long enough to drink a glass on its twenty-first birthday," said Cassie. "Anyway, love, I'm really pleased. That's wonderful news." She felt more kindly towards Primula than she had done for ages.

"What about you, Cassie?" Primula said archly. "When are we going to hear some good news about you?"

The kindliness evaporated with the speed of a genie returning to its lamp. "What?" Cassie said, with extreme chill.

Primula appeared not to notice. "It's just that Hyacinth was saying she thought you might be going to announce your engagement soon."

"This is news to me. Just for interest, did she happen to say to whom?"

"Not really."

Not really, in twin-speak, meant not only that the two of them knew all about Giles Laughton, but that they had dissected every last detail of his life, from his mother to his bank-balance, from his prospects to where he bought his socks. "Primula, I have to go," Cassie said firmly. "I have to—you know . . ."

Which could mean absolutely anything you chose it to. In Cassie's case, it meant swallowing a large slurp of her so far untouched drink. She took it out into the garden and sat on the seat which stood against the whitewashed west-facing wall of the house, waiting for the alcohol to kick in. Behind the hedge of flowering currants, the vegetables were already beginning to burgeon. She could hear frogs in the pond beyond the beds. A pair of bumble bees hung about the syringa buds, like a couple waiting for opening time.

She thought about her father. Bingo, Kipper had said. Raising money. The races. Which reminded her of another photograph she had of him, wearing morning dress, a topper on his head and binoculars slung round his neck as he smiled aloofly at the camera. Handsome Harry Swann at the races. Where was it? Somewhere in the cluttered pigeon-holes of Robin's rather fine escritoire. With her back against the solid thickness of the ancient walls, protected from the wind, she sat for a quarter of an hour enjoying the last of the day's sunshine.

In spite of the peaceful moment, however, she sensed turmoil within herself. Her father's death had emotionally disfigured her; although she knew intellectually that it was not her fault his murder had gone unavenged, in her heart she felt responsible. For too long, she had let things drift, had chosen not to question, had simply accepted. Now, with another murder so close to home, another victim with whom she empathised— even though they had never met—was she tamely going to opt out again and hope that Portia eventually received justice, where Harry Swann had not?

Or was she going to get off her fat butt and do something positive, do what she could to help?

Knocking back the last of her drink, she stood up. The westering sun dazzled her. She felt good.

She had come to a decision.

8

She dialled a number and waited for it to ring. Before it had a chance to utter more than a squawk, the phone was picked up.

"Yes?" The answering voice was imperious, impatient and belonged to Lord Wickham.

"Oh—um . . ." Cassie had expected someone else to answer. "I wondered if I could speak to—um—Jamie?"

"My butler, do you mean?" Lord Wickham made the sound usually transliterated as "pshaw." "Or, rather, my ex-butler."

"Ex?"

"That's right. He upped and left without a word of—look, who is this?"

"I'm from—uh—the—uh—" What could she possibly be from that needed to speak to Jamie but did not even know his last name? "The British Board of Flour Producers."

"Who?"

"My name's—" She looked at the fallen leaf on the kitchen windowsill and thought fast. "—Violet. Violet Mandela."

"And?"

"I'm ringing to check your butler—*ex*-butler as I now know him to be—'s surname."

"Why?"

"It's for our competition." Cassie said, attempting to give her vowels an African plumpness. "He omitted to fill in his last name on the entry form, you see. His was among the first five envelopes to be opened which answered all the questions correctly, and now, by the rules of the competition, we have to ask him one further question. If he gets that right, he goes forward to Round Two and becomes eligible for the Ford Capri or the week's holiday for two in the Seychelles."

"Fascinating. What's the question? I could do with a new car myself."

"I'm not allowed to divulge," Cassie said primly. "Only people who have filled in the form are eligible to—"

"Look, Miss Mandela, I hope you don't expect me to believe this farrago of nonsense. If you want to get hold of Jamie, he's almost certainly gone home to his mother. That's Ms. Olive Howard, as she now styles herself, though when I last had any kind of dealing with her she went under the name of the Right Honourable Olivia Grahame. You'll find her in the London phone book, I'm sure—she's living somewhere in Battersea at the moment, and going quietly mad, by all accounts. And now perhaps you'll be good enough to vacate the line. As you may have heard, my wife has—has—" He appeared to break down, his voice wavering off into nothing. "If there's anything else you want to know, ask someone else, there's a good girl." With that, he put down the receiver.

Good girl, indeed. She wished she felt sorry for him; having seen him, apparently unaffected, in the Old Plough, it was difficult to do so. As it happened, there *was* something else she would like to have known. For instance, had he murdered his wife? And, before that, had he loved her? Had he been kind to her? Or had he been one of those husbands who used the small cruelties to undermine? Had he told her she was putting on weight, asked aloud if she was going through the menopause,

openly wondered if she realised just how like her bloody
mother she was getting? Stuff like that. Men's weapons, de-
signed to humiliate a woman precisely because the answer is
nearly always yes, however much she wishes it was not.

The river sparkled below her as she drove across Battersea
Bridge. They said that dolphins sported there on summer
evenings, that you could eat without anxiety any fish hooked
from the opacity of those sludgy waters. It was an assurance
she had no wish to test. She parked without difficulty and
walked back along Prince of Wales Drive towards the mansion
block inhabited by Ms. Olive Howard, mother of Jamie Grahame, ex-butler. Beyond the gates, the green spaces of the
park gleamed: kids in back-to-front baseball caps and baggy
trousers skateboarded along the paths, office workers in short
sleeves ate sandwiches or lay with winter-white limbs spread-
eagled on the grass.

Cassie rang the bell and waited for the intercom to come
alive. Even allowing for distortion and metal fatigue, the voice
which eventually answered was unfriendly. "Yes?"

"My name's—" Did she need to stick with the British
Board of Flour Producers? "—Cassandra Swann. I wondered
if I could have a word with you?"

"What about?"

Good question, Ms. Howard. About your son's ex-employer
and the possibility that said ex-employer might have arranged
for his wife's murder. That would more or less cover it. "I'm
trying to track down Jamie," Cassie said. "I—"

"Oh, *Jamie*. Why on earth didn't you say so? He's still in
bed, actually, but come on up and I'll try and get the lazy sod
out of bed. It's the fifth floor."

Beside her ear, the buzzer sounded, the front door clicked
open and she stepped into the gloomy hall. Ahead of her
stretched the first of a series of stone stairs which wound upwards round an iron-grilled lift with a sign hung on the door
saying OUT OF ORDER.

Miles above her, a voice called, "Oh, Miss Swa-ann."

Cassie peered out and up. High overhead, someone was

peering over the steel bannister rails, like the archangel Michael at the portal of heaven. "Yes?" she said.

"I'm afraid the lift's out of order."

"I know."

"Sorry about that—see you soon."

Cassie paced herself. There was no hurry, anyway, if Jamie was still abed. When she reached the top, Ms. Howard was waiting for her, leaning against the open door of her flat with her arms folded over her chest. She was small, in her mid-forties, wearing flowered leggings and a big white shirt. A pair of revolutionary's glasses sat halfway down her nose and did nothing to hide her combative expression.

"It's good exercise," she said belligerently, when Cassie hove into view, as though forestalling any attempt to complain that her visitor might otherwise have wanted to make. "Come on in."

As Cassie followed her, Ms. Howard abruptly stopped and turned. "Who are you exactly?"

"A friend of Jamie's."

Ms. Howard frowned. "You're a bit old for him, aren't you?"

What was she implying? "I'm a *friend*, Ms. Howard. I didn't realise that involved an age qualification."

"You're right. It's just that . . ." Ms. Howard did not finish her sentence.

The flat was enormous, and in much need of decoration. It wasn't that Cassie necessarily wanted wall-to-wall carpeting and Laura Ashley curtains at every window, but a degree of comfort, of aesthetic sensibility, surely never did anyone any harm. There was precious little of either here. A hideous brown sofa with wooden arms stood against one wall, with a freeform Fifties coffee table in front of it. There were a couple of junk-shop dining chairs with tatty brown leatherette seats. A built-in unit topped with grey formica ran the full length of the room beneath windows that offered a stunning view over the park and the river to the buildings on the other side.

Cassie could take the deliberate ugliness of the surroundings. Nor was she bothered by the huge photograph of Che Guevara on the long wall of the sitting-room, staring moodily out at her from under his black beret. She could even live with the tattered poster featuring a band of workers holding banners full of cyrillic letters as they gesticulated towards the new dawn which rose somewhere beyond the frame. Much harder to stomach were the contents of the table. Posters, mostly. A huge blow-up photograph of a deer being torn to pieces by hounds which clung to its neck by their jaws while blood gleamed on the animal's dappled coat. A close-up of a terrified cat with the skin of its skull peeled back and attached to electrodes. A whale being cut to pieces by lilliputian fishermen. Posters against abortion. Posters against blood sports. Posters announcing rallies on behalf of Women in Prison, against cuts in the health services. Rain forests. Factory farming. Ozone layers. Evidently Ms. Howard had a heart as big as the Ritz, and wore it in full view on her sleeve.

Cassie felt frivolous and unworthy. The sight of Jamie, slouching in with gold stubble on his chin, and his massive lower limbs more or less concealed beneath a pair of striped cotton trousers which proclaimed as clearly as a full-page ad that he had been to India, cheered her a little. Not hugely though: he looked terrible, his eyes red-rimmed, his face gaunt.

"Don't let this get you down," he said, waving at the surroundings. "Come into the kitchen—it's more or less normal in there."

He was right. Stripped pine dresser. Bits of pottery and earthenware. A key-holder depicting a large spotted pig made out of painted tin. There was also a collection of pretty china, a string of garlic and another of onions, dried Chinese lanterns in a willow-pattern jug.

Ms. Howard, thrusting back an aggressive cloud of black curly hair, said she was too busy to join them but would love a coffee, and went back to her work in the sitting-room. Cassie sat down at the pine table while Jamie poured from a blue enamel pot into three Beatrix Potter mugs and brought one over to her. The coffee was surprisingly good: Cassie would have expected the fierce Ms. Howard to ban continental roast beans on political grounds and insist on some chicory-based substitute. Or even, God forbid, on herb teas.

While he took a mug in to his mother, Cassie speculated on which reflected the real Olivia Howard: the grungy sitting-room or the *Country Living* kitchen. "She wasn't always like this," Jamie said gloomily, coming back. "I mean, she was actually a débutante, in her time. Did the London Season, the whole bit. Coming-out party, the lot."

"What happened?" Cassie said.

"Dunno. The divorce from my father, maybe." Jamie said. "Personally, I blame the menopause."

"Don't," Cassie said strongly. She leaned forward and grabbed Jamie's wrist. "Don't *ever* blame anything on the menopause."

"Why not?" Jamie reared away from her, looking frightened.

"Because women hate it. It demeans them. It's an easy cop-out. It's the great carpet under which men sweep all the dirt they don't want to have to face up to, not just about women, but about themselves too."

"I really don't know what you're talking about."

"God, Jamie. This is *so* depressing."

"You sound just like my mother."

"I really hoped your generation of men was going to be more clued-up than the last one."

"Sorry."

Cassie shook her head at him. "Since we're talking about the menopause, let me segue neatly into why I came here today."

"I *was* wondering."

"Lady Wickham."

Jamie's face assumed an expression which hovered for a while between defiance and apprehension. Apprehension won out. "How do you mean?" he asked carefully.

"I wanted to ask you whether she and her husband were happy together. Whether she had money which her husband inherits. If he had lovers. Or she did."

"Portia? Have lovers?" The muscles on his neck swelled with indignation. "Absolutely not."

"Not even one?"

Jamie plucked at a thread on his thin pants. A mistake, as

Cassie could have told him. She knew from past experience that those Indian cottons weren't exactly good British broadcloth. "No," he said.

"Would you necessarily have known?"

"I knew pretty well everything that went on." He sat up straighter and looked her in the eye. "Anyway, why are you asking? I mean, if it's not a rude question, do you have any right to ask? Are you, as it were, empowered?"

"Not at all."

"Then why—"

"Nosey, I guess." Cassie sipped her coffee. "Just as a matter of interest, did you like Lord Wickham? I mean, apart from the fact that he gave you time off for all those important social events no British butler can afford to ignore."

"Did I like Darcy?" Jamie screwed his mouth while he considered the question. "No. I don't think I did. Not much. Not at all, actually, now I really give it a bit of thought. It was Portia I worked for: I didn't have a lot of contact with him in the normal course of affairs—events, I mean." His face reddened.

"Any particular reason why you didn't like him?"

"He was the usual arrogant sod, of course. They generally are, aren't they? Not my father, I don't mean, but an awful lot of them—"

"By *them*, are we talking aristocracy here, or what?"

"That's right."

"Your father's one of them too?"

"'Fraid so. If the Scots still count. The thing is, a lot of the time I can understand what my mother goes on about. Privilege and stuff. On the other hand . . ."

Here it came. The other hand again. "Personally," said Cassie, getting in before Jamie could. "I think it's a dirty job, but someone's got to do it. And I'd much rather I wasn't the one worrying about the costs of repairing three acres of roofs or maintaining sixteenth-century furniture in good nick, or paying the insurance costs on galleries full of Old Masters. Sooner them than me. And if you took it away from them, what would you do with it? It's hardly realistic, is it? Even if you stuck the domestic artefacts into a museum, how many of the so-called masses would come and look at them?"

"It's a point of view, certainly," Jamie said cautiously. One, she guessed, he had not been offered before.

They could hear his mother on the telephone, haranguing someone called Mary who obviously hadn't been pulling her weight over an abortion clinic in Wimpole Street. "Foetuses," Ms. Howard was shouting. "Living breathing foetuses. They're *people*, Mary. Like you and me."

Mary clearly took exception to being classed in the same category as an embryo.

"Well, if they were given the chance to grow up, they might well be," conceded Ms. Howard. "Look, are you for us or against us, Mary? I think you bloody well need to reassess your priorities."

There was a silence. Then Ms. Howard said, apologetically, "Well, if you'd *said*. Of course, if your mother's just died, that's differ—Mary, there's really no need to cry—oh, for God's sake, Mary, can't you—" The phone was slammed down and Ms. Howard gave vent to an exasperated sigh.

"The travail of a committed woman," Jamie said.

"Your mother must be about the same age as Portia Wickham was," said Cassie. "Did they know each other?"

Jamie looked down at his trousers. "They'd met. But Mum knew Darcy best. I think they had a fling of some kind when they were younger—before she married my father, that is."

"Is Darcy rich?"

"He owns a lot of land," Jamie said cautiously. A fine distinction but an important one, especially among the gentry, to whom acreage meant far more than bank balances ever could.

"What sort of land?" asked Cassie.

"Mostly in Northumbria, I believe. And other bits here and there. Some real estate in London. Some stuff in the Canaries. Or do I mean the Caribbean? Somewhere round there."

"Somewhere between Europe and America, is that what you mean?"

"Possibly. Geography's not my strong subject."

"What about Portia? Was *she* rich?"

"Loaded," said Jamie miserably. "She was the heiress to some American department-store magnate."

"Did she do anything particular with it?"

Jamie furrowed his forehead. "How do you mean?"

"Did she spend it on riotous living? Invest it in nonexistent diamond mines in Siberia? Buy art works or clothes or fast cars?"

"She did a lot of charity work."

"Did she have to keep bailing Wickham out?"

"How do you mean?"

"Didn't you tell me just the other day that you had a degree from Cambridge?"

"Yes. What's that got—"

"What I meant was: did her husband have a habit or a mad mother or five hundred dependants to support? Something like that. Something Portia might have helped him with. Until she decided to withdraw her cash." Seeing the look of amazement on Jamie's face, the mouth opening to ask some stupid question, Cassie added quickly, "I'm just theorising here." She sighed. "You're not being hugely helpful, you know."

"In what way?"

Cassie had not really expected to find Jamie confirming her own suspicions that Darcy was somehow involved in his wife's death, the motive being to get his hands on her money. She had hoped for a little confirmatory titbit, however, something rather more definite than her own suppositions which in turn were based on nothing more substantial than the conspiratorial posture of two men in a pub and the way Wickham and his chums had treated Chilcott.

Not that bloody Chilcott deserved much sympathy, either.

Thinking of him, she thought of that walk up the drive again. Was there something she had missed, some significant sound or sight she had overlooked? She had been over it in her head a hundred times and never come up with anything more than she had already told Detective Inspector Mantripp. Nor had she suffered from any of those niggles which people in detective novels regularly experience: the feeling that she had seen something of moment which hovered tantalisingly at the edge of her mind and would lead to the truth if only she could recall it—which, of course, she would not do until the final chapter.

"Tell me something, Jamie," she said. "Are you just thick, or are you being deliberately obstructive?"

"I'm thick." Jamie said.

"Right. And turkeys vote for Christmas."

"Do you think Darcy murdered her?" Asking, Jamie seemed younger and smaller. His eyes, black-circled now, and sunken, brimmed suddenly with tears.

"It had kind of crossed my mind," Cassie said. "But I don't know. You're much more able to answer that question than I am."

"I think he's perfectly capable of it."

"If he *did* kill her, can you think of any reason?"

"Like what?"

"Jealousy, Jamie. For starters."

"How do you mean?"

"To be absolutely specific, and not to beat about the bush here, did he mind the fact that his wife was screwing his butler?"

"Steady on." Jamie half stood, clutching rumpledly at the back of his chair. The side seam of the right leg of his trousers had almost completely unravelled, displaying considerably more of the muscled body beneath.

It had been no more than a guess. "Or didn't he know?"

Jamie cast an agonised look at the door, but Ms. Howard could not have overheard. She was on the telephone again, coming across loud and clear: "I'm sorry, Priscilla. Either you're with us or you're not. You're going to have to get your priorities absolutely clear. Have you ever thought—I mean really *thought*—what it's like to be a Tupamaran Indian?"

Priscilla obviously had not. Nor, judging by Ms. Howard's irritated tone, was she disposed to try. "Very well, Priscilla. If your son's ordination comes before the plight of these poor guileless people who are literally being mown down by the logging companies, that's a matter for your own individual conscience. Personally, I know where I stand, and I must say I'd thought you were—Priscilla? Pris*cilla*? Have we been cut off?"

"He didn't know," hissed Jamie.

"Are you sure?"

"Not a hundred per cent. But ninety-nine per cent. We were terribly discreet."

"She doesn't look like a discreet lady," Cassie said. "She looked like someone who enjoyed everything far too much to be discreet about it. Could she have let it slip? Or thrown it at him during a row?"

Jamie shook his head. The ring in his earlobe caught the light from the window. Someone in a nearby flat switched on a radio and a voice began to talk in measured tones about a new crisis for the Chancellor of the Exchequer and the civil war in Bosnia. "She'd never have done that," he said. "Never."

"Why not?"

"Because if he'd found out, he'd have killed her." He caught himself as the dramatic words emerged. "Not literally. I'm sure she didn't mean literally. But that's how she used to put it, anyway. He'd have killed her."

"Tell me about some of the other people there that evening. Roddy Symington, for instance." It was difficult to pronounce a name like Roddy without a class-warrior curl of the lip. Cassie didn't make it.

"He's a friend of Darcy Wickham's."

"Anything else?"

"His family owns Symingtons, the construction company."

"Of course," said Cassie. That was why the name was familiar: it was almost impossible not to have noticed the green boards with white lettering which stood on practically every building site, tower-block construction, house conversion and supply depot in the country.

"He's got a big house not too far from Halkam Court. A flat in London. Wife and three children. The usual stuff."

"Was he another of Portia's conquests?"

Jamie blushed again. "I shouldn't have thought so. His first wife died a couple of years ago, leaving him with two children, and he recently married again and they had a baby not too long ago." He looked directly at her. "Anything else you want to know?"

"What about Jeremy Marling?"

"He's played bridge at Halkam Court before. Don't know

much about him, though I think he's been involved in one or two business things with Darcy. Typical sort of well-off oik, I'd say."

Cassie would have said the same. "Any connection with Portia?"

"No. I asked her once, because she did rather like to compare and contrast, if you know what I mean, especially if they were Darcy's friends. She said she'd never met him."

"What about his partner, Jacko something?"

"Jacko Dexter? She'd never met him either. She said he was on her wish list. He's quite interesting. A whizz kid, started out doing computer sciences, went over to Berkeley to get a PhD, set up his own software production company in Silicon Valley and now he's a millionaire several times over."

"Why did you leave Darcy's employ, Jamie? It was rather a sudden decision, wasn't it?"

"Why would I stay? I told you I worked for her rather than him. With her . . . *gone* . . ." He swallowed painfully. ". . . there didn't seem to be a lot of point in staying on. Anyway, it wasn't the same without her."

"I can see it wouldn't be."

"And . . . she was always telling me that I was wasting my life being a butler, I ought to do something more constructive. I started thinking she was right."

He got up, flinging away from the table to stand drooping by the window which overlooked a patch of communal concrete at the back of the buildings where residents were able to park their cars. "I told the police what happened that night," he said. "I kept telling them. The awful thing is, I don't think they believe me." He raised his head to look at Cassie. "I think they think I did it."

"Did you?"

"This is a ludicrous question. Of *course* I—"

"Did you tell them that you and she were . . ."

"No," he said. "If I did, they might have even more reason to think I'm the guilty party."

"Which he is not, and never was." From the door, Ms. Howard addressed them emphatically as they both turned rapidly to face her. "That wretched woman."

"Portia Wickham, do you mean?" asked Cassie.

"Who else?" spat Ms. Howard.

"You knew her, then?"

Ms. Howard glared at her. "Not really. We'd met. I'm not going to say I'm glad she's dead," she said generously, "but I can't feel terribly sorry, either. The way she used my poor innocent child . . ."

"I am *not* innocent," Jamie said.

"Played with his emotions, made him fall in love with her . . ."

"I'm perfectly capable of forming my own—"

"It's disgusting—she was old enough to be his mother. *My* mother, for that matter. It's scandalous, seducing a boy half her age, introducing him to God knows what depravities . . ."

"Mother, I've lived a rich sexual life since the age of—"

"Scandalous!" An alarming dredge of blood was suffusing Ms. Howard's thin urgent face. It seemed obvious that whatever the colour of the spectacles through which she viewed the rest of the world, the ones she turned on her son were rose-coloured. Given the woman's large-hearted crusading on behalf of the deprived of this earth, there seemed to be something almost unbalanced about her attitude towards her son's involvement with Portia Wickham. Or was the crusading in fact a symptom not of compassion, but of a ruthless intolerance of anyone who deviated from her own private set of rules?

This was getting a bit heavy. A bit loaded. The vibrations were not ones which made Cassie want to reach for her own drumsticks. She looked at her watch again. "I must go," she said. " 'Bye, Jamie."

He looked at her and then at his mother, and shrugged. " 'Bye."

Ms. Howard followed Cassie to the front door. As she turned the handle to open it, she put her face close to Cassie's. "In the Middle Ages," she hissed, "Portia Wickham would have been burned at the stake as a witch."

9

He'd have killed her. It meant nothing, of course. People say it all the time, without any intention of being taken seriously. None the less, by the law of averages, some of the people who say "I'll kill you for that," must at some point go on and actually do it. The question bothering Cassie, as she negotiated the traffic streaming up Essex Road from the Angel, was whether Darcy Wickham was one of those people or not. That he was capable of homicide, she had no doubt; whether he would allow himself to lose control to the extent of murdering someone—and thus endangering himself—was a moot point.

At Highbury Corner, she turned into Highbury Fields and found a parking space in one of the residential streets nearby. It was nearly twenty years since she had last been here but the big open stretch of green still looked substantially the same. Behind the edging plane trees, the white Georgian façades gleamed, dogs and babies still cavorted on the grass, young mums still sat surrounded by blankets and balls. In one corner a football game was in progress, played by young men stripped to the waist. Not a pretty sight. Old people sat on benches and whinged gently to each other about the past.

Cassie watched for a moment. Twenty years. It seemed like last month. Was it one of the penalties of growing older that even clichés began to sound meaningful? She could remember playing on this stretch of green. She could remember walking down here, holding her mother's hand, off to her first day of school, and the wonder of a guinea-pig in a cage, child-sized chairs, the smell of the books in the little school library.

She walked towards the Holloway Road. Yesterday, it had all seemed clear: she would return to her father's pub, seek out Tony Spetz's aunt, ask her about her nephew. That was all. Now she saw that going back would need more courage than she had realised. Even though it was time she filled in the gaps in her memory, they were there for the simple reason that it was less painful to forget than to remember. Now that she was here, she wondered what she could hope to achieve by stirring up waters which, though muddied once, had long since settled and grown clear. And whether there was any point in desiring to know what exactly lay buried in that mud.

She pushed open the door of the Boilermarkers' Arms and walked back into childhood. The big gloomy bar-room had not changed: there were still the black-and-white photographs of Islington in the 1890s, still the framed sheets of newspaper pages, still the dusty tapestried cushions along the settles against the wall. For a moment, while her eyes adjusted to the gloom, she might even have believed that it was Gran behind the bar, big as a house among the bottles and mirrors which rose like a stage set behind her. But the person who nodded was a stranger; the voice asking what he could get her belonged to someone else.

"I'll have a mineral water, please," Cassie said.

The man behind the bar raised eyebrows that said he had seen it all and was not impressed by women who came into pubs and ordered water. He did some more fancy work with his eyebrows. "Would that be Evian or Perrier, madam?" he asked, with contemptuous concern. "Highland Spring? Caledonia wotsit with just a hint of apricot? There's that Italian stuff, Apollinaris, if you prefer. Or there's always your basic tap." He spoke with the air of a man used to considering himself the life and soul of any party that was going while his eyes sought, and failed to find, an audience among the other customers.

Cassie wasn't taking any of that. "How about Vittel?" she said.

"Ooh," you've got me there, dear."

"No Vittel?" On a good day, Cassie could match eyebrows and contempt with the best of them. "Pity, that's what I wanted. Perrier will have to do, then. With ice and lemon, please." Water was not what she usually ordered in pubs, but she disliked drinking in the middle of the day, and in any case, there was still the long drive back home. She certainly couldn't afford to be caught by the police with stale liquor on her breath. Or fresh liquor, for that matter. Stuck as she was, out in the sticks, she needed the car just for the fundamentals of daily life—food, whisky, soap-powder, stuff like that—let alone such frivolities as earning a living.

She hoicked one buttock on to the bar stool and looked around. Had the place been this deserted, this shabby, in her father's time? Whether because of the landlord's eyebrows or simply the recession, the place was half empty. The clientèle consisted of businessmen for the most part, plus a few young women from the banks and shops nearby. A couple of social security scroungers, beer bellies quivering beneath grubby vests as they haw-hawed over the *Sun*, sat in a corner by the window. Three bikers in leather were discussing Harley Davidsons and fingering their studs. Hunched over beers at separate tables was a handful of those small furtive men who seem to epitomise the alienation of society, men it was impossible to imagine had ever fallen in love or gone swimming or been children.

And, sitting at the end of the bar, her back against the wood-lined wall, was a woman who could only be Old Ruby. She wore a purple jogging suit picked out in green highlights, with matching flashes on her trainers. Her glasses were framed in rainbowed plastic and, behind them, her eyes had been heavily made up with pearlised green eyeshadow and lots of mascara. She couldn't have been a day over eighty-five.

Cassie had often had cause to complain about the basic unfairness Nature displays in the gender stakes. Women lose out
all along the line. There's childbirth, for a start. Menstruation.
The difficulty of growing old gracefully. The respective
amounts of booze each sex can hold. As for striking up conversations with strangers in pubs . . . men had it all their own
way. Slowly sipping her water, she tried to work out the best
way to approach Ruby without arousing suspicion.

Ruby herself had no such inhibitions. "Haven't seen you
around here before," she said, jumping straight in. Her lobes
drooped like spaniels' ears; a pearl stud hung loosely in each.

"Haven't been here before," said Cassie. Presented with this
conversation gift, she unwrapped it fast. "Not for years, anyway."

"Years?" Ruby sucked genteelly at a glass full of ice-cubes
and bubbles. "You don't look old enough to go back very far."

"Believe it or not, my father used to own this pub," Cassie
said. It was out before she had time to decide whether such an
admission was a good idea or not. There could be only one
reason why the daughter of a man who had been killed by this
woman's nephew would be sitting at the bar, and that was because she was out to cause trouble.

Ruby fiddled with the flap of the fake-leopard handbag
which stood on the bar beside her. "Who'd that be, then?"

"Harry Swann."

"Oh yes?" said Ruby, faintly hostile. She nibbled at the inside of her lower lip. "So what you doing here, then? Come
back to give the old place the once-over, have you?"

"I thought it was time to get back to my roots," said Cassie.

The landlord leaned across the bar. "Harry Swann? In't he
the one what was done in?"

Cassie nodded. "Right outside in the street." She hoped
Ruby would pick up the implicit sub-text: that Cassie had no
idea who had been responsible, nor was she aware of the identity of the old girl sitting just a few yards away.

Ruby enlightened her. "They tried to pin it on my Tony,"
she said. "People round here, I mean, not the police. I soon put
them right on that one. Tony wouldn't have hurt a fly. I'm not
saying he couldn't be a bit on the wild side when he wanted,

but knives . . . ?" She made a face expressive of disgust and twirled her glass round and round in front of her.

Since she seemed willing to talk about it, Cassie pressed on. She gave a sympathetic nod. "Give a dog a bad name," she said. Cassandra Swann, woman of the people.

"I'll say." Ruby wagged her head up and down a couple of times, looking sage. "Didn't give the boy a chance."

"Where is your nephew now?" asked Cassie. "Didn't he go to Australia or somewhere?"

Ruby stiffened. "Here, who are you?" She peered through her rainbow specs. "You really Harry Swann's daughter?"

"Yes."

"Not the police, are you?"

"No," Cassie said hastily. "I just happened to be in the neighbourhood and decided to take a look at where I used to live."

"So how come you know Tony was my nephew?" demanded Ruby shrilly. A flush laid itself along her cheekbones above the lines of rouge. "Not trying to pull something, are you?"

"No," protested Cassie.

The landlord began drying his hands on a tea-towel. "Keep it down, Ruby," he said. "Don't want to disturb the other customers, do we?"

Temporarily diverted, Ruby shoved her glass forward. "I'll have the same again, and no lip with it," she said. "I was drinking here before you was even thought of."

"I'll bet you were." The landlord held the glass up to the giant bottle of gin hanging upside-down from the wall, pressing it against the optic.

"If it wasn't for me, this place would've gone down the tubes years ago," grumbled Ruby. "Ought to get a badge of merit, or something."

"What for? Services to the brewing industry?" The man reached under the counter for a bottle of tonic water and flipped off the cap, ironic as hell.

"Nerve." Ruby clacked her false teeth around inside her mouth and moved her shoulders as though she were a duck settling ruffled feathers. "Bleeding nerve," she said. "No respect." She turned back to Cassie. "Go on, then. Tell us who you really are."

"I told you," said Cassie. By now, some of the other people in the bar had looked up from their conversations.

"Says Harry Swann used to be her father," Ruby said to the room at large. She jerked her chin at one of the furtive men. "Here, Bert. You was around in the old days. Did you remember Harry Swann having a kid?"

Bert picked up his glass and shambled over to the bar. He was about ten years younger than Ruby, wearing a shabby tweed jacket and baggy flannels. Instead of a shirt he wore a T-shirt with BORN TO KILL printed across the chest. There was a rim of dirt round the neck. "I remember Harry's old mum," he said. "Served behind the bar for years."

"That was my Gran," said Cassie. Loss, as sharp as the day she had first become aware of it, pierced her heart. There were emptinesses inside her, spaces which needed filling, maps which had not yet been drawn. What had been no more than an intellectual wish to search out something of the past had turned suddenly into emotional confrontation. Here, in the place where she had been born and spent most of her childhood, she felt isolated and, as always, an outsider. These were not people with whom she felt she had anything in common. But where exactly *did* she fit in? Certainly not with Aunt Polly's constipated middle-class gentility, any more than she did with Lord Wickham's moneyed arrogance. When Gran had been alive, she had known, without knowing she knew, exactly who she was. It had never been a question of place or class, simply a security which there had never been a need to define.

"Now I come to think about it," Bert said, pursing his lips. "I think there *was* a kid. Used to go to school down the road. You remember, Ruby. Fat little thing with her hair in them pigtails." The two of them stared suspiciously at Cassie.

"That was me." For the first year at school, her mother had done her plaits. After Sarah's death, Gran had persuaded her to have her hair cut, because of the arthritis in her fingers. Cassie could still remember the guilt as she peered down over the arm of the hairdresser's chair and saw the fine strands lying on the floor. Dimly, she had perceived it as her first betrayal of Sarah and everything she stood for.

"Didn't look much like you do, though," said Ruby, narrow-eyed.

"Can't say I'd swear to it being you," agreed Bert.

It didn't seem worth pointing out that twenty years and a lot of pain had gone by since then. And that, in any case, nobody had asked anyone to swear to anything. Cassie pressed on. "I heard that a policewoman was being beaten up outside," she said. "And that my father stepped in to stop it and got a knife in his ribs. Is that right?"

The two old people gazed at her like tortoises. Then they looked at each other. Finally Bert said, staring down into his glass, "That's about the size of it."

"Meaning what?"

"Meaning that's what happened."

It wasn't quite what Kipper Naughton had told her. Or, to put it differently, Kipper's version of events had given the policewoman a more peripheral role. Both Ruby and Bert had suddenly grown evasive, body-language shifty, eyes refusing to make contact with hers. If she was being offered a version of the truth, Cassie sensed it was the economic one.

"You're not going to go digging up all that old stuff, are you?" Ruby said.

"Sleeping dogs," added Bert. He stretched scraggy neck muscles above the belligerent message on his chest.

Ruby reached into her handbag and brought out a packet of cigarettes. She fumbled one out and lit it with a gold lighter. *Looked after*, Kipper had said. *Someone's paying her to keep quiet*, Steve had added. But who? And what did they want her to keep quiet about? Questions it was impossible to come right out and ask. Cassie smiled, looking at her watch. "Well, it's a long time ago," she said carelessly, as though it was all the same to her. She stood up. "It's nice to have seen the old place again. It'll probably be another twenty years before I'm round this way again."

She nodded at the eyebrow expert behind the bar, who made no response. When she reached the door into the street she looked back and saw the three of them, Bert and Ruby and the landlord, heads hunched together, staring at her.

There was sunlight on the streets. Outside the tube station, a newspaper vendor was barking some incomprehensible sales pitch into the swirling carbon monoxide fumes. Beside him, three black men with elaborately dreadlocked hair were arguing fiercely over a plastic carrier bag printed with the name of an Indian takeaway. Cassie was fairly sure the contents had little to do with poppadoms or chicken biryani. Further along, outside the supermarket, a young man with a dirty face sat with his legs stretched out on the pavement, holding a piece of corrugated cardboard with the words *homeless and hungry* scrawled across it while, above his head, oblivious, young mothers held a conversation punctuated with unfocused slaps at pushchairs full of whining children. The traffic was constant and noisy: whoosh of airbrakes, swish of tyres, rev of engines, screech and rattle of buses as they jerked erratically up from the Angel or King's Cross. The air smelled grubby, heavy with lung-damage. The naked city. Predatory. Hostile. Cassie loved it.

Passing the public library, she had a sudden idea. Going in, she made her way to the reference section and took *Debrett's* and *Who's Who* off the shelves. Darcy Wickham was listed in both; Roderick Peregrine Symington and James John Dexter both featured in *Who's Who*, which also gave the name of Dexter's company—New Horizons Software, with an address in Wapping. The unembellished facts bore out the information she already had. Neither Jeremy Marling nor, when as an afterthought, she checked him, Chilcott, was mentioned. She left.

Outside the police station, a man walked up and down carrying a sandwich board. HE DIED FOR YOUR SINS. A little man, with spectacles and a cap, and a nose which did him no favours. Why was it always the men like him who were so much more aware of human transgressions? Impossible to imagine, say, Harrison Ford wanting—or needing—to walk up and down a London pavement informing people that the world might end at any moment. Probably because Harrison didn't want it to, while the little man rather hoped it would.

Whose sins, she wondered, had Harry Swann died for: his own, or someone else's?

10

Cassie was hoovering up dead insects. It was not an activity she usually spent a lot of time on. A quarter of an hour per year, if that. This was the designated annual fifteen minutes. What did it say about her life that other people spent *their* fifteen minutes being famous while she sucked up wasps?

She felt, rather than heard, the doorknocker. Opening up, she found DI Mantripp and DS Walsh outside.

"Oh, it's you," she said.

"You *do* sound pleased to see us," said Walsh.

"I'm getting something wrong, then," she said.

Mantripp stepped into the cottage. He glanced around with keen-eyed suspicion, as though hoping to find half a ton of heroin on the windowsill and sixteen illegal immigrants hiding under the table.

"I suppose you've come to arrest me," Cassie said.

"Why? What've you done?" Mantripp eyed her with severity. She should have remembered that one of the requirements for joining the police force was not a sense of humour. Same with the Customs and Excise people. Which is why travellers who carelessly make jokes about bombs in their hand-luggage often find themselves up on a charge and the flight to Benidorm taken off without them.

"We wanted to go over the events of last Tuesday night with you again," said Walsh.

"I really don't think I can help you much," Cassie said. "I've been over it a thousand times with myself and I've not come up with anything new."

"Never mind. We're trained in the art of skilful questioning," said Mantripp. "Perhaps between us we can unlock the secrets of your memory."

"Well . . ." Cassie sat down and motioned the policemen to do the same. "I don't think there are any secrets to unlock—and if there were, I certainly wouldn't want you to share them—but you can try." Interrogation was less mindless than vacuuming and didn't involve the rasp of dried-up insect bodies against the plastic gizmo. That was really all you could say about interrogation.

"Dear me," said Mantripp. "You ought to water that." He pointed to a drooping asparagus fern on the table.

"I did."

"When? Last Christmas?"

"Look, could we please get on with it?" Cassie said. Bloody nerve, walking into people's houses, telling them how to conduct their lives, criticising the way they nurtured their pot-plants.

The two men sat down, Mantripp on the sofa, Walsh at the table. He reached into a briefcase and brought out a laptop computer which he set up in front of him. Once again, Cassie repeated what she had already told them about the night of Portia Wickham's murder: who had been at Halkam Court, what time they had finished playing, Chilcott putting her out of the hired car, her walk up the drive through the rain, her tripping over something on the ground, the arrival of Charlie Quartermain, his subsequent taking of her home.

"She must have been lying to one side of the drive," she

said. "Otherwise, wouldn't we have picked up her—her body in the headlights? Or, if not us, then one of the other guests?"

"Just off the drive," agreed Walsh. "On the grass. Most of her."

Cassie didn't ask what he meant. That outflung arm still haunted her.

"There was some kind of shrub there," Walsh continued, "which would have made it much more difficult to see her in the dark. And she was wearing black—a pair of those legging things and a big black overblouse. Which is why no one noticed her until daylight."

"And at no point during the evening did anyone leave the house?" Mantripp asked.

"The house I don't know about. The room . . . well, Jamie—that's the butler—must have done. And the girl who was helping him with the drinks and things. And a couple of the men—Jeremy Marling and Andrew Pascoe—had had lunch together and were moaning about a dud mussel. I should think they left the room at some point or other. In fact, most of the men would."

"Why do you say that?"

"Men always do. You must have noticed."

"Can't say I have." Mantripp began to look uneasy. "Though, talking of which, could I avail myself of the —uh—facilities?"

"I rest my case." Cassie showed him the doorway to the boxed-in staircase. "Upstairs and first on the left."

"None of these people was out of the room for very long, were they?" said Walsh.

"Not as far as I noticed."

"Though it wouldn't have taken too long to nip down to the entrance gates." Walsh sneezed very suddenly and pushed away the vase of pink and white roses on the table beside him. "The point is, you can't be absolutely certain who was in the room and who was not at any one time, is that right?"

"We were playing bridge for very high stakes. I was concentrating on my cards and the people at whatever table I was on, rather than what anyone was up to."

"Of course." Looking down at his laptop, Walsh pressed a

key and added, "You've told us already who was still in the
house when you got back, haven't you?"

"Only the ones whose voices I recognised. There could
have been others still in the drawing-room who didn't actually
speak while I was waiting in the hall. But presumably Lord
Wickham's told you who had left and who had stayed."

Walsh nodded. "We were able to establish that five people
left more or less at the same time: you and Mr. Chilcott. A
married couple called Attenborough. And Mr. Roderick
Symington. Unless we have an Orient-Express-type scenario
here, those who remained all alibi each other for the relevant
time."

"So Roderick Symington is the only one without an alibi."

Walsh leaned forward and placed a hand on her arm. Did
she imagine it, or was there a new look of interest in Walsh's
eyes? A kind of bloodhound-on-the-trail, we-always-get-our-
man look? "Is he?"

She grimaced, feeling as though she personally was setting
the noose round the condemned man's neck. "I already told
you that he came back after I did." She described again
Symington's return to Halkam Court, the rain on his shoulders, his sodden hair.

Just call me Judas.

Walsh nodded thoughtfully. "What you're saying is, he
could easily have left the gathering, stopped his car near the
entrance gates, reached for the automatic in the glove com-
partment of his car, shot Lady Wickham twice and left her
under the bush by the side of the drive, then continued blithely
on his way?"

"I'm saying absolutely nothing of the kind," said Cassie,
highly indignant. "God. If this is the kind of evidence you
build your cases on, no wonder there've been so many miscarriages of justice recently. Besides, if he *had* done all that, the
last thing he'd do would be to come back."

"Except that he'd left his briefcase behind. Isn't that what
he said?" Walsh widened his eyes. "Even murderers can be
absent-minded, you know."

Above their heads, water flushed tremendously, followed by
the long-drawn-out gurgle and slurp which was one of the

many indications of the antiquity of the cottage's plumbing system. Both of them involuntarily looked up at the ceiling and then down and away.

"And if he needed it the following day," continued Walsh, "he'd have *had* to come back. It would have looked very odd if he hadn't."

"I suppose so."

"As it happens, he isn't the only one without an alibi. Mr. James—or Jacko—Dexter left about forty minutes after the others. Unfortunately we can't find any connection whatsoever between him and Lady Wickham; no reason why he'd want to kill her. Says he didn't see anything as he drove away from the house, but that he wasn't, as it happens, keeping an eye out for corpses strewn along the road."

"Was his the customised VW?"

"Amazing, isn't it? The man's a millionaire and he drives a little car like that."

Cassie's mind moved sideways. "Did I read in the papers that Lady Wickham never appeared at her charity concert?"

"You did indeed. The point being there *was* no charity concert that night in London, as far as we've been able to ascertain. Nor have we been able so far to fill in her movements between leaving Halkam Court and being found dead in the drive."

"Is it possible she never left the house at all?"

"In that case, where's her car? We still haven't found that. And she was seen driving away from the house by at least three witnesses."

"I don't know if this is the sort of question one should ask," Cassie said, "but do you have any suspects?"

"In a case like this, the police suspect everybody."

"Which means you haven't the faintest clue."

"So young, Cassie, and so cynical."

She gave him a quizzical look. Cassie, huh? Where did he get off, using her first name like that? Fleetingly, she wondered what his was.

"Have you even found a motive?" she said, not trying too hard to keep the withering note from her voice.

"There are always motives when someone's as rich as Lady Wickham was."

"Such as?"

Walsh glanced upward again, as though worried about being overheard. Belatedly, Cassie realised that having availed himself of them, Mantripp was now taking rather a long time to vacate the—uh—facilities. Had the bathroom door stuck again? Should she go and see? Or was he creeping about upstairs, checking her cupboards and drawers to see if she'd left a bloodstained hammer lying about or inadvertently forgotten to conceal the hot tiara? Probably not, though. The floor would have creaked.

"Um—I wonder whether we should—" she began.

"The husband, obviously, is always going to be number one suspect in a case like this," Walsh said.

"Why? Does he stand to inherit the lot?"

"Not the lot. But substantial portions of it." Walsh looked down at his hands. Cassie could not help noticing that he wore no wedding ring. But he had, hadn't he, two months ago, when they first ran across each other? "And he's involved with a lot of different commercial ventures; we're looking into those, of course. But we also understand that Lady Wickham was threatening to withdraw her support from one of the charities she was involved in."

"Killing someone because she's refusing to renew her subscription seems a bit drastic."

"This is a bit more than a subscription. Apparently she'd pledged a substantial sum for the next few years. As we understand it, from pursuing our enquiries, she'd been threatening to cancel that pledge, on the ground that funds were being mishandled."

"Which charity was it?"

He snapped his fingers. "Remind me. Not the League against Cruel Sports, but something like that. Animal rights, anyway?"

"Whales? Donkeys? Chickens?"

"Or was it one of those green things? God, my mind's going."

"And how exactly was the money being mishandled?"

"Poor accounting, expenses not properly signed for, unexplained amounts vanished without trace. The sort of things which always happen when amateurs get together to try to save the world."

"Aren't our policemen wonderful?" said Cassie. "Such faith, such idealism."

"Idealists are always amateurs," said Walsh bluntly. "And because of that, when their money goes missing, it's difficult to sort out whether it's deliberate embezzlement or simple ineptitude. That's why there are so many crooks in the charity field."

"Either way. Portia didn't like it?"

"That's about the size of it. She seems, from our investigations, to have been pretty sharp where money was concerned."

Muffled banging suddenly began upstairs, followed by muffled shouting. "Sounds like the chief's locked himself in," said Walsh. "Want me to go and see?"

"One of us should, and I think he'd rather it was you than me."

While he was gone, Cassie thought again about that evening, the half-closed door of the drawing-room, overheard conversations. Most of the people at Halkam Court that evening could have had nothing to do with it, since they all had alibis, according to Walsh. Unless you went the hired killer route. Which seemed a little dramatic: this wasn't the United States and neither was Portia some eminent fighter for freedom or head of state who needed eliminating by whichever group had taken against her.

Walsh came back through the stair door, followed by Mantripp, who looked sheepish. "Sorry about that," he said. "The door of your—uh—must have jammed. Do that often, does it?"

"Never," lied Cassie. "How extraordinary. You must have been pulling the latch the wrong way."

"Surprised you didn't come looking for me, actually," Mantripp said to Walsh. "I seem to have been up there for ages."

"One wouldn't, would one, sir."

"Why not?"

"Wouldn't want to embarrass you," said Walsh. He flipped his hand this way and that, glancing at Cassie. "Could have had a duff mussel last night."

"*Mussel*?" Mantripp said indignantly.

"Or perhaps you hadn't checked the sell-by-date on your TV frozen dinner. How were we to know?"

"For God's sake get a grip, man," Mantripp said roughly. "Mussels? TV dinners? You know damn well I wouldn't touch either of them."

"Quite, sir." Walsh shot Cassie a look which indicated that he was sending up his superior. Unobtrusively, he waggled his eyebrows up and down, looking excessively comic.

"Sorted it out with Miss Swann, have you?" Mantripp said.

"What, the murder, sir? Not exactly. I mean, there *are* one or two factors still missing from the equation. Like who did it. And why."

"Don't play the fool, Walsh."

"No, sir."

The two policemen moved towards the door. "If anything else comes up, we'll give you a ring," Mantripp said.

"Or even drop by," added Walsh. "Supposing we're in the vicinity."

Once they had gone, Cassie was left with two clear choices. Either she could go back to the dead flies, or she could walk down and invite Kathryn Kurtz in for a drink that evening.

It wasn't a difficult decision. She set off down the lane. Inside her head, her brains rocked gently in a careful sea of non-commitment. She did not want to think about Portia Wickham, or John Burslake. She didn't want to worry about Steve, or wonder why her father had gone so long unavenged. It was enough to smell the fresh leaves, lean on the gate into the field that lay between her house and Ivy Cottage, and watch rabbits skitter, cows move slowly from one patch of grass to another. Almost enough. Her life had slewed off-centre and she would have to do something about it. But not at the moment.

She pushed open Kathryn's gate and walked up the little stone path between ankle-high lavender bushes then, stepping into the little porch, knocked at the door. The name Ivy Cottage was painted on a board attached to the wooden struts of the porch; she had a similar one at her own cottage. It seemed perverse that hers should be covered with ivy while this one was draped in honeysuckle. Inside, a voice shouted something in a forceful way. It sounded very much like: "Bugger off!"

Cassie listened a bit. Then she knocked again and put her ear against the panelling of the door. This time it was unmistakable. "Will you for Chrissake go away!"

Well. If that was the way she wanted it. Having come prepared, Cassie slipped a note through the letterbox and went away.

She still had two choices. Dead wasps. Or driving in to Oxford to look for a new evening dress. On Saturday she was supposed to be going to this dinner-dance thing with—gulp—Charlie Quartermain, and the police still had her old one. She gave the houseplants some water, told them she loved them and would miss them while she was gone—if Prince Charles wasn't too proud, neither was she—locked up and went off.

At six o'clock that evening, she was sitting outside the cottage again and feeling pretty good. The weather had changed, the cold front of the past week or so having given way to cloudless skies and almost Mediterranean heat. Lying on a cushioned chaise-longue, she thought about tomorrow, the first bridge class of the summer term. Eighteen people had started in the autumn, of whom twelve had survived through to this point. This was good. Even better was what was hanging in her wardrobe. Not a dress at all, but a skirt and jacket made of some silky greeny-blue stuff. "It really suits your colouring," the sales lady had said. "And your—er—shape."

She was right. The long jacket narrowed Cassie's hips, the sea-shades emphasised the colour of her hair and eyes. For once, she thought, holding it up against her when she got it home, I'm going to feel pleased with how I look. And this was despite the subtle cruelties of the changing-room mirrors. What woman dresses in her best lace panties and bra in order to try on clothes? Yet who looks particularly good in sensible knickers and workaday bra? Normally Cassie needed at least two whiskies and possibly even a small tin of anchovy-stuffed olives before she got over the depression caused by those unforgiving mirrors. But not today.

There was a glass of cold white wine in her hand. A blackbird was doing its number in the pear-tree. She had mown the lawn that afternoon and the alternating stripes stretched neatly away from her towards the vegetable garden, like something from a magazine. Even the houseplants had rallied. It wouldn't need to get much better than this to be damn near perfect.

"Hello."

The unexpected voice came from somewhere to the side of her. She leaped into the air, spilling wine down the front of herself, screaming, feeling her heart lurch into overtime.

"Whoa." The woman in front of her backed away, holding up her hands. One of them clutched a green bottle. "Whoa. Slow down. Take it easy."

"Sorry! You startled me."

"If that's startled, I hope I'm not around when something really takes you by surprise."

"Sorry."

"Jesus. Do you do that every time you have a guest?"

"I thought you were someone else," gasped Cassie. Why should she have imagined that deepish husky voice belonged to Steve? She knew he wouldn't be released for another four days. Heart still thumping, she realised just how afraid she was that he would show up here on his release.

"I'm the lady you invited round for a drink at six o'clock this evening, remember? Kathryn Kurtz. Dr. Kathryn Lamarr Kurtz, PhD, if you want the whole bit." Kathryn squinted at the watch on her wrist. "And it is now exactly six minutes past. In accordance with the precepts taught me by that flower of southern womanhood, my mother, I arrived precisely five minutes after the invited time. You can call me Kathryn. Or Kate. Or even, if you must, K.K. Just don't ever call me between nine and noon on weekdays."

"I won't, I promise." Cassie brushed at the front of her sweatshirt. "That's why you yelled at me this morning, right?"

"Right. Though if I'd realised it was you and not some bible-carrier trying to persuade me to join the Church of the Latter-Day Saints, I probably would have opened up."

Cassie poured wine, found nibbles, moved chairs around. The white cat appeared at the edge of the grass and stepped delicately towards them, followed by a tiny tortoiseshell kitten. When all four of them were settled, Cassie said, "How are you liking it here?"

"Liking? Listen, I'm loving it. I'm a wannabe Englishwoman. I'd have been great at tromping through far-flung corners of the Empire in a tweed skirt and an umbrella. I'll tell you, if some English guy came up and asked me to share his life, I'd be hard put to it to turn him down."

"I don't like to disappoint you, but English guys aren't usually that spontaneous. They generally like a bit of time to get to know a girl before they propose."

"To see me is to love me," Kathryn said. Her upper teeth protruded slightly, giving her a goofy kind of face that lined up somewhere between a Walt Disney chipmunk and a dolphin. She was probably a year or two older than Cassie. Her hair was a pale ginger and she looked like she'd been put together by Pinocchio's dad during a hangover.

"What do you like about England?"

"Not the food, I have to say. And I really miss my swimming pool. And baseball on the TV." Kathryn sipped her wine and pushed her protrusive teeth even further forward. "I guess it's the way you English sit so comfortably with yourselves. And if occasionally you don't, you don't bore other people with it. Back home, we're all so self-obsessed, so concerned about fulfilling our potential and finding the real us, and digging down into our psyches., I mean, look at those kids of Woody Allen's: into psychotherapy at the age of three, for God's sake."

"With parents like that, I should think they need all the help they can get."

"Three years old? Is that sick, or what?" Kathryn wore tight trousers and a big loose shirt which did nothing to disguise the fact that with a sack of melons in her hand she probably hit the scales at around seven stone. "And it's not just that back home people *do* all that twelve-step programme stuff, they also *tell* you about it. They're all suffering from toxic shame and they want to make damn sure you *share* it with them. You wouldn't believe how many times I've practically nodded my head off my shoulders while some neurotic creep tells me all about co-dependency. Jesus."

"Brits have problems, too."

"But you don't talk about them all the damn time. Anyway," Kathryn said, "what problems do *you* have?"

"Where to start," said Cassie.

"You look like you've got it made. Nice house, nice cat, nice kitten, nice body."

"Nice body?" Cassie arched her eyebrows. "How kind."

"How kind," Kathryn echoed, repeating the words under her breath, nodding as though she were an anthropologist making a note of some quaint native custom. She smiled at Cassie. "I mean it."

"Well," Cassie said, embarrassed. "The house isn't mine, neither is the cat. Nor the kitten. As for hang-ups . . . how long have you got?"

"How long do you need?"

"For starters, I'm being emotionally harassed by a red-headed farmer and psychologically threatened by a psychopath. On top of that, the police drop by to interrogate me at all hours of the day and night."

"Apart from that, Mrs. Lincoln . . ."

"In addition, someone I know has just killed himself and someone I don't know but would have like to has just been murdered."

"That's one hell of an agenda. What do you do for a living—sell ferry tickets across the Styx?"

"Basically, I play bridge"

"My two brothers put themselves through school playing bridge," said Kathryn. "I guess that's why I never learned. Too much gender-politics going on in my family."

"I'll teach you, if you'd like. Maybe you don't have time. I don't really know how you spend your days."

"My days? Mornings I work at home. Afternoons I work at home. Evenings I work at home. Nights, I tumble into bed. It's real interesting."

"Work on what?"

"I'm a professor back home. I know I don't look like your

average professor but that's what I do: teach in the modern history department. But I always wanted to come and live over here, so I put in for this special scholarship I saw advertised in one of the journals. Gives you just about enough money to survive on if you stick to beans and rice and never turn on the central heating. Plus visiting rights at one of the colleges in Oxford, and a chance to eat there once a fortnight. Oh, and you have to take a few seminars here and there. But it's not a heavy load. And it gives me a chance to get on with the novel I've always been convinced I could write if someone would only allow me the freedom."

"Were you right?"

"I haven't had the time to find out yet." The tortoiseshell kitten jumped down from Kathryn's lap and sauntered over to the white cat which lay snoozing on the warm flagstones. It began to bat at one of the delicate pink ears with its tiny paws. "Did you know there was a murder a few days ago, not far from here?"

"It's probably the same one that's bothering me."

"How're you involved?" The kitten tried to scramble up on the white cat's back.

"Peripherally." Cassie went through the whole story again, while Kathryn asked questions. As she did so, Cassie found that she had one or two questions of her own. She remembered again the feeling she had had that something in Lord Wickham's library was not quite right. Was it because Kathryn's questions were different from Mantripp's questions? Or Walsh's?

Although the white cat was at least twice as big as the kitten, it was not prepared to argue. It was easier for it simply to get up and go somewhere else where there weren't any irritating females with needlelike claws and no idea how to relax. As it walked off and slid beneath the hedge, Cassie heard a car pull up in the lane. A car door slammed. Not Charlie Quartermain, she prayed. *Please*. Giles Laughton came round the side of the house, looking gloomy.

"Giles," Cassie said. "How nice to see you."

"I came to take you out for a drink," he said.

"Have one with us instead."

Kathryn reached out a lanky arm. "Hi. I'm Kathryn."

"How do you do."

"I'm from the States," said Kathryn.

Giles spoke in his most Eeyore voice. "I don't suppose by any chance you'd like to marry me, would you?"

"Jamie," Cassie said. "Look at me."

He looked up from his walnut-and-Stilton salad. "What."

"There's something you haven't told me, isn't there?"

"I don't know what you—"

"And if you haven't told me, it's a fair old bet you haven't told the police either."

His handsome face crumpled for a moment. Yesterday, watching the interplay between the tortoiseshell kitten and the white cat, Cassie had experienced a moment of revelation. Jamie, for all his looks and upbringing, was like the white cat: easy prey to a determined woman. She was well aware of the irony of having used the same phrase to describe herself vis-à-vis Steve. Jamie had plenty of determined women in his life, from his mother, to Portia Wickham, to the girlfriend who changed her mind about going round the world. Cassie felt no compunction in adding herself to the list.

"Let me ask you another question instead," she said. She

had rung him up the night before and told him in a determined fashion that she would buy him lunch today. He had, not at all to her surprise, agreed to be there at twelve-thirty and had only been fifteen minutes late.

"What is it?" He sounded sulky.

"Portia was found wearing leggings."

"So?"

"But she'd told her husband she was going to a charity concert. She was even seen driving off in her car."

"Exactly. I was one of the people who saw her."

"I bet you were the only person who knew where she was really going."

He stared at her without speaking. After a few seconds, his jaws crunched together over the forkful of walnut and lettuce he had just delivered to his mouth.

"Which wasn't, and never had been going to be, a charity première," pursued Cassie.

"What makes you think so?"

"Partly because the police told me there wasn't a charity concert on in London that evening. And partly because, although no-one else seems to have noticed the fact, if she *had* been going to a concert, she wouldn't have been dressed like that. So where was she going?"

"I don't know."

Cassie drew in a deep breath. It was Sartre who said that hell was other people, and even though she'd never found it easy to emphathise with a sexist old fart like Jean-Paul, some of the time she understood exactly what he meant. "OK. Here's another question. Possibly unrelated. Possibly not. Where were the butler's quarters at Halkam Court?"

"There's a staff block at the back," said Jamie. "Converted from the stables. The housekeeper sleeps there."

"And you?"

He squirmed. "They gave me a couple of rooms at the top of the house."

"They?"

"Portia." Jamie seized his wine glass and swallowed boldly. "Let me ask you a question now."

"What is it?"

"Why're you so interested? You never met Portia, you've no idea what she was like, and in any case, the police have the investigation in hand. I mean, it's not like you're the talented amateur sleuth who's been hired by the victim's family because the police have decided it's suicide or got the wrong man or something like that."

"Why am I interested? Good question." Cassie had once heard a famous Canadian authoress answering questions from the audience and been impressed by the way she slowly repeated each enquiry in a low thrilling voice to give herself time to think up an answer. "Why am I interested?" she said again. She was not going to tell Jamie about the unresolved guilt which had haunted her since she first learned of Portia Wickham's death. "I'm interested because although, as you say, I never met her, I felt that she was very like me."

Jamie nodded. "That's true. And not just to look at."

"I don't for a moment think I'm finding out stuff which the police have missed. I certainly don't see myself as some kind of Miss Marple. It's just . . ."

Momentarily, her attention strayed. At the next table a tiff was developing between the two men who occupied it. Wine carafes were being pulled this way and that, tempers were fraying.

". . . I think I have more in common with her than the police do. Also, I was there the night she died, which they weren't, and I feel—perhaps quite wrongly—I have a kind of proprietorial interest. Plus a certain sensitivity to whatever vibrations were going on at the time. I can't put it any better than that."

"Remember what happened last time you had too much to drink, Neville," one of the men said crossly.

"What?" Neville said, as though truly interested in the answer.

"Embarrassed? I didn't know where to put myself."

"I certainly knew where to put *myself*, ducky," Neville said, looking roguish. As the one currently in receipt of the carafe, he took the opportunity to hold it out of his friend's reach while he refilled his glass.

"And did, too," said his friend waspishly.

Neville winked at Cassie. "You know you loved it," he said, his voice over-loud.

"Do you *mind*, Neville?"

"To get back to what we were talking about," said Cassie. Although she spoke authoritatively, what she said was based on pure guesswork. "There was another place, wasn't there? Somewhere else she used to meet you, away from the house."

Jamie picked at his roll then made a resigned face. "Yes."

"Is that where she was headed that night?"

Jamie nodded disconsolately. "I told her it was quite impossible for me to get there that evening. She said that just because Darcy chose to alter his arrangements at the last possible moment, there was no reason for the butler to change his plans, too. It was supposed to be my evening off, you see. And the housekeeper was away."

"And you didn't agree with Lady Wickham?"

"Not really. Noblesse oblige and all that. Darcy was a decent enough employer and I didn't want to let him down if people were arriving from London for the evening. I told Portia I'd try and get there later, when they'd gone."

"There?"

"She used this cottage on the edge of the estate. Over towards Market Broughton. I'm not sure Darcy even knew about it."

"And did you go later?"

"You saw yourself what happened. First you came back. Then Symington. Most of the others stayed on late. I drove out after Darcy had gone to bed, but by then there was no sign of her."

"Was her car there?"

He sighed. "I hadn't expected it to be. She didn't like waiting."

"Where did you think she was?"

He shrugged. "She could have gone anywhere."

"And you've not told the police any of this?"

The hunted look reappeared. "Of course not."

"There's absolutely no reason why they'd think you did it."

"Except that nobody saw me between you and the others leaving, and you coming back. I was around, in the kitchen, but Tamsin had—er—gone by then. Darcy and his chums were busy finishing off the sandwiches and knocking back whisky in the drawing-room, and they didn't need me for anything. I could easily have run down the drive and shot her."

"Why would you do such a thing?"

"Maybe they'd think we'd quarrelled."

"Had you?"

"No!"

Neville at the next table looked over and wagged a reproving finger. "Temper, temper," he said. "Shouldn't shout at Miss Marple, old boy. Fri'fully bad form."

"Neville!" hissed his friend.

Jamie lowered his voice. "We'd exchanged a few brisk words on the subject of my intransigence at fulfilling the terms of my contract—who exactly was paying whom, and what exactly they were paying for—but nothing more than that."

"Did anyone overhear this?"

"One of the cleaning women came in while we were talking. I don't know how much she took in."

"I still can't work out why Portia would be walking up the drive that late at night, in the pouring rain. Why not use her car?"

"She could be very impulsive," Jamie said. Suddenly, to his own intense embarrassment, he began to cry. "I miss her," he said. "I loved her."

"That's what you have to remember." Cassie reached across and squeezed his hand tightly. "None of the other stuff matters. Given or received, love is always a plus. Especially given. Hold on to that." At the next table, Neville opened his mouth to make some comment. "Shut it, Nev," she said. She felt immensely protective. Almost maternal—or as she imagined maternal might be. It felt good.

Later, she was able to establish that Jamie had seen nothing, heard nothing. The cottage had been dark when he arrived, and after a quick check to establish Portia was no longer there, he had come home and gone to bed until woken by the housekeeper, at which point he had put on a dressing-gown and gone down to be informed by the postman about the discovery of the body.

"Who identified the body?"

"Officially, I've no idea. Darcy, I should think. But the postman knew who it was. And so—so d-did I. There was no mistaking her." His voice shook.

"How did Darcy take it when you told him?"

"Stunned," Jamie said. "He was absolutely stunned. There's no other way to describe it."

"Did that surprise you?"

He thought about that, raising underdone pink pigeon-breast to his mouth and chewing it thoughtfully. Eating seemed to calm him down. "Not really, at the time. Anyone would be stunned to learn that their wife had been murdered." He raised his eyebrows. "I chose the word carefully, by the way. He didn't burst into tears, or seem shocked and distraught. He was, like, bowled over rather than saddened. If that answers your question."

"Were they a close couple?"

Jamie shook his head.

"Did you bring that address I asked for?"

"Yes."

Having paid the bill, Cassie stood up and leaned over Jamie. "Want some advice?"

"No, thanks"

"Tell the police all this. Whatever you think they think about you, if they find out for themselves—which they will—it'll look much worse for you."

"I'll see you all next week," Cassie finished. "You've done well during the Easter break, not forgotten too much. Just to keep everybody up to scratch, I thought a couple of weeks from now we'd have a min-tournament. Establish the Archbishop Cranmer Upper School Pairs Tournament."

The members of the evening class groaned pleasurably at the thought and began to tidy away their notes, pass the plastic wallets of duplicate hands forward for Cassie to collect, set chairs up on tables to make things easier for the cleaners. She had been surprised to find that both Kathryn and Giles had joined the class: even more so to find that they had arrived together.

"Coming for a drink, darlin'?" Charlie Quartermain appeared at the table where she was packing up her gear.

"You're going to be really good, Charlie," she said, sidestepping the question. Somehow, without her knowing quite how, going to have a drink after class with Charlie had evolved over two terms into a habit it was hard to break. "The way you played that third hand was brilliant." She was trying to keep the relationship on a professional basis, but it was difficult.

"We're coming, too," Giles said, stepping up behind Quartermain. "Aren't we, Kathryn?"

"Try and stop us," said Kathryn. "After using my brain like that for two hours, I need strong liquor."

"How did you enjoy the class?" Cassie said.

"Extremely informative. You're a good teacher," Kathryn said. "One of these days, I might even be able to take on my brothers, at last."

"If she can teach me to play bridge," Quartermain said, with a note of fond ownership in his voice which irritated Cassie almost to kicking-point, "she could teach pigs to fly."

"Sometimes," Cassie said, "I wish I'd stuck to ballet."

They ended up in the Old Plough at Market Broughton. With a number of unnecessarily emphatic gestures, Quartermain insisted on buying the first round, even though nobody was arguing with him. The other three found somewhere to sit. The two small dogs reappeared and snuffled round the ankles of Giles' corduroys. The Character at the bar was doing her shtick, slapping her vast sides and shaking with laughter at some witticism of the landlord's. It must have been a good one, because Quartermain was doing it too.

When he'd finished demonstrating some high-quality amusement, he returned, plonking down their drinks and hoicking bags of salt'n'vinegar-flour crisps out of his pockets. Before Cassie could say that she hated flavoured crisps, he said, "Hang on, darlin'. I brought some cashews with me. I know you like those."

"Cashews!" exclaimed Kathryn. "Gimme." She tore open the plastic packet and poured some of the contents into her hand.

"So," she said. "Are you two—you know—going together, or what?"

"Who," said Cassie. "Me and Giles?"

"Giles? No. You and Mr. Quartermain here."

Cassie was about to open her mouth and make her position with regard to Mr. Quartermain here absolutely clear, but Kathryn went on, "I mean, he obviously wants you to have his children."

There was a quiet pause, during which Kathryn realised that she had somehow alienated one-third of her audience and discomposed the second. The other third was sitting there with a shit-eating grin on his big face, nodding like a buddha.

"I can see why you're a professor, luv," he smirked.

The pause might have gone on for some time, except that the door opened and Lord Wickham came in with Roddy Symington.

Giles, whose face had gone red, moved the upper half of his torso towards the centre of the table round which they were clustered. "That's Darcy Wickham," he said in a low voice.

"Do you mean the one whose wife was murdered?" Kathryn said. Her face, too, was flushed.

"Yes."

"How do you know?"

"My mother plays bridge with him sometimes," Giles said.

Kathryn shook her head. "Doesn't look to me like a bereaved spouse."

"Much more like a man who's got two successful deals going down and is hoping by the end of the evening there'll be a third," said Cassie. Talking about Wickham had the edge over the thought of bearing Quartermain's children, but only by a hair.

"One of his companies is trying to take over some big wine-producer in Australia," Quartermain said, his voice a fraction louder than it ought to have been. "I read it in the *Financial Times* a couple of days ago."

Another theory about Darcy Wickham's guilt leaped into Cassie's brain on hearing this. He needed his wife's money to expand and she had refused to lend it because, as a lifelong teetotaller, she abstained from drinking and disapproved of those who—but Portia was not the kind of woman to abstain from anything, and besides, Walsh had indicated that Wickham had no money problems.

"The other one's called Symington," she murmured.

"Symington? Is that the construction company? I was reading about them the other day," said Charlie. "Something to do with floating shares in a company which wants to build leisure complexes in seaside resorts."

"What?" said Cassie

"I think that's what it was," Charlie said.

Cassie stared at Roddy Symington, eyes narrowed. It would be too much of a coincidence, wouldn't it, if he turned out to be the man behind John Burslake's problem. Symington was leaning on one elbow, displaying several inches of wrist and a thin watch on an effeminate gold strap. From here, it seemed to have the right complement of numbers, and no diamonds. But that didn't necessarily mean anything. A man like Roddy—a man who allowed himself to be *called* Roddy—would probably have more than one watch. She wondered whether she should pass any of this on to the police. It couldn't have any bearing on the murder of Portia Wickham but it might lead belatedly to some kind of justice for Burslake.

The bolder of the landlord's two tiny dogs rested its nose on Kathryn's jeans. Giles leaned over and stroked one of its ginger-brown ears. Cassie could see that what he was really doing was stroking Kathryn's knee. She could also see that Kathryn didn't mind. Was this one of the faster courtships on record, or had she simply gone to sleep and woken up to find that two people she thought had been introduced fewer than forty-eight hours ago had in fact been dating for six months? And why wasn't she more pissed off that Giles, who'd been badgering her to marry him for some weeks, seemed to have turned his attention to the American professor without the slightest sign of regret? Why didn't she mind?

"Cassie," Quartermain said.

"Because I don't love him," she said. "That's why."

"What?"

"Nothing."

"About Saturday."

"I bought a dress," Cassie said, still watching Giles and Kathryn and not pretending very hard not to.

"What time shall I pick you up?"

"I can drive myself."

"I've organised a driver. Much easier all round if I come and get you."

"What is it exactly we're going to?"

"It's a dinner-dance at the Randolph. That's why I want you to come along, so you can add a touch of class."

Cassie ignored this. "The Randolph Hotel in Oxford?"

"Yeah. So we can all get acquainted."

"Acquainted?" What with? she thought rudely. Grief?

"With the other interested parties." At Cassie's blank look, Quartermain added, "I told you I was going into business with someone, didn't I? Three of us. Could be a nice little earner, if we get it right. A money man, an ideas man, and a man with expertise. That's me."

"Expertise in what?"

He looked at her reproachfully. "I'm a master mason."

"I know." Where did he get off, Cassie asked herself, coming on all reproachful? Had she ever asked him into her life? Ever given him the faintest encouragement? "What kind of business is it?"

"I told you that, too. It's like landscape gardening, only with a difference. It won't make our fortunes, but it'll be bloody satisfying." He smiled at her. "I'm a lucky man, Cass. I earn my living doing something I really enjoy, and not too many men can say that."

"Nor women." Cassie smiled back. "I'm the same."

"I know, girl. It's why I fell in love with you."

The smile faded. "I just wish you'd fall out again," she said coldly.

"I shan't do that, luv," Charlie said. "Not ever."

Cassie lifted her head and looked over to where Wickham was sitting. He was staring at her, and the expression on his face made her feel extremely uncomfortable. Had he realised who Violet Mandela was? Did he know that she had been questioning Jamie? Was he aware that she had actually tripped over his wife's body and, by doing nothing about it, condemned the poor corpse to a night in the rain? She wanted to march over and confront him—but what about? However much she might feel that he was involved in his wife's death, she had absolutely no proof, and very little basis for believing it. He caught her eye and she smiled tentatively; he did not smile back. Perhaps he didn't recognise her. Perhaps he did, but chose to pretend he did not.

She wondered whether Walsh might stop by one of these days and return her dress. If he did, perhaps she could ply him with whisky, promise him sexual delights such as he had never even dreamed of and, in return, get him to reveal his professional secrets. It was hard to assess to what extent he might be susceptible to such offers, but it could be worth a try. Or maybe she could just promise him sexual delights, without bothering about the *quid pro quo*. One of the things you couldn't ignore about Detective Sergeant Walsh was the fact that he was no ordinary policeman. Another was that he was definitely sexy.

Meanwhile, there were one or two things she wanted to check. For instance, Jamie's mother had indicated that she scarcely knew Portia. Yet, from the information Cassie had easily obtained by making a couple of phone calls, she and Portia had served on not one but two committees together. Wasn't it likely, therefore, that they must have been more than passing acquaintances? And what about the open animosity with which Ms. Howard had spoken of her son's employer's wife: wasn't that also a dead giveaway? That kind of dislike could have come only from intimate knowledge.

"Listen," Kathryn said, "it's my birthday next week. Why don't we celebrate? A party at my place?"

"Sounds good," said Giles. "How old will you—"

"Don't ask," Kathryn said, leaning forward and putting a finger across his mouth.

"Aren't we supposed to be proud of our age, these days?" Cassie said.

"You may be: I'm not. There are too many things I've never got round to doing and now I probably never will." Kathryn smiled at Giles. "Why didn't I get out of Nebraska years ago?"

"What day, then?" Quartermain said. "Can't be Tuesday because Cassie teaches at the prison. Can't be Thursday, because of her evening class."

"And here I thought I'd left my talking diary at home," said Cassie, trying hard not to show her annoyance.

"Since Wednesday is the actual day, let's make it then." Kathryn looked round at them. "Feel free to bring a couple of friends each, if you want. I might even bestir myself and cook something—not that the kitchen in Ivy Cottage is up to much—but all contributions gratefully received."

"I'll bring some champers." Charlie grinned at Cassie. "Gotta mate with a champagne shop. He'll see us right."

"I'm branching out, trying to revive some of the local cheeses," said Giles. "I'll bring a selection along."

"Great!"

While the others chatted together, Cassie thought about tomorrow. Her usual Friday morning bridge game had been cancelled, since Naomi Harris, one of the regulars, was in the John Radcliffe Hospital in Oxford for medical tests, and Lucinda Powys-Jones, another regular, was off in the afternoon for a weekend course in stencilling, and could use the time saved to organise her husband, children and dogs so that they managed to cope during her absence.

With a free day, Cassie wondered if it might be a good idea to start thinking about a replacement for Gran's ratty old fur. Or, at least, start talking to someone who might be of some help. And if she was going to do that, she might as well go straight to the top.

12

The board announcing Fairline Farms Ltd was set amid a
confusion of dark green shrubbery beside an unmade-up lane
which veered sharply back on itself from the road. Cassie
turned cautiously in. The tangle of boskage was of the Jurassic
Park variety: luxuriant and menacing. Any moment, a rabid
mink might leap in through the open car window and sink its
fangs into her arm. She rolled up the window, telling herself
she was an idiot. After a while, she came to a one-storey
building and pulled up in front of it.

Could this possibly be the domicile of Mr. and Mrs. Winston Griffiths? If so, they lived in a house for which the word
"shabby" might have been coined. Without actually being a
shack, it none the less managed to convey the impression that
if it had its rights, it would be. Surveying it from the interior of
her car, Cassie decided that Early Dustbowl didn't really catch
the architectural flavour of a dwelling which seemed, at least

from the outside, to be the very last place she would have expected Melissa Griffiths to inhabit.

She got out and pressed the bell at one side of the door. After a while, she could hear someone shuffling around inside. After another while, punctuated with the sound of chains rattling and keys being inserted into deadlocks, the door opened to reveal something Cassie had never seen before, though she had heard Aunt Polly use the phrase often enough about certain of Uncle Sam's unmarried parishioners. If they'd been advertising for a slattern, this woman would have fitted the job description head and dandruffy shoulders above anyone else.

"Yer?" she said. Ash dropped on to her shoulder, and without disturbing the fag in her mouth, she blew sideways at it. Years of practice, obviously. Behind her, a couple of adolescent boys materialised and stared at Cassie with the hardened insolence of habitual criminals.

"My name's Cassandra Swann: I was looking for Mrs. Griffiths," Cassie said.

"Wha'?"

"Mrs. Melissa Griffiths?" Cassie said in a voice as precise as polka-dots. Momentary panic gripped her. She could hear the authentic tones of Aunt Polly in her throat. A mixture of superciliousness and disgust. Like, get thee behind me, grunge.

"Oh, 'lissa," said the slattern. She scratched her head vigorously. Two purple plastic curlers rode above each ear. Friday is payday, right? Looked as though she was getting ready for a big night out. "You'll find her up at the big house." She jerked her thumb over her shoulder. "Further on, dear." One of the boys started grinning and whispered something to his brother.

"Ah." As a trailer to draw people on to the delights of Fairline Farms Ltd, this place was a definite disincentive. One look, and most punters, rather than wait for the big feature, would drop their popcorn and run.

"You can leave your car here if you want," the woman said.

And come back to find the tyres gone? Or the car itself? No jolly fear. "Thank you," Cassie said. "But I might as well drive up there."

"Suit yourself." The woman sniffed and dragged a wrist

along her upper lip. It was so much in character that for a moment Cassie wondered if she was being set up here. Briefly she imagined some pin-striped mogul inside the house looking up from his *Financial Times* and saying, "There's that blasted doorbell again, Fiona. Why don't you go and give them your slattern, old girl?" But no. Green ankle-socks set into disintegrating trainers, chapped legs, a dipping hemline, bra-less boobs barely contained in a home-knitted sweater which had been the victim of many unskilful washings: this was the genuine article, all right.

She drove further down the private lane. Trees and bushes—alders, for the most part, interspersed with brambles and dog-roses—hung over it, creating an air of rampancy. She tried to remember why the name of the place, although she had been given the address by Jamie only the previous day, was one she had heard before, and recently. Where? Why?

The alder gave way to a stretch of rhododendron and euonymus. Rounding a bend, she found herself drawing up in front of what might have once been a Victorian gentleman's residence. Not pretty, but eminently respectable. Red brick. Green woodwork. Slate tiles. A turret or two. And big. Plenty of room there for the children and their nursemaids, governesses, lady's maids, cook-generals and housekeepers, as well as the footmen, housemaids and tweenies without which no respectable Victorian household could have functioned. Shrubbery spread on either side of the house, concealing what lay on the other side. She pulled up behind a top-of-the-range Merc, a four-wheel drive and an old Metro. Getting out of her car, she could hear various layers of noise. Close at hand there was a considerable amount of cheerful clucking going on, indicative of hens contented with their lot. Behind that, someone was singing along to an old Dylan number—never the easiest thing to do at the best of times—and banging metal buckets about. And, further away, there was an almost inaudible but constant hum.

Cassie lifted the brass door knocker and let it fall again. Someone approached behind stained glass inserts and opened up. Bette Davis lipstick, tight skirt, high heels and a hoover: since it wasn't Melissa, it all added up to the woman who helped Melissa with the house. Disconcertingly, she could have been the slattern's twin sister, despite the differing approach to personal presentation.

"Mrs. Melissa Griffiths?" Cassie said, guessing that this was the owner of the Metro.

"What about her?"

Fair enough. Cassie realised that though she had arched her eyebrows enquiringly, she had not in actual fact framed a question. If Madam Literal here wanted to make something of it, she was game. She took a step forward. "Is Mrs. Griffiths in?" she said.

"In where?"

In the bloody house, where else? "Is she at home, receiving visitors, available, free, around, able to see me? My name's Cassandra Swann and she met me a week or so ago, at Lord Wickham's house."

"Him," said Madam Literal. She held the door so that Cassie could enter. "You'd best come in and I'll see if they're free. What name was it again?"

"Cassandra Swann."

A door to one side of the wood-floored hall opened, and an enormous man of Afro-Caribbean descent, carrying a book, came out. Seeing Cassie, he stopped. "We have a visitor," he said.

"Yes," said the help, with an audible sigh. Perhaps she felt she had a monopoly on literalism.

"All right, Mrs. Valenti," the big man said. "I'll take care of it." Surging towards Cassie, he held out his hand. "Winston Griffiths. And you are . . . ?"

"Cassandra Swann." After so much repetition, her name was beginning to take on a lunatic meaninglessness, so that it could just as well have belonged to a new kind of cheese or been a synonym for the sexual act. "I was hoping to have a word with your wife."

"My wife." He looked round the hall as though wondering what he'd done with her. "She's out somewhere. I'm not sure where."

"Out as in outside? Or out as in gone from this place?"

He smiled gently at her. "As in the first. Come." He put down his book. "Follow me."

Cassie was happy to do so. He walked fluidly back through the door he had just entered by, across the room so revealed and between a pair of long open windows, which led out onto a terrace. "There she is," he said. At the far end of a long shrub-enclosed stretch of lawn was a paved area beside a pool. On it were set a number of cushioned chaises, a white plastic table with an umbrella inserted down its centre, three matching chairs and two women. Melissa. And Mother.

Oh God, no, Cassie thought. The last thing she wanted to do was to end up as the No-Man's Land in the Battle of the Bitches. Was it too late to withdraw?

"There you go," Winston said. He had a great smile, and a rough London accent, a shell-suit in mostly white, and a flat-top. "What do you want to talk to Liss about?"

Not much hope of lying here, nor of pretending to be something other than she was. Especially when standing directly under God's blue heaven. Cassie had always found it much easier to tell lies indoors, as though ceilings and roofs somehow blocked the airwaves between her and her Maker. "Uh. It's to do with a charity I'm—uh—interested in," she said.

"Charity? You're not one of those troublemakers, are you?"

"I hope not."

"Because we've had enough of them. Coming down here, telling us how to run our business. I mean, I'm as humane as the next bloke, love animals and that, but I've got a living to earn like everyone else, kids and so forth."

"No, I really wanted—"

Winston appeared to have segued from affability into instant fury. "I mean, who the hell do they think they are, demonstrations out in the road, passing the bad word, letters to the Press, just because those rich bitches have got connections? Christ: don't they realise? I've sunk everything I had into this venture, and a lot I didn't, I'm not going to lie down and let it all go down the tubes because of some bleeding-hearts who don't have a blind bit of trouble stuffing pâté de foie gras down their throats, and never mind how the French produce *that*. Have they ever seen what force-feeding does to the bleeding geese?"

"Uh—"

"None of what they wrote in the papers was true, anyway," said Winston, passionately. "The Inspectors are down here regular, see we run things right. There was one shed—*one* shed—where they found a spot of bother, but I got rid of my manager on the spot."

Yeah, and the dog ate my homework, thought Cassie. She nodded encouragingly.

"Can't be doing with staff who don't keep their eye on things," Winston went on. "Like I say, it's a fine line between good business practice and respect for the product you're dealing with. So whatever you've come about, it better not be about my eggs, thank you very much."

"It isn't," Cassie said faintly. How had she ended up talking about eggs, when she'd come here to discuss mink? The reason why the name of the place had been familiar suddenly clicked into place. Although she didn't spend a lot of time memorising the names on the tops of her egg cartons, Fairline Farms had recently been singled out as the target of a campaign by one of the animal rights organisations, which was seeking to do something about the way eggs were produced. There'd been a series of photographs of battery hens being reared in conditions of utter misery. Details returned to her: claws which had grown right round the bars on which they stood, beaks removed, wings clipped off. Horrible stuff. Which explained Mother's ovarious jibes.

She started to say something about having made a mistake, but Winston wasn't listening. "I told that last woman I'd have her if I saw anything in the papers," he said. "Sue her for libel."

"Which last woman?"

"That one came down from London. Boadicea type, waving banners and papers at me. I told her to get lost. Who the hell do they think they are, anyway? Sitting in their fancy flats in Battersea, trying to stop people earning an honest bob or two. 'Listen, sunshine,' I told her, 'I've made my way up in the world without any help from anybody, started out with nothing, grew up in the back streets of London, thank you very much, nobody handed me nothing on a plate, not like you lot with your titles and your butlers and what the hell else. So don't you come down here trying to take away everything I've built up, because you'll regret it if you do.' That's what I told her."

"How did she take it?" What fascinated Cassie was the way Winston could open his mouth and speak whole paragraphs without drawing breath. Even though what he was saying was knee-jerk rhetoric obviously produced many times before, it was amazing that he seemed to show no need to fill his lungs from time to time. Then something he had said knocked at the door. "Battersea?" she said.

"That's where she came from. The leader of the demonstration. Had the nerve to come in here one afternoon, say she was in the neighbourhood and would like to see over our nesting-sheds, if I didn't mind. 'Don't mind?' I said. 'I bleeding well do mind, thank you very much.' Told her to sod off." Winston paused to wipe a fleck of foam from his lower lip.

"And did she?"

"Yes, after giving me her business card. Can you believe that? SW12: I'd like to give her SW-bleeding–12. Oh, yes: she went off all right. Came back later, though. Brought a crowd of other sluts with her, too. Handing out leaflets in the town, bawling through megaphones. And then picketing all the local supermarkets and hotels, chucking stones through the windows. Breaking into our distributors' warehouses. They even stopped one of our delivery vans and threw the entire consignment into the road. Christ: the amount of business we've lost. We'll barely break even this year, and if anything big happens, anything major, I'm going to be hard pressed, I'm telling you."

Why exactly *was* he telling her. Cassie wondered. Did he always spout off like this, to complete strangers, or did he take her for someone who was somehow involved?

"We've had the RSPCA down here," Winston went on. "They couldn't find anything to complain about. I do my best, given the competition. But you know what really gutted me? What really got me riled?"

"No."

"One of them—*one* of them—was none other than Portia bleeding Wickham. Whose husband is a friend of my mother-in-law's. Can you believe that? Can you bloody well believe that? Talk about loyalty. I told her to get off my property and not come back. I told her if I ever saw her again, she'd better make damn sure she wasn't alone, because . . ." He pulled himself up. "Not that I meant it, of course. Just the sort of thing you say in the heat of the moment." Belatedly, he'd remembered that Portia had been murdered only a few days ago. "Not that the business has suffered *that* badly," he said, glaring at Cassie, forgetting, or choosing to gloss over, that he had just said the opposite. "And any publicity's good publicity, eh? People've got very short memories: they remember the name but they aren't sure why."

Just like me, thought Cassie. "Have the police spoken to you?" she said. Not that it was any of her business.

"What about?"

"The local murder."

He stared at her, as though trying to sort out which of the many local murders she could possibly be referring to. "Lady Wickham, do you mean?"

"That's the one."

"Not me. I didn't have nothing to do with it," Winston said quickly. So quickly that she began to wonder whether he'd ever done time. That instant refutation of any blame which might be going was a con's habit. After all, nobody had accused him of doing anything in the first place. "The wife. The cops had a few words with the wife. But she was in the clear. Why're you asking? What's it to do with you?"

"Absolutely nothing. I came down here to ask you about fur coats."

"Fur coats? What you on about?"

"I was under the impression that you were a mink farmer," said Cassie. "Now I discover it's eggs."

"Got you," Winston said. "I once managed a mink ranch. Gave it up, though. Couldn't stand those horrible little creatures baring their teeth every time I walked past them. Began to take it personal, know what I mean? You don't get much of that with chickens."

"And the chickens don't get much of anything, right?"

"You what?"

"Winston! Who's that you're talking to?" Melissa raised her bones languidly from the chaise and stared in their direction through mirrored sunglasses.

"Someone come to see you, honey-bunch," Winston said.

Melissa smiled. She stood up and began walking across the grass towards them. Cassie could hear her bones grinding together with each movement. Beside her, Winston looked at his watch and then at his wife. "Mmm . . ." he said, like someone choosing dessert off the trolley, so much under his breath that Cassie was sure he didn't even realise she had heard. She looked where he was looking but clearly saw something different. Just Melissa, wearing a shiny yellow bikini. Between top and bottom was a considerable amount of tanned skin covering amazingly little flesh. Was that daylight she could see through Melissa's body, the vague outline of the chairs and table behind her, or was it a trick of the light?

"Darling," Melissa said, removing her glasses and twining herself round Winston like the serpent round Eden's apple tree. She looked over at Cassie and frowned. "You're— um . . ."

"Cassandra Swann."

"Didn't we—um . . . ?"

". . . play bridge together the other night?"

"Yes."

"We did," said Cassie.

"I think she wanted to have a word with you about something," said Winston. He had pushed his hand down inside the bottom half of Melissa's bikini and was cupping one of her thin buttocks. And why not? Cassie asked herself. Better him than someone else. Especially when Melissa was so obviously turned on by it. She could see, looking at the two of them, why such an unlikely pair had come together. There was a sexual electricity about them which made her want to find the nearest cold shower. Or warm man. No wonder Mother was so bitchy.

"It's all right," she said. She had, after all, found out less than she had wanted to know, but at the same time something more.

For all his protestations of innocence, Winston had good and sufficient reason to wish Portia out of the way. Was it not at least feasible that, driving up to Halkam Court to collect his wife and mother-in-law, he had seen Portia, architect of at least some of his troubles, stumbling through the rain and, seized by another of his short-fuse rages, had seized a gun and shot her? People who lived in the country, people like Winston, often had guns. If she checked, she would almost certainly find that he had a licence. But for a Baby Browning .22? It wasn't very likely.

The trouble with that theory was that, assuming she *had* stumbled over the body, Portia was already dead when she herself had finally arrived back at Halkam Court, but Melissa was still there, still banging on about asking for Aces. She had heard her quite unmistakably. Which meant that Winston had not yet arrived to take her home, unless he had, for some reason, having killed Portia, lurked somewhere for a while. Why would he do that? To provide himself with an alibi? But, at that stage, he'd had no idea that he might need one, no idea that Cassie Swan would be able to establish the time by which the body was already there.

She tried for a long shot. "Actually," she said to Melissa, as Winston removed his hand from his wife's pants and enclosed her narrow waist with his arm, "I heard your husband talking about a woman from Battersea who came down here to demonstrate, and wondered if by any chance it was someone I know."

"Liss," Winston said, and the lust in his voice was unmistakable. One of his huge thumbs began furtively to massage Melissa's nipple.

"I don't know who you know," Melissa pointed out. Now *she* had her hand down the back of *his* trousers.

"My friend, who's into demonstrating and stuff," Cassie said apologetically, "is called Olivia Howard. Actually, she's Jamie's mother."

"Who's Jamie?" asked Winston. The whites of his eyes seemed to redden slightly.

"Don't be silly, Winston," Melissa said. "Who *is* Jamie?"

"The butler," said Cassie. She couldn't believe they didn't know. "Lord Wickham's butler."

"Oh, is that what he's called? I'd never seen him before that night we played bridge," said Melissa. "My mother goes to Halkam Court from time to time, but I've never been invited before. In fact, I only went this time on the strict understanding that that bitch who's been causing us so much trouble wasn't going to be there."

"Bitch?" asked Cassie.

"Portia Wickham," said Melissa. Her eyes sought her husband's and she smiled fondly up at him. "Not that I give a damn who invites me to their houses and who doesn't. I've got all I need right here at home, haven't I, darling?"

"You betcha," growled Winston throatily.

Down by the pool, Mother was staring wistfully at her daughter and son-in-law. Cassie made an excuse, which neither of them heard, and left.

Food for thought. Which reminded her rather acutely of food for sustenance. It was definitely lunch-time, especially for those who had skipped breakfast. She decided that in the interests of her waistline she would wait until she got home again and then make herself an improving salad. Tomorrow was Charlie Quartermain's dinner-dance and she needed to look her best. Whatever that was.

Passing through a village, she saw a bow-fronted house facing on to the High Street. She slowed down. A sign across the top of the window read JAGO'S. Wasn't that the new vegetarian restaurant she had read about in the foodie column of the Sunday paper a couple of weeks ago? Hadn't the columnist spoken in awed tones of sun-dried tomatoes, a savoury fetta cheesecake, roasted pepper salads? And weren't all of those exactly the sort of thing a woman who wished to look her best ought to be lunching on? It was the work of a moment to nip off the road and into the carpark behind the restaurant, of but three more to find herself seated at a table inspecting a menu which could have been written by an archangel.

Having ordered, she replayed her recent conversation with

Winston. Was she jumping to conclusions to assume that the Boadicea-type he had mentioned, who lived in Battersea, was Olive Howard, aka Olivia Grahame? She had seen, now that it was brought to mind, a pile of posters on Ms. Howard's formica-topped table relating to battery-reared hens, hadn't she? Whether they specifically mentioned Fairline Farms by name she could not recall. But it seemed likely. Especially when the weighty presence of Portia Wickham was included in the equation. Add to that the fact that Portia and Olivia were on a couple of the same charity committees, and the lines of connection made it more and more feasible that Olivia had roped Portia in as a bit of local ballast during the protest demonstration against Fairline Farms.

If she was right, she thought, trying a delicate salad of rocket-leaves, pine-kernels and sun-dried tomatoes, discreetly sprinkled with a lime flavoured dressing, it made it all the stranger that Olive Howard should have implied that she barely knew Portia. *"We'd met,"* she had said. But if she had enough leverage to persuade Portia into coming over to the other side of the country in order to picket the home of a man whose mother-in-law played bridge with her husband . . . Which in itself was a socially dangerous thing for even the reckless Portia to have agreed to. While not a particular fan, Cassie knew enough about living in the country to know that, just as in prison, it was vital to maintain the social networks, that the system would start to break down if too many rules of etiquette were flouted. A good old-fashioned feud, with families not speaking to each other and solicitors' letters passing, was one thing. But, at the lower levels, order had to be maintained. Country dwellers were much more dependent on each other, especially in the winter, than townies.

She considered what she knew about the former Olivia Grahame. Born and married into a class she had rejected. One child she obviously saw as a cross between Sir Parsifal and a pearl above rubies. Going quietly mad, according to Darcy Wickham—and her own son—and there was no reason in that particular conversation to imagine that he was grinding any axes. Hung up on older women having sex with younger men. Possibly hung up on sex altogether. And into every possible

cause going. Being so involved with so much of the foul un-
derbelly of contemporary living, wasn't it likely that your
weltanschauung grew a little distorted? Might you not want to
start cutting through the proper channels, the bureaucracy, the
red tape? And might not something of the same apply when
you saw your child being, as Olivia had put it herself, introduced to God knows what depravities? They might not seem
like depravities to anyone else, but to a woman with a chip of
mirror-glass in her eye . . .

Go over it again, Cassie said to herself, as she tucked into
the savoury cheesecake, trying not to faint with delight.
Olivia/Olive suddenly can't stand any more of Jamie having it
off with Portia, jumps into her car and heads for Halkam
Court. Perhaps she's telephoned Jamie first and established
that Portia will be out that night. She hides her car, and lurks
about near the house until she sees or hears Portia's approach.
Then she comes up behind the woman and shoots her but
nerves have made her hand shake and the bullet goes into Portia's back, forcing her to have another go. This time, the bullet
goes into Portia's brain, and Olive makes off, back to London
and no one the wiser.

No. Too many ifs and buts. There was no possible way
Olivia could have known that Portia would arrive back on
foot. And though she might have had access to a gun while
living with her former husband up in Scotland, the chances of
her having one in Battersea were minimal.

On the other hand, it might explain Jamie's evident apprehension, which amounted to something more than his grief at
Portia's death, if he thought his mother was responsible . . .
Cassie wondered whether Olivia had a history of violent action.
Certainly, if she was breaking into warehouses and hijacking
delivery vehicles, she wasn't your average stay-at-home miss,
was she?

But why stop at Olivia? What about Jeremy Marling as villain? Or Jacko Dexter? Or Symington?

Suppose, for instance, that Marling was a Mr. Big in the
drugs field? And suppose Portia did drugs, the way she did
everything else. Had she failed to fork out for her delivery of
Acapulco Gold and Marling had decided to show her what

was what? But wouldn't it make much more sense for her sup-
plier—Marling—to keep her hooked than to kill her? Especially when the police had said she had no financial problems,
any more than her husband had. Could she have been blackmailing Marling, then? Had Portia discovered what Marling
really was, the reality of how he funded his glittering lifestyle;
had she threatened to expose him?

Cassie wrote down "glittering lifestyle" on her paper napkin
and then added a couple of question marks. How did she know
whether Marling's lifestyle glittered? What exactly constituted
glitter, anyway? Fancy cars? Perfumed women? A string of
racehorses? Several residences, at least one of them on a
Caribbean island?

They were much more the sorts of things you'd expect from
Jacko Dexter, the computer-whizz millionaire with the place
in Wapping. On the river, no doubt. Very trendy. Very expensive. Did his story about striking gold in Silicon Valley have
any basis in reality? It probably did, given the fact that he had
a software company which people knew about. But it might be
worth asking Detective Sergeant Walsh, next time he showed
up. If he did.

Or could it be that the charity Walsh had mentioned, from
which Portia was threatening to pull her money, was one of
Olivia's pet causes? Just on the basis of phone-calls overheard
while she was in the Battersea flat, it was obvious that Ms.
Howard was having a hard time keeping her troops rallied. The
loss of significant amounts of cash might be disastrous. It
was also something Cassie could check with the police. Perhaps even telephone Walsh about. It was as good an excuse as
any to get in touch with him. Not that she was particularly interested in making contact.

Swallowing the last delicious morsels of the cheesecake
base, she reminded herself that she was not a detective, and
nobody had retained her to look into anything. She wasn't
even that inquisitive by nature, and anyway, the police were
probably doing a meticulous job of sifting through the information they had received. So what the hell was any of it to do
with her? The excuse she had given Jamie, of a fellow-feeling
with Portia, was thin enough; to start pinning murder scenarios

round the neck of innocent citizens because of it was going much too far.

Drinking coffee, she told herself none of it was her business. Not really. A few months ago, she'd got involved in a spot of snooping, but that was simply because her own livelihood had seemed threatened. Which was not the case here.

None the less, she hoped Walsh and Mantripp dropped in again soon.

Correction. To be absolutely honest, she hoped Walsh dropped in again soon.

13

That afternoon, she sat at her computer and once again went over the financial projections for the conversion of the outbuildings behind Honeysuckle Cottage. Whichever way you hacked it, they came out depressing. Even with Robin willing to stump up for a large portion of the costs, there was still a considerable shortfall. What they needed was a backer. It was infuriating that the promising relationship with Chilcott had foundered, and all because he had played like an idiot and wasn't man enough to admit it. Though perhaps someone as lacking in equilibrium as Royston was not a good person to have as part of a team. She shook her head: the whole business of his chucking her out of the car was so bizarre, even in retrospect, so out of character. But then, she had never really known him.

At four o'clock she went into the house to put on the kettle. Outisde, a car door slammed, and looking through the windows, she saw the burly frame of Detective Sergeant Walsh walking up the path. If ever she had been given a sign that though strait is the gate and narrow is the way, it was worth treading every time . . . Obviously God had noted the way she had avoided the temptation to lie while at Fairline Farms earlier in the day, and had seen fit to reward her substantially for it. Because, from the way Sergeant Walsh's shoulders moved under his white shirt, there could be no doubt that he was substantial, and, at that particular moment, more of a reward than she could have hoped for.

He stepped inside the cottage, bending his head to avoid smashing it on the beams. "I really like this place," he said.

"Me, too."

"Did you buy it from that old poofter who used to live here?"

"No. He's moved to France and I'm just looking after it for him. He's my godfather." Cassie watched with malicious pleasure as Walsh slowly turned red.

"When I said old poofter," he said. "I meant—"

"—old poofter," said Cassie. "I know what you meant. So would Robin, if he was here. On the other hand, the police force is in enough trouble already. Judgmental statements of that kind don't do much to improve the public attitude towards the police, you know."

Walsh rallied. "It was a statement of fact. I wasn't necessarily being judgmental."

"And I'm Mother Teresa," said Cassie. "Can I get you something? The kettle's on. Or you could have a glass of white wine."

"I'm not supposed to drink on duty, but—"

"Or off it. Not if you're driving."

"One glass won't hurt," Walsh said.

They sat outside. Since Portia's murder, the lilac had swelled and coloured, although the blooms were not yet fully out. There were thick buds on the roses, and in the hedge, a self-seeded laburnum hung its brilliant yellow flowers over the grass. "Did you come for any specific reason?" Cassie asked.

"Yes." Walsh turned his head and looked at her. As noted last time he came to the cottage, his eyes were somewhere between brown and green, a colour difficult to analyse without a certain amount of deep-gazing which she thought might be a mistake, given the way he was staring at her.

When he did not enlarge on this, she said, "What was it?"

"Oh, and I also came because I thought you might be interested to know that we've located Lady Wickham's car."

Cassie was still trying to work out the precise meaning of that "also" and how precisely it modified, if it did, what he had just said. "Where did you find it?" She looked at his beautiful mouth and felt an internal sigh fill her lungs. Some things were not meant to be. If Walsh had been just another Joe Blow, they might have been able to get it together. But he was Authority and she was Witness. Maybe even Suspect. The relationship was, and unfortunately would have to remain, strictly professional.

"In Nottingham," Walsh said. "An alert patrol-car noticed it standing in a side street. Not that it needed a degree to figure out that a four-wheel Daihatsu in that particular area was a little unusual, to say the least."

"Nottingham? I wonder why."

"Turns out one of the lads from Moreteyne Hall was on the run and nicked it. Didn't take him thirty seconds to break in and get it going. All that lot're accomplished car thieves by the time they reach double figures. We picked him up at the same time as we collected the car. Mind you, we were already on to Nottingham ourselves."

"How?"

"Some bright spark down at the station put two and two together and came up with a missing Daihatsu. Suggested we might try looking for a runaway in Nottingham—which was where the lad's Gran lived—and possibly our missing vehicle at the same time. Turned out to be right. When we picked him up, he said it was her birthday." Walsh gave an unsympathetic snort of laughter.

"And where did *he* find it?"

"Standing outside one of the cottages at the edge of the village," said Walsh. "Apparently Lady Wickham—uh—spent a lot of time there. She'd gone there the evening of her death—obviously to meet someone." He jittered his eyebrows about meaningfully.

"Are you suggesting it was a love-nest?" Cassie hoped she sounded sufficiently surprised.

"Exactly. Although it belonged to the Wickham estate, it wasn't in use. At least, not as a residence. The absconder couldn't believe his luck—nasty wet night, car standing there, radio, four-wheel drive, the lot. All he had to do was jump in and drive off to wish Granny many happy returns of the day."

"So you're assuming that Lady Wickham was there that night?"

"With her car parked right outside, wouldn't you?"

"But you don't know whom she'd gone there to meet?"

"Not yet. But when we do, we might well have solved the case."

So Jamie still hadn't confessed his role. "How?"

"Obvious, isn't it?" Walsh turned his eyes on Cassie again. Definitely hazel, she thought, mostly brown with a few green flecks and one that seemed almost black. "Lover boy shows up, they have a row, he drives her back home and shoots her when she gets out."

"For God's sake," said Cassie.

"What?"

"Why would he drive her when she had her own car there?"

"Don't forget hers had been nicked."

"OK. How would he make her get out halfway up the drive? And anyway, why wait until he got to the drive; why not do it along the road somewhere? Or even in the estate cottage where they'd had their row? I think it's much more likely that whoever was supposed to meet her that night just didn't show up and when she got tired of waiting, she discovered her car had vanished. Which explains why she was traipsing up the drive in the rain." Cassie looked thoughtful. "Do you think Wickham did it?"

"Mantripp does. He's still hung up on this contract-killing caper."

"But you're not?"

"It's too obvious, isn't it? Too pat." He stretched, turning his face up to the sun. "It's the modern-day equivalent of the passing tramp or the homicidal maniac. On the other hand . . ." He stared up at the sky, scratching lightly at his jaw, ". . . the detective novel with its multiple suspects and motives is old hat. These days, the contract killer is increasingly the weapon of choice, and the problem for the police is proving who was responsible."

"You can't be serious."

"I am."

"But suppose I wanted to bump someone off: I wouldn't know where to begin finding a gun for hire."

"There's plenty who do. I'll tell you what I think: whoever actually pulled that trigger—and it couldn't have been Darcy Wickham because we know he didn't leave the room—it was intended to make us think it was him."

"Any reason why it shouldn't have been? The simple answer is often the right one."

"How would he benefit? Her money doesn't go to him. And anyway, he's got plenty of his own. We've looked into his finances: it's trust funds and inheritances and land which's been in the family for generations. And he's a shrewd investor, too. If there's anything dodgy in there, we haven't been able to find it. So what would be his motive?"

"Another woman? Or maybe he wanted an heir."

"So why not go the divorce route? That lot don't think twice about it."

"How would he—or anyone else—have known she'd be walking up the drive at that moment? Even though you've explained about her car being nicked, I can't work that out."

"I'll tell you what I can't work out," said Walsh.

"What's that?"

"Why someone like you is living alone. I'd have thought you'd have been snapped up years ago."

"Leaving aside the rampant sexism in that statement, I was."

"What happened?"

"Just about the same as in your case, I should think."

"You walked out on him?"

"More or less."

"I hope it didn't hurt him as much as my wife's leaving hurt me."

"God," said Cassie, "you really need re-educating, don't you?"

"Why?"

"You haven't even bothered to ask why I baled out. Or how much he might have hurt me before we finally broke up. You imply not only that it was no more than a whim on my part, but also that he was the only one who was hurt."

"Hey." Walsh leaned over and took her wrist between his thumb and first finger. "Did I say that?"

"You didn't need to. It was implied by the way you phrased your remark. Anyway, why did your wife leave you? Or didn't you bother to ask her either?"

"Any more of this wine?" said Walsh.

"Most of the bottle. It's indoors, in the fridge."

He stood up and took hold of Cassie's hand. "Come inside and show me where the fridge is, will you?"

"I thought you policemen were trained in the art of detection."

"We are."

"See if you can detect that big white thing in the corner of the kitchen."

Walsh pulled her to her feet. "I was just looking for an excuse to make you stand up."

"Why?"

"Because it's easier to kiss you standing up."

"What?"

"I've been wanting to, ever since the first time I saw you. That's really why I dropped in. I could easily have telephoned you about finding the car." He touched her lips with his lovely mouth. She shivered. "I thought it would be more fun to come round in person."

"Suppose I'd had a visitor."

"I'd have gone and had lunch and come back later."

"Do you want something to eat now?"

"Yes, please." He held her close to him and lightly ran his tongue over her lips.

"Oh, Lord," she said. "Are you on duty?"

"Yes. But I'm entitled to a break for lunch."

"Help yourself," Cassie said.

♠ ♥ ♣ ♦

He turned out to be adept at kissing women. Or perhaps it wasn't women, just Cassie. He was also adept at making them feel that if he didn't take them to bed in the next few seconds they might melt into a pool of lubricious juices. But then again, that might also just have been Cassie. And, once in bed, he proved to be particularly adept at touching and holding, tasting and feeling, loving and moving and murmuring and joining and, finally, at bringing matters to a mutually satisfying end.

When she was next capable of coherent speech, Cassie said, "Is this what they call conduct becoming to a police officer?"

He raised himself up on his fists and smiled down at her. "What do you think?"

"At this precise moment I couldn't think if my life depended on it. But it seems pretty becoming to me."

"I'll tell you what I think."

"What's that?"

"You're not a bit like Mother Teresa."

"How would you know?"

He leaned down and kissed the tip of her nose. "We had her down at the station once. Picked her up for soliciting."

"I hope that's not an example of your ready wit," Cassie said.

"It's not my wit which is ready." He moved the lower half of his body against the lower half of hers.

"Goodness," she said.

Later, she said: "*Did* you ask your wife why she was leaving?"

"The milkman," Walsh said briefly.

"The milkm—?"

"Not literally. The bloke she worked for. Ran his own plastics business, which gave him plenty of time for himself. And her. The CID isn't often that lucky." He stroked her shoulder, then bent his head to kiss her breast.

Cassie closed her eyes. She had not felt this good for quite a while. Fetta cheesecake at lunchtime, and Walsh for tea . . . mmm-*hmmm*.

After a bit, Walsh said, "Time's up. I have to get back."

She looked up at him. "Don't tell me we've been screwing at the taxpayer's expense."

"Just the last time. Not the first two."

"Talk about dereliction of duty."

"I know. Are you in tonight?"

"Yes."

"I could drop by on my way home."

"What time is that?"

"Eightish. There might be further information to give you. Or a breakthrough in the murder case which you should know about."

"Even if there isn't," said Cassie.

When he'd gone, she lay in the bed for a while longer. She tried not to think of the silkiness of his skin, the smile which transformed his face as he looked down at her, the way his eyes lingered on her body. Turning her head, she could smell him on the pillow; if she shut her eyes she could . . .

She forced him out of her mind.

If there was now an explanation for why Portia had been walking up the drive to her own front door in the rain, it still did not answer the question of how the murderer could have known she would pass at that particular time. Her death could not have been a random killing: even in the most rural of areas, murderers did not, on the whole, stalk the country roads with guns in their hands, loosing off stray shots at anyone who passed. Particularly in the rain. And Portia had been inside her own grounds, not wandering along the road.

Having had one problem solved for her, the second seemed all the more intractable. In the normal course of events, Portia Wickham would have arrived back at her home by car. However much you subscribed to chaos theory, you could not, as a murderer, possibly have envisaged a scenario involving a delinquent lad-cum-car-thief. Still less, counted on Portia's date for the evening not showing up. You couldn't have actually *planned* it.

She realised she had forgotten, what with one thing and another, to ask Walsh the name of the charity from which Portia had been threatening to pull out, and whether it had any con-

nection with one of Olivia's causes. More importantly, she realised she had forgotten to ask Walsh what his first name was.
To make love with a man whose name you didn't know
seemed amazingly decadent.

She got up, stretched, brushed her teeth.

She went out into her vegetable garden. She forked compost carefully into the asparagus bed behind the hedge. It
was late for this: already there were green shoots showing. In
the greenhouse, which had been little more than a ruin when
she arrived, her spring onions were coming along: next week
she could probably gather the first ones before planting them
out, along with the first of the radishes. There were also the
lettuces to thin out in their seed-boxes, and her different
herbs to organise.

Later, she had a bath. It was seven-fifteen. In three-quarters
of an hour, Walsh would be back. Running a hand down her
legs, she decided that although she had only done them two
days ago, she'd better do them again. If she had been a more
commited feminist, she wouldn't have bothered—no one expected men to shave their legs, leg hair was just as much part
of a woman's physique, if they don't like the natural me, they
know what they can, blah blah blah. But when a man was
making love with a woman, he didn't want to wonder suddenly if he'd stumbled into a recently harvested cornfield, did
he? Face it, stubble wasn't exactly a turn-on. Not that Walsh
had appeared to need one.

Her razor, she recollected, was in her bedroom, where she
had taken it to try and excise the brown bits which had appeared on some of the leaves of the *spatiphyllum* which stood
in a pot on the broad windowsill. Her amateur surgery didn't
seem to have helped much, she saw, as she padded naked
across the carpet; the leaves stretched towards her like
wounded suppliants.

"Sorry, guys," she said. Picking up her razor, she glanced
idly out of the window, which looked over the front stretch of
grass and the lane. The garden was taking on a pleasantly cot-
tagey aspect: the crab-apple blossom was gone but the last of
the bluebells and forget-me-nots were still quietly rioting, and
sweet williams and wallflowers were in bloom. Behind the

hedge, tucked in well to the side of the lane so that it was almost hidden, she could see the roof of a black car. Was this
yet another instance of the Bath Syndrome—someone showing up the minute she stepped into the tub? If so, who? There
had been no knock at the door, no voice calling.

She frowned. Why was someone parked there? It couldn't
be anyone she knew; none of her friends drove a black car.
Her mind immediately flew terror-stricken to Steve, then
calmed down—he wasn't due out until early next week. So
who was it? There were no footpaths on the other side of the
lane, no woods where people might come to go walking. Directly across from her was a field where the farmer was holding his young bullocks prior to the summer sales. To the right
of that, towards the village, was plough, drainage ditches,
hedges and more plough. Further to the left, almost opposite
Kathryn's cottage, was more scrubby pasture with sheep in it.
None of it invited the enthusiastic rambler. And nobody came
down here except deliberately, since it was a dead end.

For a moment she stood irresolute, staring at the palely
transparent moon which hung like a piece of tissue paper in the
still daylight sky. Should she go and see? But that would mean
getting dressed again. And there was nothing much she could
do to prevent anyone who wished to from parking in the lane.
In the end, she went downstairs and made sure all the doors
and windows were locked.

At half-past eight, the telephone rang. A woman's voice
said, "Detective Sergeant Walsh for you."

"I can't make it tonight," Walsh said, his voice angry and
preoccupied. "Something's come up."

Cassie sensed that this was not the moment for ribald ri-
postes. "I'm disappointed."

"You and me both," said Walsh, sounding fairly perfunctory about it. "Look, I'll try and call you in the morning."

"Fine." Cassie felt ridiculously hurt by his brusque manner,
though she was perfectly well aware that the man on the other
end of the line was speaking to her as policeman and not as
bed-partner.

"Sorry." Walsh rang off before she could say anything else.

Ah well. Win a few, lose a few. At least her legs were smooth for tomorrow—not, heaven forbid, that there was any question of Charlie Quartermain running his hands or anything else down them—so she hadn't wasted her time.

It was just, she wanted to see Walsh again. She'd like to have asked him a couple of things. Like, among others, what the hell his first name was.

14

"You really don't mind?" Kathryn said.

"I *promise* you."

"Because I'm not the sort to come in and take someone else's—"

"Shame on you," said Cassie. "I can't believe you're coming out with such sexist talk. Giles is a big boy and perfectly well able to make up his own mind."

The two women were sitting under the ramshackle pergola halfway down the garden of Honeysuckle Cottage. Vine leaves trailed erratically over the half-rotten framework. The sun blazed, the air was soft and warm. All around, birds trilled and butterflies danced. At the end of the garden, beyond the hedge, a tall pear-tree stood against the sky, its branches already laden with small unripe fruit.

"In my wildest dreams, I'd never have imagined this," Kathryn said. "Me falling for an Englishman. An English *farmer*. My mother will have a fit."

"Aren't farmers respectable in the States?"

"They just have a different image. More bib-front overalls and plaid shirts than good suits and silk ties. Not that Giles wears those to work in. God! To think I'm in love with a man who wears one of those flat tweed caps. I can hardly believe it."

"And he's a pillar of the bench, to boot."

"A pillar of the bench," sighed Kathryn. She sucked in the sides of her mouth so that chipmunk pouches formed in her cheeks. "I don't have the foggiest idea what it means, but my mother will fall over on her nose. Look: are you absolutely sure I haven't taken him away from you?"

"Kathryn, this is the Nineties. You're talking like a woman's magazine in the Sixties. And I thought American women were supposed to be in the vanguard of the move towards independence and liberation for their sisters."

"Not this babe."

"Even if Giles were mine for you to take, he wouldn't have gone if he hadn't wanted to, for heaven's sake. We once had a thing going, admittedly, but it reached the end of its natural life some time ago." Cassie exaggerated for Kathryn's sake, not adding that Giles had more than once suggested they get married, nor that she had more than once considered adopting the suggestion.

"You know, I really thought at my age that I was one tough old broad," Kathryn said. "I mean, with the breaks life's thrown at me, I had to either get tough or get out. So all this is simply . . . love and everything." She looked across at Cassie. "You aren't just being stoic, are you?"

"No."

"Hiding your broken heart behind a façade of false cheer?"

"No, Kathryn."

"Laughing that you may not weep?"

"Not in the slightest."

"Because if you were, I'd—"

"I'm *not*, OK?" It was about the fifteenth time Kathryn had said this or something similar. "I'm delighted you're so happy. So what are your plans, if any?"

"For the moment, I'm just gonna lie back, enjoy the adrenalin jolt, let the chemicals surge. A farmer!" Kathryn said ecstatically. "Me!"

"Have you met Giles' mother yet?"

"Oh God! Don't you just love her?"

"Well . . ."

"I mean, she's a total eccentric. My parents are so staid and respectable."

"Sometimes I think those are my favourite flavours."

"Where I come from, even the house-pets are staid and respectable. I can't tell you what a relief it is to meet a really weird person like Mercy." Kathryn looked over at Cassie. "What about you and that big chap—Charlie? Are you an item?"

"No, we most certainly are not."

"That's a shame."

"Is it?" Cassie knew that one of the things she had picked up from Aunt Polly was an ability to fill two words with more frost than a supermarket freezer cabinet.

"I won't say another thing."

"Do I detect a faintly negative tone in your voice?" Cassie asked aggressively.

"No. I just thought he was kind of nice."

"And I'm a bitch, right? The thing is, Charlie Quartermain has worked out this nice little routine of the faithful lover, which makes everybody think I'm some kind of hardhearted witch for not going along with it."

"You're going out with him tonight, I understand."

"I've agreed to accompany him to some business function, yes."

"Be sweet, Cassie."

"Thank you for reminding me, Mother."

"He's a great character. And so unusual."

"Isn't he, though?"

"And obviously adores you."

"This is true, Kathryn."

"He told us that he'd win you round eventually."

"If Charlie Quartermain was the last man on earth, I'd demand a recount," Cassie said loudly. "Could we *please* change the subject?"

"Right."

They sat in silence for a moment, relishing the day. Cassie closed her eyes, thinking of Walsh, awash with longing to see him again. A thrush landed on the mossy brick floor of the pergola and began to beat the hell out of a snail, like an olden-days washerwoman at the river's brim.

In the house, the telephone began to ring. Heart beating like an adolescent's, Cassie raced to answer it.

"Yes?" she said breathlessly.

"Detective Sergeant Walsh to speak to you," a crisp female voice said.

"Cassie?"

"Yes." The smile on her face felt as though it was easily wide enough to engirdle the earth.

"Are you free tonight?"

"Any time at all. Oh, but—" Cassie recollected that she was engaged to go to the Randolph Hotel with Charlie Quartermain that evening. "No, I'm not," she said slowly. "I'm afraid I'm doing—I have to do something else."

"Can you change it?"

"No." Much as she would prefer to be with Walsh, there was nothing more despicable than a person who let other people down at the last minute because something better had come up.

"Damn it," said Walsh.

"Sorry."

"Cassie."

"Yes."

"Yesterday was—" Walsh's voice softened.

"For me too."

"I'll ring you tomorrow."

"Right. By the way—"

But he had gone.

"You look like a million dollars," Quartermain said.

"You look pretty good yourself." Cassie cast a critical eye over him but could find no fault. In evening dress, he cut an impressive figure, no doubt about it—but then most men did. What would Walsh . . . but she was not going to think about him this evening. She had made a conscious decision to be gracious. to behave like a lady—that legendary creature invoked by Aunt Polly whenever Cassie had made any bid for individuality. Useless to point out that the kind of clothes the twins wore looked ridiculous on someone of Cassie's size and shape. Useless to point out that she was physically uncoordinated, so that the tennis and ballroom dancing lessons were a waste of money. Useless to say she hated horses and loathed the sea; way back in Aunt Polly's rearing someone had decreed that tennis and dancing, riding and sailing were suitable accomplishments for a modern well-bred girl. Bridge, luckily, had also been deemed acceptable.

It might not have been if Cassie had ever described to her aunt the kind of bridge she and Dad and Gran used to play, with a friend of one or the other making up the four, Gran with a fag in her mouth and a pint of stout to hand, Dad eating fish and chips out of greasy newspaper and laughing his head off, and Cassie allowed a sip of his beer every now and then, just to get used to the taste. Nor had she ever told Aunt Polly that she was a demon snooker-player. Well-bred girls definitely didn't play snooker. The day she left to go to university at the age of eighteen, she had shaken the Vicarage off as though removing a pair of deeply uncomfortable corsets. Although she was grateful to her aunt and uncle—even loved them, in a way—she had never since spent more than forty-eight hours in a row in their home.

The trouble was, having renounced one habitat, she had not yet found another to take its place.

"Class," Charlie said. "That's what you add."

"I've told you before that, however much it may disappoint you, I am *not* class," said Cassie. "Far from it."

"Compared to me, darlin', you're the bloody aristocracy."

Yes, well, compared to Charlie . . . but she did not let herself finish the thought. She had promised Kathryn she would be sweet. "My father was a member in good standing of the great British working class," she said patiently. "I grew up in a pub in the Holloway Road." Which, as Aunt Polly had never tired of pointing out, was something we don't talk about, dear.

"And look how classy you turned out, girl."

She breathed deeply. What was the point of trying to explain to a man who refused to listen? "Who else did you say was coming tonight?"

"The money man and his wife, the ideas man and his girlfriend, and a couple of other odds and sods. Should be fun. They do a good nosh at the Randolph, and I like dancing."

"Great," said Cassie. She could see it so clearly: an evening with a bunch of men discussing their Flymo lawnmowers and their central heating systems while their thin wives talked about their holidays in Florida. Followed by Charlie, holding her much too tightly, crashing about on the dance floor. Should be fun, as he said. And she could have been with Walsh. But that wasn't Quartermain's fault. And as he would undoubtedly be among the first to point out, time flew, did it not, when you were having fun?

The big banqueting room of the Randolph Hotel was crowded. Quartermain led the way across the floor and Cassie followed. At least she *looked* classy. Even Aunt Polly would have had to concede that.

There were four people already seated at their table, with a couple of unopened bottles of champagne sitting in front of them in silver buckets. Quartermain began introducing them. "This is Spencer Pritchard and his wife Stella—he's in printing, and she's gorgeous, aren't you, Stella, my love?"

Stella seemed to like this sort of thing, judging by the smile she gave Charlie.

The second pair consisted of an untidy young man accompanied by a woman of about Cassie's age wearing close to a dozen different shades of red, some on her feet, some on her fingernails or mouth, some at her ears, several clothing her body. "This is Gareth MacPhail," said Charlie, "and Siân." Both of them shook Cassie's hand. Gareth wore a dinner jacket, a dress shirt and a black bow-tie. He also wore jeans. Probably some kind of fashion statement.

"You might have heard of Gareth," Charlie continued. "He's just won an award. The Sweetbread Prize for Poetry or something."

"Whitbread, Charlie," murmured Siân.

That Gareth MacPhail? The one who'd been in all the newspapers recently, on all the chat-shows and literary radio programmes? The one whose use of foul language had turned the four-letter word into a symbol of the decay eating at the heart of our decadent society and of almost anything else you cared to apply it to? But who had also, in the process, produced some breath-catching poetry? "Congratulations," Cassie said.

"I like the idea of a sweetbread prize," Gareth said, consideringly. "I wonder how exactly it would be administered." His accent was strongly Scottish, his eyes of a celtic blue. Easy to imagine him in a kilt, calling the yowes to the knowes or something similar. He indicated that Cassie should take the seat beside him. "When I won this prize, see, I was of a great expectation that it would consist of barrel after barrel of the finest brew. And instead, it was money."

"Rather a lot of it," Cassie said, "from what I read."

"I'm not sure about the whole notion of prizes," said Gareth. He tossed a fistful of curly black hair back from his brow. "Isn't it invidious to select one man above another and say, this wee feller is a better poet than that one?"

"Of course it is." And very easy to make statements like that after you've won the prize, thought Cassie.

"I'll bet you're thinking how easy it is to mouth off like that after you've banked the cheque," he said, turning his blue eyes on her again. "Let me tell you that I have absolutely no intention of returning the cash. My principles are no more than skin deep, if that."

"What's your role in this enterprise of Charlie's?" Cassie said.

"I advise on the inscriptions," said Gareth.

"Inscriptions? I'm not entirely sure what the idea is."

"Och well. One of these days you'll have to travel north of the border and see for yourself."

"See what?"

"My garden."

"I've got one of those."

"Ah, but does yours stretch across several acres of hillside?"

"No."

"Does it incorporate peat-bogs and natural pools?"

"We're a bit short on peat-bogs in the Cotswolds."

"Heather? Rowan-trees? Broom?"

"There's a broom in the garden shed."

"Not a vicous yellow one, bright as a lemon, is it?"

"How did you guess?" Cassie said.

"No, seriously though . . ." Gareth glanced across the table at Siân, who was chatting animatedly with Charlie and Stella, while Spencer got stuck into opening one of the champagne bottles. "The idea behind our business is that we produce landscape gardens with chunks of granite or slate or limestone strategically placed here and there with some of Charlie's lettering on. The man's a genius, isn't he? Such beautiful work. His affinity with the oneness of . . . He carved an R which quite literally made me weep when I saw it."

Cassie was beginning to think she had got trapped in some kind of three-dimensional Pseud's Corner. Gareth fumbled down by the side of his chair, and brought up a portfolio, the contents of which he proceeded to spread across the damask cloth, sweeping aside the table settings in cavalier fashion. "Look," he said, producing photographs. "Is that not beautiful?"

At first sight, it just looked like an R cut into a flat slab of slate. But the more Cassie stared at it, the more she was drawn. So stark, so simple. Who would have thought that a single letter of the alphabet could be so aesthetic?

"Put that beside a pond," Gareth said. "Some purple flags to one side, a curl of white gravel. And, behind them, the immensity of trees, the clamour of hills. Think of it. Man imposing himself on nature in the subtlest of ways. Letters are the most profound symbols of our civilisation that it is possible to find, don't you think?"

"Apart from the word 'fuck,' do you mean?"

His answer to this was drowned in the arrival of two more couples. One of them, to Cassie's immense surprise, was Jeremy Marling, accompanied by his wife, both wearing the expressions of people who unexpectedly wake up from a nightmare in which Jim is fixing something for them to find that in fact he is doing just that. The other two were a short and unassuming pair, Fred

Mills and wife. Fred, Charlie assured them and most of the tables round them, was the kingpin, the brains without which the whole enterprise would never get off the ground.

"Gardening expert," Marling confided to Cassie. On seeing her, his face had dropped its look of disdain and grown guarded. Perhaps he was embarrassed at not having telephoned her; perhaps he was afraid she would remind him of this in front of his wife. He had seated himself firmly next to her, leaving his wife, a pleasant woman dressed in an unbecoming shade of red which matched none of those Siân was wearing, to find her own place at the table.

"Fred Mills—of course," said Cassie. "I've heard him on that gardening programme on the radio."

"Runs a small school for would-be landscape gardeners down in Devon," said Marling. "I don't mind telling you I'd have been much more reluctant to come aboard if he'd turned us down. He's got all the contacts, all the horticultural expertise. There's a waiting list four years long to engage his services and even longer to enrol in his school."

"Sounds as if your enterprise is off to a flying start."

"With Charlie in as well, yes, I think we are. You know his work, of course?"

"Of course," Cassie said smoothly. She felt ashamed of herself for being so dismissive of Quartermain—but it was the man who annoyed her, not the craftsman. If he didn't always come on so strong, she would have been able to evaluate him more fairly.

"Futhorks," Charlie said loudly, leaning over the table towards her and, in the process, nearly capsizing one of the silver buckets.

"What?"

"Futhorks. Runes. What Gareth was showing you just now. Lovely things, aren't they?"

"If futhorks is what they are, then yes," Cassie said, meaning it.

At her side, Marling said, "I must tell you it's something of a surprise to see you here."

"Small world," said Cassie.

"But not that small. Which is why it seems odd to have

bumped into you again so soon after the first time. Anyway, what's your part in all this?"

"I haven't got one. I came with—" Cassie hated having to say this."—With Charlie Quartermain."

"I see." Marling lowered his voice. "That was a pretty traumatic end to the evening last week, wasn't it?"

"Especially for Lady Wickham," said Cassie.

"Presumably the police have been on to you."

In more than one sense, as it happens . . . "Yes, two or three times."

"Luckily I've only had them round once. Rather frightening experience, really. I'd hate to think what it would be like if I was actually guilty. I had a chap called Mantrap or something similar: is that who came to see you?"

"Yes."

"They don't seem to have got very far in their investigations," said Marling.

"They told me they were pursuing various lines of enquiry," Cassie said.

"Which means nothing."

"Exactly. They seem to think she was murdered for her money, but they can't work out by whom."

Marling pulled out a small diary and fiddled with the gold pencil which ran down its spine. "They told me she had lots of lovers. Not having met the woman, I wasn't able to be much help." The straight lines of his fair, slicked-back hair had wavered slightly towards the crown of his head.

"The cops told *me* that they were looking quite hard at Darcy Wickham, and that in cases like this, the husband is always a number one suspect."

Marling nodded, thoughtfully. "I could well believe Darcy had a hand in it. But I wouldn't go so far as to say that he actually pulled the trigger on his wife."

"How far would you go?"

"Let's say, if the police discovered that he'd paid someone to do it for them, I wouldn't be totally surprised."

"Is he a friend of yours?"

"I've known him for some years," said Marling cautiously. "He's older than I am, but we've been business colleagues at various times. Just because I believe him to be capable of murder doesn't mean I like him the less. Nor that I necessarily think he did it. Simply that if it turned out he did it, it wouldn't be all that much of a shock."

"What exactly do you do?" asked Cassie. Boring question, but then Marling didn't give out too many clues.

"Buy into small companies like this one." Cassie despised herself for the way her expression immediately became ingratiating. But why not: maybe Marling was the saviour she and Natasha had been looking for. "Sail a bit," he continued. "Race a bit, climb a bit, gamble a lot. You've heard of the idle rich? That's me."

"You can't be that idle or you wouldn't have anything to gamble with."

"I'm afraid I can. There was a trust waiting for me when I turned twenty-one."

"Just like Darcy Wickham."

"What?"

"He had one of those, too."

Marling seemed slightly disconcerted by this piece of information. "Yes, well, there are a lot of them about," he said. "And then I had the good sense to marry a woman with money. My wife's not what you'd call stinking rich, but she's certainly comfortable. Which spares me the necessity of bringing home the bacon. On top of which, my great-aunt died and left me quite a bit of money. I was at the Stock Exchange at the time and it wasn't too difficult to double it fairly quickly. Since then, I've been able to indulge myself." He smiled at her and made a deprecating gesture with one hand. "I'm afraid self-indulgence is frightfully bad for the character."

It was easy to see what Jamie had been talking about when he spoke of revolutions. Jeremy Marling seemed custom-designed for standing up against a wall and being shot. The public-school arrogance, the upper-class accent, the easy carelessness, the unspoken assumptions: she thought of John Burslake, of Kipper Naughton, of Rastaman and Ginger. Even of Steve. Yet there was nothing unpleasant about Marling, nothing that spoke of a deliberate desire to take what rightfully belonged to another, or of major character flaws. He was as much a product of his birth and upbringing as they were.

"As a gambling man," Cassie said, "if you had to put your money on someone as the most likely person to have murdered Lady Wickham, who would it be?"

He thought about it. "I haven't got a lot of form to go on. I suppose I'd probably bet on Darcy as the favourite. Put money each way on one of her current lovers, presuming she had one, with maybe a current lover's wife as an outsider. But let's not talk about Portia. It's all so desperately sad."

"What would you rather talk about?"

"How about sailing. Do you sail?"

"I have done," said Cassie.

"Oh." He raised sandy eyebrows which, from this close, looked as though they had been combed into position. "I'll bear you in mind next time I'm making up a crew."

Cassie smiled. "Don't. I hated it." The twins had enjoyed it: perhaps that was why she hadn't. By the time she had struggled into foul-weather gear she looked even huger than usual, whereas they just looked like two cute little pixies in their yellow sou'westers. Sometimes she wondered whether her adolescence would have been easier to bear if the twins hadn't been twins.

Across the table, Quartermain knocked over a glass of champagne. People began dabbing at it with napkins. Waiters were loudly called. Banter ensued, most of it from Charlie. "So what do *you* do?" Marling asked. "Apart from play a lot of bridge?"

"Teach it, mostly."

"Where do you teach?"

"At evening classes, or to private fours. I sometimes organise bridge weekends in hotels or on cruises. I also, at the moment, teach in the local prison."

He screwed up his eyes. "What's that called—HMP Bellington, is it?" She nodded. "Isn't that a bit tough?"

"Not really. Most of the inmates are rather pathetic: it's just occasionally there's one you genuinely wouldn't want to meet on a dark night."

"Big brutes, do you mean?"

"The big ones are often the nicest. It's the hard ones who really worry me. For instance, there's one at the moment who's . . . I know it sounds melodramatic, but who really scares me. He goes round slashing women with a Stanley knife."

"I hope he's been put away for a good long time."

"Not nearly long enough. Actually," said Cassie, realising how close it was, "he gets out next Monday." Saying it out loud only emphasised how much Steve had become a permanent low-grade worry. She suspected that, next week, low-grade would shift upwards to high-grade.

Marling raised his eyebrows. "That seems to frighten you."

"It does. Partly because every time I see him, he says he'll drop in on me once he's released. He even seems to know where I live. Not that that's difficult to find out: they have access to telephones and directories even in an old prison like Bellington."

"It's probably just talk."

"I hope you're right."

"Do you ever feel that there are men in there who shouldn't be?" Marling said. "You read about these miscarriages of justice, and I sometimes wonder just how innocent the victims are. I mean, even if they didn't do what they're accused of, they've probably done something else."

"What are you: in charge of your local lynching party?"

"I'm only asking. It's what a lot of people think."

"You don't often meet people whom you feel are innocent, although they all tell you they are. But there is—*was*—someone in there." Cassie said slowly. "I'm convinced he was set up. Not by the police: by the people he worked for."

"Ever felt tempted to take up the cudgels on his behalf?"

"I've thought about it. But where would you start?"

"If you were part of the legal profession, I suppose it would be easier. Or a journalist."

"True." Cassie said. "Mind you, Burslake—this chap—did say one or two things. Perhaps I should pass them on to his lawyer. Not that it makes much odds now."

"Why not?"

"He died recently, in a road accident, while he was being transferred from Bellington to serve his sentence in Durham."

Charlie Quartermain was tapping the side of his glass with a fork. "Quiet, everyone," he said. "Let's have a toast, shall we?"

"What to?" Gareth asked.

"Us. And since you're the bloke with the silver tongue," said Charlie with a wheezy laugh, "why don't you say a few words?" He looked round at them all. "Everyone agree to that?"

They indicated that they did.

"Noisy fellow, isn't he?" Marling said under his breath. Although she had been thinking the same thing, Cassie resented him saying it. Who was he to sit in judgment on those who had not had his advantages? Not everyone came into trust funds when they reached their majority: some people had to work for it. Quartermain was a better man than Marling would ever be—to her surprise, she found herself gazing at the big man with something approaching fondness. At that moment, Charlie looked at her and caught the soft expression on her face before she had time to wipe it off. Dammit. What exactly was going on here? Why was she thinking fondly about someone as irritating as Charlie? And did the fact that she had done so—briefly —indicate that Charlie's long-term strategies of breaking down her resistance were working? She shuddered. Never!

"Ladies and gentlemen," Gareth said, holding up his glass. "I might be exaggerating if I said that rarely in the history of mankind has such a wealth of talent been gathered round one table. But it would not be beyond the realms of truth to declare that rarely have such diverse talents as we see here tonight joined together in a single common weal. Weal, as you all know, being a word in which prosperity is implicit."

"I'll drink to that," roared Charlie, banging on the table and setting the maître d'hotel's Adam's apple twitching.

"A professional gardener," continued Gareth. "A master mason. A craftsman printer. A rich dilettante," he pointed his glass at each person in turn. "And a humble poet. What a combination! So, may I ask you to drink to the success of Mills &

Runes, the new concept in landscaping. And just before you raise your glasses to your lips, I'd like to add that our order books are already prebooked until the middle of the year after next. Gentlemen: we cannot fail!"

They drank.

Later, dinner over and cigars fouling the atmosphere, Cassie found herself chatting with Jeremy Marling's wife. "I've never learned to play bridge," Mrs. Marling said. Although she had the tan of someone who had spent several work-free weeks in the sun, she seemed unassuming, almost diffident. "My parents played a lot, but it always seemed to me to be a game for puce old buffers home from India." She laughed. "The sort who retire to Cheltenham and write indignant letters to newspapers."

"The image has changed a lot," Cassie told her. "More and more young people play these days. In the States, people put themselves through college by playing bridge, and my evening classes always have a good proportion of people in their twenties."

"I'm so thick I'd probably need special coaching," Mrs. Marling said. "But it could be useful. Jeremy and I have this little house in France, and it would be rather fun to sit outside under some vine-covered arbour, playing bridge with other thoroughly lazy people like ourselves."

"The best kind of fun," Cassie smiled at her. Never one to miss an opportunity, she added, "I'd be happy to help you get started."

"Would you?"

"It's part of what I do: private coaching. Do you have any friends, two or three others, who might be interested?"

"Definitely."

Before she could offer Mrs. Marling her business card, Charlie reached across the table and grabbed Cassie's hand. "How about a turn round the floor, light of my life?" he said.

If she hadn't enjoyed the evening so far, she might have started chewing the tablecloth at that one. Instead, she gave him a big smile.

Despite her fears, she had not heard a single word about either Flymos or small-bore central heating. MacPhail was witty and irreverent, with enough sense of humour about himself to be able to mock the wilder flights of pseudery to which he seemed unable to stop himself from giving vent. On her other side, Marling too proved an entertaining companion. Though she had pumped him further about the Wickhams, he had not added anything to what she already knew.

Quartermain swept her into the middle of the dance floor. Like many big men, he was light on his feet, and, she soon discovered, an excellent dancer. "You shouldn't be smoking them things," he said reprovingly.

"What things? That cheroot I had?"

"They're bad for you, girl."

"What about you? I didn't notice you holding back when they were handing out cigars," said Cassie.

"I'm a lost cause, darlin'," said Charlie. "You're not."

"Listen, Charlie," she started, meaning to tell him that she would go to hell in whatever handbasket she found congenial without any interference from him. And that, anyway, she smoked no more often than three or four times a year. But he held her closer to his broad chest and turned her in a swooping circle, using a series of small fast steps, and the words were lost in trying to concentrate enough to keep up with him.

At the end of the number, they stood together, waiting for the next dance. Cassie felt faintly ridiculous with her hand trapped in his huge paw but it would have meant an unseemly wrangle if she had tried to wrest it away. The orchestra swung into something slow and smoochy: the lights dimmed a little. Oh God. If Charlie got a hard-on and started pressing her against his crotch, she really would leave the floor and never mind unseemliness. There were a few things she hated more than being someone else's involuntary masturbatory aid. It would have been different if he had been DS Walsh—but he wasn't.

Charlie, however, behaved like a gentleman throughout the next set, and the one after that. Finally, he said, "I'd like to go on dancing with you all night, girl, but I'd best let some of the others have a go."

The sentiments were Neanderthal, but she let them pass. "Thank you," she said formally. "I enjoyed that."

"So did I, Cass." He tried to give her a meaning glance but she refused to meet his eyes. When they returned to it, their table was empty except for Siân and Marling. Charlie led Siân off to dance and Marling immediately turned to Cassie, an enquiring look on his face.

"Any chance of your playing bridge with me next week?" he said. "I can't remember if I explained that my wife doesn't play and the chap I usually play with will be on holiday. A commercial proposition, of course. How much does Roy Chilcott give you?"

"Quite a lot."

"I'll match it."

"It depends what day you're talking about. Presumably you play in the evenings . . ."

"Yes."

". . . in which case, next week I'm booked up on Tuesday and Thursday. And," she remembered, "Wednesday."

"Doesn't leave much choice. How about Friday."

"Sounds good, though I'd better check my diary. Where?"

"London. You don't mind coming up? I'll pay your travelling expenses, of course." He reached towards one of the candles on the table and held it up to his mouth to light a fresh cigar. The numerals on his expensive watch—a Rolex Oyster—glinted momentarily, and she remembered poor Burslake, as much a victim as Portia. If she tried, would she be able to find the offices in Swindon where he had gone, and from there, track down a man on the strength of nothing more solid than an unusual—and probably equally expensive—watch and the fact that he played bridge? And would there be any point? Even if she managed to do so, it was too late for Burslake.

". . . meet you somewhere central?" Marling said. He had his diary out again and was making a note.

"You tell me."

They made tentative arrangements. Cassie was pleased. One door closes, another opens. The loss of Chilcott as a partner was going to mean a definite drop in income—not that she would ever be foolish enough to start relying on such haphazard sources of funds—and it would be extremely useful if Marling were to take Chilcott's place. He might even have friends in a similar position who were prepared to pay for a professional partner. In that case, she would eventually be able to consider giving up the prison, which was not only stressful but also poorly paid. Or could she? Wouldn't she feel as though she were abandoning them all if she did that? Perhaps she could talk to the Education Officer about switching to morning classes so as to leave her evenings free . . .

Charlie sat beside her in the back of the hired car. "Enjoy yourself?"

"Very much indeed," Cassie said. "Thank you for asking me."

He took her hand and patted it. "Thank you for coming."

"I hope Mills & Runes is a hugh success."

"It doesn't matter that much if it's not, as long as it doesn't actually land us in the red."

"But surely you don't get people like Jeremy Marling backing things unless they're going to make money, do you?"

"He's a funny lad, is Jeremy. Dunno where he gets all his dosh, but he seems to have more than he knows what to do with. He likes putting it into things like this."

"Inheritances and trust funds," said Cassie. "That's why he's loaded."

"That figures. Gawd: could've done with a trust fund or two myself when I was starting out. Would've made things a lot easier."

"How did you get into partnership with him?"

"Someone introduced us: we belong to the same club."

"What's that?" The Hot Girls à Go-Go? Cassie thought.

"The Reform," said Charlie. "I must take you there to dinner some time. Right up your street, that'd be."

Cassie had a hard time not demonstrating ugly snobbish amazement. Uncle Sam was a member of the Reform. So was Robin. It was difficult to imagine three more different men, even more so to envisage them all together in the splotched brown marble halls of the Reform.

"You're full of surprises, Charlie," she said quietly.

"Yer, well. It's part of my charm, innit?"

At her gate, the driver stopped the car. "Do you want to stay the night?" Cassie asked, preparing to get out. "I mean," she added quickly, "the bed's still made up in the spare room from the last time you were here."

"Thanks, darlin', but I've got to pop over to Cologne on an early flight tomorrow morning. It's easier to get to Heathrow from my place." Charlie opened the door on his side. "Come on. I'll walk you up the path."

"When do you get back?"

"Why? Will you miss me?"

"Don't push your luck, Charles. I was thinking of Kathryn's birthday party on Wednesday."

"I'll be back for that. It might be nice to have a bed for the night then, if the offer still stands."

"I'm—uh—not sure," Cassie said awkwardly. She had been thinking about inviting Walsh to come with her to the party at Ivy Cottage, if he were free.

"See how we go, eh?"

In the porch, she unlocked the front door and fumbled for the switch. Quartermain followed her in.

"You ought to leave some lights on when you go out," he said. "And draw the curtains. Shouldn't give the villains the impression that there's nobody home."

"It's safe enough round here."

"Don't you believe it, girl. It's easy enough to use timer switches. Tell you what: I gotta mate with a timer-switch shop. I'll bring a couple with me next time I'm passing." He looked round the room, then walked towards the kitchen. "I'll just have a quick look round before I leave."

"I'm perfectly capable of looking round myself, thank you," Cassie said.

"Ever taken one of them self-defence courses?"

"No."

"You should. These days, the villains don't mind who they knock over. Kids, old folk, women, it's all the same to them, long as they get what they came for."

"There's no need for you to go upstairs," Cassie said, but not as firmly as she ought to have done. Truth to tell, she was rather relieved to have him checking the place over, even though she did not begin to believe that some mad rapist was lurking under the beds. "I'll make sure it's all—"

"But I want to take a leak, darlin'."

"Would you please stop calling me 'darling.'"

"Sorry, luv."

"That, too."

She heard Charlie walking about upstairs. When he came down again, she followed him to the front door. As she opened it, he turned. "You're a feisty little thing, aren't you?" he said, clamping his big hands round her shoulders. "I like that."

The last time anyone had called her a little thing, she had been eight. She rolled her eyes at him but none the less reached up and kissed his cheek. "Good night, Charlie," she said softly.

And if he read anything into *that,* she could not be held responsible.

The little light on her answering machine was flashing. When she pressed the Play button, she heard Walsh's voice.

"I wanted to say goodnight, Cassie." There was a pause, and she smiled, eyes half-closed, remembering the way their bodies had been together. "And also to say that the Mounties aren't the only ones who always get their man. Because we've nailed the bastard who blew Portia Wickham away!"

15

She had immediately rung the station, only to be informed by the enquiry desk that Detective Sergeant Walsh was not available. It was difficult to determine whether that meant he was there but couldn't talk to anyone, or had gone home for the night; the enquiry desk was not prepared to spend any time on helping her sort this one out. Not that it mattered; even if he had been calling her from his home, she had no means of getting in touch with him there, since his number would not be in the telephone directory. Policemen never were, any more than prison officers or people who worked for the probation service.

In the morning, she phoned again, to find that Walsh was still unavailable. This time she did not give up so easily and was eventually put through to the CID Control room. "I understand an arrest has been made in connection with the Portia Wickham murder case," she said.

The CID officer who took her call was cautious. "I'm afraid we can't give out that information."

"But won't it be in the papers?" She was about to tell him what to do with the cloak of secrecy, since she already knew that someone had been nailed for it. Just in time, she realised that perhaps Walsh should not have told her.

"I suggest you ring back later for an update when the officer concerned is here," the polite CID person said, po-voiced.

"And when might that be?"

"I'm afraid we can't tell you precisely."

"So there's not much point ringing back, is there?"

"That's up to you, madam."

Thanks a lot.

At news time she switched on the radio, but there was no announcement. Whom could they have taken into custody? Darcy Wickham? He was the main and obvious suspect. Jamie? Unless he had come to his senses and made a belatedly clean breast of things to the police, he must also be a suspect. By now they would certainly know of his liaison with Portia, and his silence on the subject would not have been helpful to his case. Not that Cassie thought him capable of killing anyone. There was also his mother, certainly fanatic enough, in Cassie's opinion, to commit murder for a cause, whether it be her own son or a minke whale.

There was Winston, too, but after her visit to Fairline Farms, she could not really see him trying to knock Portia off on account of a few smashed eggs and a bit of aggravation. He could have been one of her conquests, of course. But having seen him with his wife, she would have put him down as a one-woman man—and Portia was not the woman.

So what about Symington? He was the only one who had obviously been out in the rain, the only other person without an alibi for the vital fifty minutes or so. Mantripp and Walsh had told her that the others had alibis, and, in any case, no motives. If Symington had simply run from the house to his car and done the same in reverse when he returned for his briefcase, it was difficult to see how he had got quite so wet. Thinking about it, he grew in stature as a murder suspect. In spite of the ageing effect of the half-moon specs, he wasn't in bad shape and had a considerable amount of his own hair left. Who said sexual desire, infatuation, luv, call it what you will, didn't strike the over-fifties?

Take Jamie out of the equation and substitute Symington. Suppose, late in life, he falls heavily for Portia. Perhaps he sees it as his last opportunity before the yawning grave— though a man as loaded as he must be able to take his pick from any number of those career bimbettes with the big tits and the bigger hair, despite the wife and new baby Jamie had told her about.

OK. So he's not only suffering from testosterone poisoning where Portia is concerned, but also from heart burn. And then she gives him the push. What would a man as rich and powerful as Symington do, a man used to having his every last wish fulfilled whenever he wanted, a man who had never been denied a thing in his entire life—what would he do? Would he seize a gun and scream, "If I can't have you, nobody else can either!"?

It was hard to imagine. Cassie tried, but as a concept it didn't jell. He didn't look anything like a rejected lover. And if he'd had murder in mind that night at Halkam Court, he must be a pretty cool customer: he had played some excellent hands without showing any sign of nerves. But she still liked him for it. As a good bridge-player, he would know how to present a deceptive front and, however unlikely it might seem, perhaps beneath that snooty exterior he was a seething mass of passion. On top of everything else, he was the one she had seen in the pub with Darcy Wickham only days after Portia had died. Wouldn't a guilty man agree to go along with whatever plan his friend suggested, just so as not to look guilty, especially if he had just murdered the man's wife? She wondered how deeply the police had looked into him and any connection he might have had with Portia.

All right: for the moment push Symington on to the back burner. Look instead at Jacko Dexter. Could he be implicated? He didn't have much of an alibi, which almost argued his innocence, unless it was a double bluff and he knew that innocent people often had no means of proving where they were at any given moment. But even if he had the opportunity, why on earth would he want to shoot Portia? The same reasons might apply to him as applied to Symington, but it was pretty thin.

She thought again about the charity from which Portia had been planning to withdraw her support. Suppose Portia, by all accounts a lady who didn't stand much nonsense, had looked through the charity's financial statements and seen clear evidence of wrongdoing on the part of, say, the treasurer, the accountant, the auditor, whatever. What would she do? She would threaten to expose him/her, wouldn't she? Thus making herself a prime target for murder by someone unwilling to spend the next decade in prison.

Cassie mulled over that one. It had definite possibilities. She would, therefore, have to look into the charity concerned. Once she knew what it was. On impulse, she dialled the number of Jamie's home in Battersea.

"Yes?" The voice was Ms. Olive Howard's, as was the haste with which the phone had been snatched from its rest. Today the sharp tones were overlaid with something stronger than mere impatience.

"It's Cassandra Swann."

"Jamie's friend? I'm afraid he's not here," Ms. Howard said in a high taut voice.

"Actually, it was you—"

"He's being questioned about Portia Wickham's murder, as it happens." Ms. Howard was trying to sound as if she didn't give a toss, and not doing a good job of it.

"Oh, my God." Mantripp and Walsh had decided it was *Jamie*?

"I'm—uh—I'm . . ."

Distraught was probably the word Ms. Howard was looking for. "Did he go to the police voluntarily?" Cassie asked.

"No. They just showed up here last night, asked him to accompany them, and bundled him off before I realised what was happening. I haven't seen him since. They've taken him to some police station near where—where it happened." Ms. Howard suddenly dissolved into racking sobs. "He didn't kill her! I know he didn't. Jamie wouldn't hurt a fly."

It was the standard cry of a murderer's family, as though the use of a fly-swat inevitably signalled homicidal tendencies. "Is someone with you, Ms. Howard? Does Jamie's father know?"

"He's flying down from Scotland tonight," sobbed Ms. Howard. "Oh, God. That dreadful woman. This is all her fault."

A natural if uncharitable sentiment. "Has Jamie actually been charged with murder?"

"I don't *know*," Ms. Howard wept. "I don't know *any*thing. Every time I try to find out, they say they have no further information at this time." She snorted loudly, trying to stem her sobs. "I told the police it had nothing to do with Jamie, but they wouldn't listen to me. I *know* he didn't do it."

"The trouble is, he doesn't have an alibi, does he?"

"Who needs alibis?"

"The police quite like them. And then—"

Suddenly Olivia was off into New Age ramblings: "Wholeness . . . Wellness . . . positive energy . . . the meaning of soul . . . the meaning of Meaning . . ." She was moving towards crystals and Oneness when Cassie interrupted.

"Has Jamie got a solicitor with him?"

"Yes. My former husband contacted the family firm immediately."

"Then he'll be all right," Cassandra soothed. She hoped it was true. At the moment, Jamie's problems seemed to focus more on a parent who was rapidly losing it than on a possible charge of murder. She did not for a moment believe that Jamie had killed Portia Wickham, and wondered why Mantripp and Walsh did. Had they found new information which pointed towards the young butler or were they acting on circumstantial evidence? Either way, she wished that Walsh would get in touch with her again.

Meanwhile, was there anything she knew which could exonerate Jamie? Had she missed something which would point to his innocence? For innocent she knew him to be, though she would be hard put to it to say exactly why. Certainly it was more than a mere gut-feeling. Just as she was used to assessing the opposition when it came to playing bridge, summing up their weaknesses and strengths, watching for the mannerisms which betrayed their tensions, the minute signs that might give away the whereabouts of a high card or the gaps in a suit, so she had assessed Jamie from the first time she had met him and come up with a young man who lacked ruthlessness. Looking back at her further meetings with him, she saw no reason to change her mind. Jamie was simply not capable of murder.

But wouldn't they have said that about Christie? About Dennis Nilsen? About any number of human beings who suddenly stepped out of character?

Not wanting to go down that road, she returned to the evening of Portia's murder. Did she know something which could point suspicion away from Jamie to another direction? Had she observed anything which could help clear him? Especially in view of the fact that she had felt a certain disquiet, a sense of things being not quite right, long before it was known that Portia was dead.

She sat down and began to lay out a game of Patience. It was always easier to concentrate with the cards in her hands. Although she had several times been over the events of that evening with the cops, she relived them once again, this time for Jamie.

It was amazing how the questions formed themselves into logical order, how everything began to sort itself out in her mind as the cards dropped in their calm unchangeable sequences. Red Jack on black Queen. Red eight on black nine. Ace out. King up. Turn over and find a home. Black two on red three . . . She was laying them out yet again when a car pulled up outside in the lane, then footsteps sounded on the flagged path. Someone called her name.

She ran to open the door, and Walsh came in. He put his arms round her and held her close. "God, I've missed you," he said.

"It wasn't Jamie," said Cassie. "You've got the wrong person."

"What?"

"Jamie didn't do it. He couldn't have done. He loved her."

He stepped away from her, his face falling into lines of disappointment. "Are you talking about James Grahame? The Wickham case?"

"Yes. Isn't that why you came?"

"I've driven halfway across the country to get away from the job for an hour or two, not to get stuck deeper into it. In order to be with you, Cassie." He smiled down at her. "Maybe, even, to persuade you to go to bed with me."

"He's at the Bellington station, is he? Have you charged him yet?"

"Jesus, Cassie. After the other day, I thought you felt the same about me as I do about you."

"I do, but this isn't the right moment. I'm more concerned about poor Jamie."

"What is this: blackmail? No nooky until you let poor little six-foot-two Muscle Man Jamie walk free, is that it?"

"That's a crude disgusting thing to say," Cassie shouted.

"But it's true, isn't it?"

"Don't be so ridiculous and unreasonable." She stared at him, and her gut dissolved with longing. She made an effort to soften her tones. "Look. Can I see him? There are some things I'd like to—"

Walsh grabbed her and kissed her. "Cassie," he murmured, his mouth against her lips. "Cassie, I've thought about nothing else but you since I was last here. It's playing hell with my concentration."

Much as she wanted to kiss him back, Cassie wrested herself away from him. "Have you charged him?"

He drew a long breath in through his nose, his expression furious. "Not yet," he said through gritted teeth.

"Do you think you will?"

"I don't know."

"What's the name of the charity which Portia was threatening to pull out of?"

"Do you think it was easy for me to get away at this stage of the investigation?" he demanded exasperatedly. "Aren't you glad to see me?"

"Ecstatic," Cassie said. "What's it called?"

Walsh rolled his eyes. "It was one of those anti-logging, save-the-bloody-trees ones," he said angrily. "Deadbeat, or something. No: Drumbeat."

"Another thing," Cassie said, aggressive as hell. "Don't you think it might be a good idea to let Jamie's mother know what's going on?"

"He's assisting us in a murder enquiry, *that's* what's going on. And she does know. Grahame telephoned her himself this morning."

Cassie was tempted to let it go at that. How simple it would be to take his hand, lead him to the bedroom, let him undress her slowly—or fast, depending how they both felt. But . . . "Assisting?" she said. "Your message on my answering machine said you'd got the person who killed Portia. You don't seem so sure now."

"We were at the end of a long hard slog. Do you know how many people we've talked to? How many statements we've taken, how many I've personally read? I've had about six hours' sleep since I last saw you, most of that sitting at my desk. Last night, it seemed as though we'd finally cracked the case."

"What on earth made you think Jamie could have done it?"

Irritably, Walsh ticked points off on his fingers. "One, he was heavily involved with Lady Wickham. Two, he was right there at the scene. Three, he admits he went down the drive at the relevant time. Four, he is known to possess—and use—a shotgun. Five, he's also known to be a good shot."

"What's that got to do with anything? You don't need medals from Bisley to walk up behind someone in the dark and stick a gun to their head. You said so yourself."

"When did I say that?"

"And, anyway, not one of the things you've mentioned amounts to a row of beans," Cassie said indignantly. "Either separately or together. They prove *nothing*."

"They're enough to provide a pretty good scenario for murder," said Walsh.

"In that case, what's the motive?"

"They quarrelled. She wanted to give him the old heave-ho and he didn't want to go."

"Jamie wasn't her only lover: the same could be true of any of them. Did you find a gun anywhere? Anything you can link to him?"

"Not yet. He admits he had one, but says his mother

snatched it away from him last time she saw him with it and chucked it into Loch Ness or somewhere." Walsh gave a grim chuckle, "I've heard some fairy stories in my time, but—"

"You obviously haven't met his mother."

"I'll agree," Walsh said, in an obvious attempt at mollification, "that your chum Jamie doesn't look as good for it as we'd originally expected. But give us a few more hours, and things might change."

"You mean, you'll fit him up?" Cassie said bitterly. "Isn't that how your lot does it these days? Pick on a suspect, suppress the bits of evidence which don't suit your theory or make them up if you need to, disorientate him until he agrees to anything you say, just to get you off his back, and then—"

"You sound exactly like my bloody wife," Walsh said coldly.

"And you make me realise why she left you."

They glared at each other. Then Walsh turned and walked out of the cottage and down the path. Watching him go, Cassie could read his hurt in the set of his shoulders. Her eyes filled with tears; her chest seemed full of painful air which it was difficult to breathe. What she had just said to him was unpardonable.

The local team of bellringers swung into action. From the village church came the sudden joyous sound of bells.

Perfect timing, boys. Slowly Cassie closed the front door as Walsh's car started up in the lane and drove off in a burn of black rubber.

After several more games of Patience, she carried her cordless phone into the sitting-room and dialled a number. Perched on the window-seat which looked out over the front garden, she waited for it to ring. Through the unruly box hedge that separated Honeysuckle Cottage from the lane, her eyes were caught by the glint of sunshine on chrome. A car—was it the same one she had noticed a couple of days earlier?—was parked in the lane. A black car. She just had time to think "twitcher"—it was the obvious answer to why someone would park in a dead end in broad daylight—when the phone was lifted.

"Natasha? It's Cass," she said.

"Cass!"

"I've heard from Robin. He's got that planning permission we were after."

"That's terrific. Wonderful. Now all we need is some money."

"It might be a good idea to go over the figures again. I could bring the papers over if you're likely to be home this afternoon. "

"Come to tea. The kids have some friends coming round, so I've just done some baking."

"Flapjacks?"

"As always. And some of those chocolaty biscuity things the kids adore. And a lemon cake, believe it or not. Must have been meant."

"How soon can I come?"

"As soon as you like."

"I'll set off in a couple of hours. Oh, and Tash . . ."

"Yes?" Natasha said cautiously.

"Chris will be there, won't he?"

"He'd better be: he's got a lawn to mow."

"Would he be allowed time off to look up something on one of his databases for me?"

"I'll think about it."

Chris and Natasha Sinclair were the kind of couple that magazines devoted to country living write articles about. Originally an executive in a PR company, Chris had moved into freelance work as soon as he had built up enough contacts, and eventually begun his own highly specialised company, organising fund-raising events for a widening circle of affluent clients. Natasha was a former model, half Russian and half Sri Lankan. Why such an exotic should have fallen for Chris, who came up to her shoulder, whose girth was Churchillian, whose own mother wouldn't have recognised him if he'd turned up with hair, was one of those mysteries which could only be ascribed to love. He and Natasha had been popular and assiduous partakers of the NW3 scene, but the hazards of living in the city had been brought sharply home to them when the youngest of their four children developed asthma, which the doctors attributed directly to traffic fumes, and another was beaten up on his way to school by a gang of youths shouting racist taunts.

"It's not that we don't think there's racism in other places," said Natasha, explaining to Cassie why they had decided to sell up and move out of London. "As the products of a mixed marriage, we always knew the kids might have problems. It's just that we hope that, in somewhere more rural, they'll have more chance of not getting kicked half to death while listening to their mother being called rude names."

"Let's hope you're right. How is Dima, anyway?"

"Still hobbling about with a stick, which didn't stop him going to a disco last week with some of his mates. But poor little Daisy's had a couple of terrible winters: even before Dima got on the wrong side of those other kids, we'd been thinking about moving."

After searching for six months, they had finally settled in Larton Easewood, a village twelve miles from Cassie. Chris, born and raised in Liverpool, had taken enthusiastically to country life. Thanks to fax machines, modems and electronic mail systems, he was able to work as efficiently from Larton as from Hampstead. Natasha, too, had been happy until Daisy started at the local primary school. But with no children at home, she had found time passing too slowly.

"Chris is stuck into his machines," she said to Cassie once. "And the children love it here, the big garden and so on. But frankly I'm not domesticated. I don't want to get a full-time job, not with Daisy still getting wheezy from time to time, but I do want an interest of some kind. Some sense that I'm worth something in my own right and not just as somebody's mother or wife."

"How about a shop?" Cassie.

"I've thought of that. There's a definite commercial streak in me: I think one of my ancestors must have been a carpet-seller. But what sort of shop?"

"Fashion?"

"Give me a break. I spent my entire working life in fashion and I wouldn't mind if I never saw a designer dress again in my life. Let alone a designer."

"Interior decor?"

"Please!"

Now, at last, it looked as though their bridge sundries might actually be about to become reality.

Cassie passed the village grocery shop, which stood on one side of the narrow High Street. As well as a number of fine houses ranging from Tudor to High Victorian, the street boasted a church, complete with its own vicar, a couple of pubs, two antique shops, and a greengrocer which also sold local produce: home-made jams, honey, cheeses, cut flowers in season, fresh herbs. England as engraved on the ex-pat heart.

The Sinclairs lived in a Queen Anne house just beyond the post office. Cassie parked in front of the house which, linked to its neighbours, gave no hint of the large garden behind.

"Chris," Cassie said, fingering the last delicious crumb of flapjack from her plate, "I need some information, and I'm hoping you can get it for me."

"Am I allowed?" Chris said to Natasha.

"Since it's Cassie," said his wife. "But the grass will still need cutting."

"Bloody stuff. Why doesn't someone invent grass which doesn't grow?"

"They have. It's called Astroturf," said Cassie.

"I shall order an acre of it tomorrow," Chris said, getting up and leading the way to his office. "What exactly are you looking for, Cass?"

"You've got access to details of all the registered charities in the country, haven't you?"

"In the *world*, darling." He sat down, booted up, watched the screen as the computer went through its various good-morning-and-how-are-we-today routines before finally declaring itself ready to get to work.

"I'm interested in one called Drumbeat."

"OK." He logged on to one of the many databases he subscribed to and then downloaded the information on to a disc in his own computer. "Shall we print it out, or do you want to read it off the screen?"

"All I'm interested in is the names of the people on the board. But thanks: a printout could be useful."

Although she was already half convinced that she was right, it was with a feeling of satisfaction that she saw the name of Roderick Symington flick into existence on the screen. And, as Chris scrolled down at her request, that of Portia Whitbread. Seeing the two names there gave solidity to her theory about a connection. Now all she had to do was establish what it was.

If not sex, was it that other great motivator: money? It seemed strange, somehow, that Symington would need to abuse his position vis-à-vis the charity in order to add what must surely to him be peanuts to his bank-balance.

So, stick with the charity but dump the cash angle: what other malfeasance could Portia have discovered? It would not matter whether it was large or small: just the taint to his reputation might be enough, were it to come out that he had abused his position. Cassie remembered reading recently about Amazon Indians who, in return for cash, had promised not to go on felling their mahogany trees, but whose head man had none the less continued to do so at the demand of unscrupulous furniture-makers—for more cash, of course.

"What do you know about Roderick Symington of the construction company Symingtons?" she asked.

"Funnily enough, I was looking at him the other day," Chris said, leaning back in his office chair and stretching his shoulders. "Someone in Ireland wants to set up an operatic trust to enable young singers to experience professional opera, and Symington's a likely prospect for donations, since he's known as an opera-lover. What exactly do you want to know?"

"Tell me about him first. I know about the new wife and baby."

"The company's doing fine, even in the recession. There's always a need for construction, even when domestic housing is on the skids. Symington himself? Let's see . . . He's an only child, inherited the business from his father, never had any financial problems. Father was made a life peer under the Heath government: our Symington could reasonably expect the same honour some time fairly soon. Not only expects, but very much wants. From what I've read about him, he's a man who's spent his life trying to get out from under Daddy's shadow. Old Symington's dead now, but in his time he was a hell of a character: used to own horses in the days when racing was still a sport for gentlemen, sailed at Cowes with Prince Philip, grew orchids, kept exotic mistresses, that sort of thing. Always a colourful column or two to be got out of old Lord Symington. So Roddy's desperate to become a star in his own right, overtake Daddy if he can." Chris smiled and swung his short legs up onto the windowsill, rubbing his hands together. "Which makes him fair game from my point of view: he'll support anything that he perceives as helpful in building up his profile."

"And if it were discovered that he'd been involved in something a bit shady, would it scupper his chances?"

"Heavens, yes! Too many governments have found themselves getting into bed with the wrong people recently. Maxwell wasn't a great advertisement, any more than Anthony Blunt. Makes those crusty old colonels in Tunbridge Wells who returned their OBEs when the Beatles got them look like idiots, doesn't it?"

"They always looked like idiots."

"People like Ceausescu being feted by heads of state didn't do anyone much good, either. And that disastrous Honours List of Harold Wilson's, if you can remember that far back . . . No: these days you have to be squeaky-clean inside and out." Chris rolled backwards on his chair so that he could look out of the window to where his wife stood beneath a large chestnut tree gesticulating at a child hidden among the leaves above her head. "Don't let it be said that I'm prying, but do you have anything—you know—" he made delicate movements with his hands, "discreditable . . . on Symington? It would be useful for my files if you do."

"Nothing. Just wild theories," Cassie said. "If any of them are confirmed, I'll let you know. There's another thing: ever heard of a girl called Tamsin? She lives more or less up the road, in Marsh, I think."

"They're all called Tamsin these days," said Chris. "How old is this one?"

"Seventeen, eighteen. Doing her A levels this summer. Helps out a bit at Halkam Court from time to time."

"Oh, my God." Chris straightened up, putting his feet down on the floor. "You don't mean Tamsin the Leather Queen, do you?"

"I don't know. Do I?"

"Just a minute." Chris got up and left the room. Cassie heard him shouting up the stairs, and then, as there was no other sound but the whump-whump of a bass speaker from the top of the house, muttering curses to himself as he bounded up the stairs. Minutes later, he reappeared with Dmitri, his eldest son.

"Ask Dima about Tamsin," he said.

Cassie repeated her question. "Yeah," said Dima, fourteen years old last birthday. "Tamsin Dark. She's ace. She goes on the bus to school with us because they won't let her ride her bike."

"Roads too dangerous, are they?"

"*She*'s too dangerous. She crashed into a car once at seventy miles an hour and did nine hundred quids' worth of damage."

"Seventy miles an hour? She must have terrific leg muscles," Cassie said. "Or are we talking about motorbikes?"

"Get real," Dmitri said scornfully. "Tamsin wouldn't ride a *bi*cycle."

"Sorry. Tell me some more about her."

"Everyone at school's well scared of her," said Dmitri, with a wide smile. "Last term she had a fight with another girl, with *knives*."

"I thought you moved out of London to avoid this sort of thing," Cassie said to Chris.

"So did I." Chris shrugged, looking at his son with unconcealed pride.

"What was the fight about, anyway?" asked Cassie.

"Oh, some boy Tamsin was mad about at the time. She thought this other girl was bonking him."

"Dima, do you mind?" Chris said. "You're too young to know about such things."

"Don't you believe it, Dad." Dima's voice was still break-

ing, and at this piece of insincere braggadocio it soared briefly
into an upper register.

"So she's a bit of a toughie, is she, this Tamsin Dark?" said
Cassie.

"Yeah. She's got about twenty rings in her ears. *And*
through her nipples."

"That's *tough*," said Cassie, wincing slightly. "Are there
any other Tamsins at your school doing A levels next term?"
If there were, Dmitri would probably know them, since the
catchment area for the comprehensive in Bellington embraced
both Larton Easewood and March.

"Only her. There's others, but they're in the year below."

"I don't think we can be talking about the same girl," said
Cassie. "The one I'm thinking of has dark hair and blue eyes,
and freckles. Very pretty." It was difficult to imagine the de-
mure waitress at Lord Wickham's bridge evening with rings
through her nipples.

"Same one," Dmitri said. "She comes and baby-sits sometimes, doesn't she, Dad?"

"Arrives on her bike," agreed Chris. "And I'm telling you,
punk or no punk, you have never committed an impure act in
your heart until you've seen Tamsin in leathers. It's a sight to
gladden an old man's eyes."

"You wouldn't like her, Dad," Dmitri said. "She's much too
butch for you."

"Anyway, she probably wouldn't look at an older man if
you paid her to."

"Dunno about that," said his son. "She's been going out
with this really old bloke who's twenty-six or something."

"That's dis*gusting*!" Cassie cried.

"Isn't it, though?" Chris screwed his face up with mock re-
pugnance. "That tender young body next to his wrinkled flab.
That sweet innocence befouled by some drooling lecher of
twenty-six. It doesn't bear thinking about."

"Was this ancient by any chance someone from Halkam
Court?" Cassie said.

"Yeah. Butler, or something," said Dmitri.

"Ah." It was what Cassie had been half expecting to hear. "I don't suppose this Tamsin knows anything about guns, does she?"

"Probably. The cops are always round her house because her brothers are always being done for nicking stuff." Dmitri gave it some thought. "Yeah. Bet they've got dozens of guns—they're the sort." He moved carefully to the door of the room and added, "Know what they say about her at school?"

"What's that?" asked Cassie.

"She's so tough, she keeps her knickers up with drawing pins."

"The way you've described her, I'm surprised she wears any."

"She's so tough," Dima went on, "she kick-starts her vibrator."

He dodged quickly out of the room while his father roared: "Dmitri! Come back here immediately."

"Jesus," said Cassie. "Whatever happened to childish innocence?"

"Television chewed it up and spat it out in their poor little faces," Chris said.

"If it ever existed."

Chris shook his head in mock despair. "Do you realise that kid'll be swapping dirty stories with me down the pub before I know where I am?"

"He's probably already forgotten more than you ever knew."

On the way home, Cassie played with a new theory. Tough Tamsin, dead keen on Jamie, decides to eliminate her rival, Portia Wickham. Perhaps she even tries to force him to choose between the two of them. He opts for Portia. After he takes her home on the night of Portia's murder, she jumps on her bike and zooms back to Halkam Court, gun stuffed down the front of her studded leathers. To her surprise, she encounters her employer's wife trudging up the drive in the rain. Trained by her rough-talkin', hard-shootin' brothers, she pulls out her weapon and pumps a bullet into the older woman. It misses, and she fires again. This time Portia slumps dead to the ground, and young Tamsin zooms off back home, there, no doubt, to pull out her notes on Sylvia Plath or Philip Larkin, and catch up with some of the A level revision she's missed.

As a theory, it had all the ring of inauthenticity. It was, none the less, perfectly feasible. Tamsin was a local girl, she not only knew Portia but was aware of the liaison between her and Jamie; from what Dmitri had said, she was plainly a girl who went after the things she wanted, and one of them was Jamie. Easy prey.

As for the young butler: while savouring the delights of the more mature Lady Wickham he was obviously, in his turn, not averse to Tamsin's youthful charms. And who could blame him? Perhaps it would have been more pertinent if the police, instead of wanting to know what he was doing at the time in question, had asked whether he practised safe sex.

16

Cassie stood naked on the scales, beating her head against the bathroom wall. How come she weighed so much more today than she had yesterday? Two flapjacks and a slice of lemon cake couldn't have translated into three pounds of unsightly fat already, could they? No one's metabolism worked that fast.

She stepped off the scales and found a towel. Before she could sink into suicidal despair, reason asserted itself. If they had, so what? This was her, this . . . *woman* . . . was Cassandra Swann.

She tried it out loud. "This is me. This is Cassandra Swann."

Hmm.

Cassandra Swann, like it or lump it. Though, to be fair, there wasn't all *that* much lump. Nobody had yet mistaken her for the European butter mountain or Durham cathedral. No one had tried to climb her because she was there. Nobody had said she was clinically obese—and she'd bloody well like to see them try.

So why did it matter? Would she be happier if she was a stone lighter? Would she earn more, achieve more, be more beautiful, save the world, if she stayed within the parameters of her acceptable weight range—that arbitrary computation involving height and age and number of clothes the victim was wearing at the time?

Big question: *would she be able to keep her houseplants alive?*

And underneath those queries lay another, more serious, one; would she give a damn about her weight if Sarah had lived, or if she had grown up with Dad and Gran, loved, if she hadn't been so rudely transplanted from one growing medium to another?

Aha! She glanced at the pathetic spider plant which lay gasping on the bathroom windowsill. Was that early personal re-potting and her own subsequent failure to put down roots the *real* reason why all her philodendrons and Busy Lizzies snuffed it? Was this life imitating life? Could it be that all those untimely vegetative deaths were nothing more than a transferred metaphor?

Before she could start pouring Baby Bio down her throat, the telephone rang. She willed it to be Walsh. Since he had walked out the day before, she had alternated between despair and indignation, but she knew that if he rang to suggest he came round that evening, she would have a hard time not dropping to her knees and shrieking "Yes! Yes!" If he said he was sorry—but even on such short acquaintance, she sensed that this was unlikely. Walsh was not a man who apologised for much, nor needed to. It was an ability she envied him.

"Hello," she said guardedly.

There was no reply. She listened for a moment but heard only the absence of sound. She shrugged. A wrong number, most likely. She looked at her watch.

She felt restless. Outside, an unseasonable wind was shaking the lilacs and scattering the last wallflower petals in the front garden. She sat down in the gloomy sitting-room with a

pen and a pad of paper and tried once more to marshal her
thoughts.

Inevitably, they drifted again to Walsh. His hands, his eyes,
his lovely mouth. The way his skin felt, the scent of his
hair . . . men had such different odours from women, even
their smells were more assertive. Was it Napoleon who was
supposed to have sent a message to Josephine saying he'd be
arriving on the following day and she was not to wash? And
what connection, if any, was there between that and his other
on dit: "Not tonight, Josephine."?

Come on. Cassie. Think.

Walsh had said that DI Mantrippp still liked the idea of a
contract killing to account for Portia's death. If you agreed
with him, then the person who set it up could be anyone:
someone who was at Halkam Court that night, someone who
worked with Portia, someone back home in her native
Texas—absolutely anyone.

Hold on to Texas! Without being too xenophobic, weren't
the Yanks much more into contract killing than we were? Was
this a trail Walsh and Mantripp had gone down? She tried to
imagine a tall lean Texan with rangy hips and weathered fea-
tures swinging into town to pay his advances to the lovely little lady at Halkam Court. Or a black-hatted gamblin' man with
lace at the throat and eyes like Clint Eastwood. No. She shook
her head. In the local villages, he'd have stuck out like sun-
cream on an Ozzie batsman's lips. Someone would have told
the cops.

She wrote down Motives on her pad. Then added the word
Money, and under it, Sex.

Take money: it must be fairly easy to establish who had
most to gain with Portia out of the way. The cops would have
been into that, and it was fairly obvious that they had con-
cluded financial gain was not the motive or they would not
have arrested Jamie.

So move on to sex: if it were a *crime passionel*, the Texas
Connection sank right back into the obscurity from which she
herself had dragged it. Portia had been in England for a considerable time, too long to make it feasible that a rejected
Texan was likely to show up with murder in mind.

Knock out the contract killer, and you also knocked out most of those present that evening, since many of them were able to provide alibis for each other. Common-sense argued that the murderer had to have some connection with those who were there that night. Which of them had no alibi? Symington. Tamsin. Marling. Jacko Dexter. Jamie, of course. And Cassandra Swann. Except that she had no reason whatsoever to wish Portia dead, and anyway could not have anticipated being around to kill her, even supposing she had the faintest idea where to get hold of a gun.

Why should Portia have been murdered that particular evening? There had to be a reason. And thinking this, she began to realise that she might be on the right track at last. A glimmer lit the dark obfuscations in which the whole murder scene had hitherto, both metaphorically and literally, lurked.

Why that evening? Briefly she returned to the notion of the hired assassin. Suppose Jeremy Marling had done the hiring. What were his connections with Portia? Cassie fetched the printout of the charities Portia supported or had worked for, along with the names of her co-supporters, which Chris had given her the day before at Larton Easewood. If she found one with which Marling was also involved . . . But she did not, and if she had, it wouldn't have proved a thing. She didn't find one with Dexter on it, either.

None the less, she continued to think about Marling. He was obviously not one of the super-rich. If he were, he would certainly not be investing in small companies like Mills & Runes. Nor did he seem to be living at a high level. The wife had spoken of a small house in France: it had sounded like nothing more ostentatious than a standard middle-class aspiration. And Marling himself had been engagingly frank about not doing much except enjoy himself because there was so little financial necessity. Plus the fact that he had the advantage of a well-off wife. *Not what you'd call stinking rich, but certainly comfortable,* he had said. Cassie, a Capricorn, could not imagine anything more horrific than spending her life doing nothing, but perhaps Marling had been lucky enough to be born under a less demanding sign.

The problem continued to worry her. Gambling? Could Portia have gambled away her fortune and now be at the mercy of the loan sharks? Was Marling—or Dexter or Symington, for that matter—a loan shark? Had they killed her to make an object-lesson of her? But it was hardly something you could advertise: Hey, sucker: we killed her because she owed us, so if you know what's good for you, you'll pay up pronto. All sucker would have to do to get them off his back would be to inform the local plod. And anyway the police had been into Portia's financial status and found it healthy.

She thought about Chilcott, but not for long. His name certainly didn't figure anywhere on the print-out, and besides, he hadn't known the Wickhams before that evening. Nor would he have kicked her out of his car if he was behind Portia's murder: he'd need all the corroborative evidence he could get.

She looked at her watch again. A bare hour had crawled by. At her age, she was not going to sit about hoping for the phone to ring. Before she could change her mind, she picked up her car keys. Why should she wait for Walsh to telephone when there were still people she could go and talk to?

About to lock the front door behind her, she paused. Monday was her free evening.

The hell with pride.

Back inside the cottage, she telephoned the nick. "I'd like to speak to DS Walsh," she said.

"I'm afraid Detective Sergeant Walsh isn't available."

"What exactly does that mean?"

"It means I can't reach him at this time, madam."

"Suppose I had important information to give him concerning the current case he's working on."

"Which particular case would that be?"

"The Wickham murder."

"Is that the lady who rang the other day? Another officer will be glad to speak to you, madam, if you'll just hold on."

Cassie rang off, feeling like an idiot.

The land was rich with barley and wheat. Poppies thrived along the edge of the fields, and the hedgerows were thickly tangled with willow-herb, loosestrife, Queen Anne's Lace and grasses. On the busier roads, the hedges were kept fiercely pruned and the ditches sprayed to eliminate the profusion of wild flowers, but in the back lanes, it must still look much as it had a hundred years ago. Cottages built of buttery stone, honey-coloured churches, lichened roofs, dry-stone walls: although the city was her natural habitat, Cassie was prepared to concede that this was indeed beautiful. Beyond the flat ground, the rounded Cotswold countryside lifted gently towards a pale blue sky. Today, there was little sun and the trees seemed weighed down, as though the greenness of their leaves was almost too heavy a burden for their branches to carry.

The village of March consisted of little more than a thoroughfare bisected halfway down by Market Street and, further along, by the road which led towards Burford. The twentieth century had successfully been kept at bay in the main street, which was lined with ancient cottages of pale Cotswold stone, only a few of which had been translated into antique shops, places selling traditional craftware and cafés offering Cream Teas. Beyond the exploitation of the tourist traps lay a raw new housing estate, all aggressive red brick and dark-stained wood. There was a Spar here, a BP garage, garish and ugly, and tacked on to it a warehouse labelled Auto Spares, with a huge tyre spinning slowly on top of another out in front.

Easy to condemn, Cassie thought. Easy to wonder what progress was all about when you set these cramped modern houses against the aesthetic appeal of the old cottages. But set that appeal against the brutish lives the cottagers used to live: the infant-mortality rates, the consumptive lungs, the lack of hygiene, and the equation became very blurred.

At the garage, she pulled in and went into the attached shop.

"I'm looking for some people called Dark," she said to the woman behind the till. "Do you know where they live? It's somewhere round here."

"I'm from Bourton, myself," the woman said. "But Terry's local: I can ask him." She picked up a receiver and spoke into it in a low conspiratorial way; at the same time, her high-pitched heavily amplified voice blared behind a wall of soft drink refrigerators and shelves of cassettes.

Somewhere, Terry picked up a receiver and responded. "Go down that road there," the woman said, pointing as she repeated what he said. "Take a left turn at Falcon Walk. First right is Curlew Way. Just off Curlew Way there's another turn into Robin Crescent, and the Darks live at the end, number 16 or 17, Terry's not sure which."

"Thank you very much."

The receiver squawked some more, and the woman said; "Terry says, if you're looking for Shane, he's on holiday at the moment, and if you want Darren, he's not there."

"Thanks," Cassie said. She bought a paper and a Diet Tango, and got back into her car. If Dmitri Sinclair's information was to be trusted, it sounded as though at least one of Tamsin's brothers might currently be sampling Her Majesty's hospitality.

She parked in Robin Crescent and got out. Both 16 and 17 were neat and well maintained. Both had a central concrete path with flower-beds on either side, stuffed with flowers of a shrill orange interspersed with clumps of intense blue lobelia. There were frilled draped net curtains at both sets of windows, and each had a fake carriage-lamp of black-and-gold tin beside the front door. Neither looked like the kind of household where the inmates wore nipple-rings and carried guns. Each had an integral garage: the one at No. 17 was open so that she could see the usual clutter which gathers when a house does not have enough storage space. Plastic laundry-baskets, milk-crates full of beer bottles, garden tools and furniture, a broken industrial bag spilling cement powder, a straw wreath with some withered sprigs of holly and a faded red ribbon still attached, cardboard cartons of junk, a playpen, a standard lamp trailing electrical flex, paint-cans, a tool-box, an old armchair with a torn Bri-nylon slip cover. Detritus, for the most part, the sort of stuff that ought to be thrown away but which inevitably hangs on even in the best-regulated household, losing more and more excuse for being there, until the occupants eventually move or die.

The clincher, for Cassie, was the three motorbikes leaning against the wall of No. 17. She walked up the path and pressed the buzzer: inside, door-chimes ping-ponged.

After a short wait, a neat woman with a ravaged face opened the door.

"Good afternoon," Cassie said politely. "Is Tamsin at home?"

Briefly the woman closed her eyes. Opening them, she said, "Who wants to know?"

"My name's Cassandra Swann. It's a purely personal enquiry."

"What sort of enquiry?"

"Are you her mother?" The woman nodded. Cassie could tell that Tamsin's mother was afraid she was from the police, the probation service, the education authority, an insurance company. She had the look of a woman who is used to opening front doors and finding accusatory representatives of some body or other on the doorstep. Anxious to reassure, Cassie said, "I'm a friend of a friend of hers."

Mrs. Dark relaxed a little. "She won't be home for another hour at least," she said. "No. Today's Monday: she won't be home until well after six. She does a couple of hours at the supermarket on Mondays."

Keeping yourself in motorcycle spares and nipple-rings while you were still at school obviously meant hard graft. With A level revision on top, Tamsin had set herself a heavy timetable. "Is that the one in Bellington?"

"Tesco, yes." Mrs. Dark suddenly looked anxious. Cassie wanted to put an arm round her thin shoulders, tell her that, this time at least, there was nothing wrong, it was simply that she had a couple of questions to ask, and thought Tamsin might know the answers.

"I'll pop in there on my way home," she said. "See if I can see her. It's not important." She began to back down the path, still smiling encouragingly.

The supermarket was surprisingly busy. Entire families strolled up and down the aisles, stopping every now and then to take something from the shelves, read the packaging and then either put it back or place it in their trolley. In here, it was easy to believe that supermarket shopping was the great new family entertainment of the masses; one that could be sustained even in the face of recession. The only difference between now and the affluent Eighties was the amount of stuff you finally wheeled up to the checkout.

Cassie took a basket from the pile by the revolving door and wandered over to the fruit shelves, keeping an eye open for Tamsin. Something exotic, she thought. A paw-paw, Cape gooseberries, fresh dates, mangoes. Those spiky things like yellow hedgehogs. Star fruit. The good thing about fruit was that there was not an ounce of cholesterol in any of it. And the good thing about living in the Nineties was that you didn't have to take a cruise to the South Sea islands in order to buy a paw-paw.

She swung on down towards the bread, turning her head and thinking of England as she passed the cream cakes in their cold cabinet, shutting her eyes as she moved swiftly by the wrapped Battenburgs and apricot Swiss rolls, the chocolate brownies and bread pudding, the ginger cakes and pecan pies and crumpets and English muffins. "Buy me," they whispered at her insistently. "Buy me. Just one of me. I won't hurt you."

It was hard. But made easier by the fact that she knew most of them would taste shitty when she got them home, and helped even more by seeing Tamsin stuffing the frozen-vegetable shelves with giant bags of frozen corn and garden peas. She wore a red-and-white check overall and looked as demurely pretty as she had in her black frock the week before, though this time without the hint of mislaid undergarments. But she was paler now, and there were shadows under her eyes.

"Tamsin," Cassie said.

The girl looked up, half recognised her, frowned. "Yes?"

"You probably don't remember me . . ." Cassie began, but Tamsin interrupted.

"You were at that bridge do of Lord Wickham's, weren't you?"

"That's right. But before that—"

"—you taught biology for a couple of terms, didn't you?"

"Yes."

Tamsin nodded. Then she said quickly, keeping her head down; "I keep thinking about it. Her lying there in the drive, dead." She shuddered. "Jamie and I might have driven right over her. I'm sure I remember . . ." Her voice drifted off into silence, and she looked down at the trolley full of frozen vegetables, her gloved hands reaching out to add more to the already bulging shelves.

"Jamie told me he asked you at the very last minute if you could come and help out that evening."

"Yeah. He rang me at my house the night before."

"Did you always have such short notice?"

"No." Tamsin didn't seem to think it was odd that Cassie was asking questions. "There'd been a change of plan. He wasn't too pleased about it, because it was supposed to be his night off. He said he'd only just been told that they were going to play at Halkam Court instead of the usual place."

"Where was that?"

"London, I suppose. I don't know."

"Were all those people originally going to London to play?"

"I don't know. Some of them, I suppose. And some *came* from London."

"Does Lord Wickham often have evenings of bridge at his house?"

"Yeah. About once a month."

"But you usually had more notice than you did that night?"

"Yeah. They're arranged two or three weeks in advance, usually." Tamsin shrugged, and at the same time stacked more packets of peas. "I didn't mind too much. I'm more or less on target with my revision—I've got A levels coming up—and I needed the money."

"Saving up for your holidays?" Cassie said, with what she recognised as a horrible Aunt-Polly waggishness.

Tamsin shook her head. "No. I'm hoping to go to university, but these days, even on a full grant, it's difficult to survive. You read about these kids who go on the game and that, in order to support themselves, or have to give it up because they can't afford it. That's not going to happen to me, I'm not dropping out. No way." She sounded vehement about it.

"What subjects are you taking?"

"French, German and economics," Tamsin said. "And philosophy." Once again she bent, brought up an armful of the floppy packages of corn and stuffed them into place. "The philosophy's just for fun. The rest's so I can get a job somewhere in Europe, so I can get out of this bloody awful country."

"We're not the only ones in a financial mess," Cassie said.

"I'm not talking just about the economy," said Tamsin. "I'm talking about pride. I know they've got problems in continental Europe—look at the Neo-Nazis in Germany, for example—but they don't tolerate the things we do, like the dirt and the yobs and the kids running wild and nobody telling them off or teaching them to behave. Their educational systems are *much* better than ours, and they haven't lost the excitement of intellectualism, the way we have. I mean, in France, people sit for hours over a bottle of wine, talking about *ideas*."

Cassie nodded encouragingly. It was not for her to spoil the dream.

"And *our* government's actually considering knocking Shakespeare off the curriculum because it isn't relevant to black kids in the inner cities. If you're a kid who wants to get on, who's brainier or more ambitious than the rest, you have to keep dead quiet about it or they'll get you after school, beat you up, try and muck up your notes and essays, that sort of thing." She shook her head as she stowed away the last of her bags of frozen kernels. "Unless you can show them you're tougher than they are, you've had it."

At the end of the aisle, one of the managers, a spotty creature in a Tesco-issue suit, stood watching Tamsin, frowning slightly and tapping his clipboard with a pen. "You sound as if you're speaking from experience," Cassie said, trying to look like a customer enquiring as to the whereabouts of the frozen stir-fry vegetables.

"I find that's usually the best way," the girl said in a level voice.

Was ambition what lay behind the motorbikes and the body-rings? Were they no more than necessary props to help Tamsin escape from an environment which tried to stop her from realising her potential?

"Anyway, I'd better get on." Tamsin said. She gestured towards the yoghurts.

Having paid for her fruit, Cassie walked down the main street of Bellington and went into W. H. Smith, where she bought a substantial book token. She scribbled a message inside: "Enjoy university." It had all been easier in her own time. In a society which was currently proposing to make students pay for the privilege of their higher education, apparently blind to the fact that they were the seed-corn for the future and should be carefully nurtured, perhaps it was a forlorn hope, particularly for the other Tamsins out there. She wrote Tamsin's name on the envelope and went back to the supermarket, where she handed it to one of the supervisors.

"Could you please make sure this reaches her?" she said.

"I'll take it now." The woman smiled; it was all part of customer relations. Cassie watched her walk towards the dairy products section before she left.

She had time to think on the way home. There had been an accident along the Bellington by-pass, and it took half an hour to travel less than a mile. As she passed the flashing blue lights, the police cars and the emergency services, she could see the cause of the delay. One vehicle, a transit van, was a complete write-off, the front portion totally demolished. The other, a Vauxhall Cavalier, sat upside-down on the hard shoulder, its windows smashed and seatbelt webbing trailing through the wrecked doors.

The fact that the bridge game had been moved so suddenly from London to Market Broughton had to have some significance. Jamie had mentioned it before, but Cassie had not attached any particular importance to it at the time. But if there was a connection between the change of venue and Portia's death, had she died because of the alteration? Or had the alteration been made in order to achieve her death? Either way, Lord Wickham must be implicated.

She wondered whether Walsh was aware of the change of plan that evening. If so, whether he thought the two were connected. But they had to be. It was otherwise too great a coincidence. Frustrated, she banged her steering wheel. How much easier it would all be to figure out if she had been present at the interviews the police had conducted.

But certain factors were proving more and more insistent. A

couple more pieces of information, and she might be able at last to reconstruct what had happened that night.

As she turned into the lane approaching Honeysuckle Cottage, her heart began to thump. A white car was parked beside the hedge with a blue lamp clamped to its roof. That meant police. More specifically, it meant Walsh.

Didn't it?

The car was empty. She maneuvered round it and pulled up in front of her shed. If it was Walsh, where was he? She got out and walked around the side towards the back door.

"You should never leave your house unlocked," he said, as she came round the corner of the cottage. He was sitting, with a glass of white wine beside him on the slatted table, reading an old copy of *Lucky Jim*. "Anyone could just walk in."

"It looks as though they already have," said Cassie.

"There was an ugly-looking customer hanging about on a motorbike when I arrived," Walsh said. "He saw I was police and took off like a bat out of hell. If I hadn't arrived when I did, you might have had half your stuff nicked."

Why did this information make her feel suddenly cold? "Burglars don't use motorbikes," she said slowly.

"True." Walsh raised the glass to his mouth. "Unless they're opportunist thieves. Perhaps he was only after the portable things: jewellery and so on. Anyway, why don't you join me in a glass of this excellent wine?"

Deciding it was all the apology for his walking out that she was going to get, Cassie did so.

"You'll be glad to hear that we had to let your chum go," Walsh said. He stared out across the garden towards the buddleia by the pergola.

"It was the only sensible thing to do," Cassie said neutrally.

"Mmm."

"Did he give you any further information?"

"Not really."

"Did he explain why that bridge evening was set up at such short notice?" Cassie too stared at the buddleia, where tortoisehell butterflies were clustering round the purple spikes.

Walsh put a hand on Cassie's thigh and pressed it. "He said that Wickham had come down to the kitchen and explained that there'd been a change of plan, that instead of going up to London, as arranged, people would be coming to the Court."

"What was the reason for the change?"

"He didn't say."

"You mean you didn't ask."

"At this stage, we're more concerned with *what* happened than why."

"But there has to be a connection. The change of plan and the murder: I don't believe they just randomly occurred on the same night."

"You think that Wickham set it up?"

"Don't you? What else is there to think?" Cassie said slowly. She recalled the Vauxhall which had flipped over on its roof. Perhaps it was not the only thing which was upside-down and back-to-front. Perhaps she had been approaching all this from the wrong angle.

Pushing thoughts of the murder from her mind, she turned to Walsh. For the moment, the fact that he was here was all she needed. Behind his head, a mottled butterfly hovered, then flew off. He was looking at her, and his eyes were the same colour as the butterfly's wings. She opened her mouth to ask him a most important question but before she could speak he was kissing her and she was kissing him back and somehow one delicious thing led to another and it was the morning and his car was driving off down the lawn before she realised that she still did not know his first name.

17

"Straight up, miss," Kipper said, rolling himself an untidy cigarette. "He threw himself under that TIR. No question about it." He lit up and squinted through the smoke at the cards in his hands. "Uh—pass."

"No bid." Haslam-Jones leaned judicially back in his chair. "Sometimes death seems preferable to a fate worse than death."

"Is the system really that inhumane?" Cassie asked.

"It's not the system Burslake was worried about," said Eddie Taylor. "Um—pass."

"Leastways, not the system the Home Office knows about," Kipper said.

"Wouldn't the officers have seen Burslake was all right?"

"With what was waiting for him in Durham?" said Taylor. "Not a chance."

"They'd have done him one way or another," Kipper said.

A shred or two of flaming tobacco fell from the end of his cigarette on to his score-card.

At the other table, Leslie said, "He didn't dare talk. He'd already been duffed up in one nick and cut in another."

"Who by?" Cassie said. "It's your bid, Nigel."

Rastaman looked up from his cards. "I know, miss, but I'm
still figgerin' it out."

"Three passes to you, so far," said Cassie.

Haslam-Jones peered over the top of his rimless glasses.
"Three noes and only a fool goes."

"Say what?" Rastaman shook his big head, made doubly
huge by the great weight of his dreadlocks netted inside a tri-
coloured beret of crocheted wool. "You sayin' Rastaman is a
fool? Just 'cos I don't got no degree in lawyering, that don't
mean I is stupid."

"I'm merely repeating what Miss Swann has told us several
times in the past," Haslam-Jones said. "I wouldn't dream of
calling you a fool."

"Not unless you like hospital food," said Ginge, who was
partnering Leslie at the other table.

Kipper looked impatiently at Rastaman. "Pull yer finger
out, mate."

"Uh—two hearts," said Rastaman.

"What exactly do you understand by that?" Cassie asked his
partner.

"Rasta's off his bleeding trolley?" suggested Ginge.

The big black man pushed back his chair, his round baby-
face ferociously screwed into a high-intensity glare.

"I understand," Haslam-Jones said smoothly, "that my partner, however unlikely it might appear, has twenty to twenty-
two points and a five-card suit."

"And have you, Nigel?" asked Cassie.

"Yo."

Cassie looked at his cards. "So you have. All right, what is
your partner going to reply?"

"If I followed what you told us earlier this evening . . ." said
Haslam-Jones.

"And we all know you did," muttered Leslie.

". . . then my response, given my poor hand, should be two No Trumps."

"I'm goin' for it, man," Rasta said. "I say four Hearts."

"Your lead, then, Mr. Naughton," said Haslam-Jones.

"Me? Why me? I didn't bid nothing," Kipper said.

"You, dear boy, are sitting on the right hand of—"

"God," said Leslie. They all roared with laughter at this sally.

"—Dummy. Therefore you are the first to lead."

"Here, miss," said Taylor. "We made up a joke for you the other day. *And* it's clean."

"Did you? Let's hear it, then."

"Tell her, Ginge," said Taylor.

"Um. What's the difference betw—"

"No, you wally," said Leslie.

"Why's it *me*'s got to tell this fucking joke, anyway?"

"Language," said Taylor.

"Get a bloody move on, Ginge," someone said.

Ginger sucked in deeply on the end of the thin cigarette he was smoking. "Why is this nick like a bid of seven Hearts?" he said, after several seconds' thought.

"I don't know," Cassie said. "Why *is* this nick like a bid of seven Hearts?"

"Because they're both grand slams," said Ginge. "Get it, miss? Grand slams? They're both grand slams."

His fellow bridge-players fell about in appreciation of the witticism.

"Slam," Haslam-Jones said kindly to Cassie, "in case you were not familiar with the term, is an abbreviation of the word slammer, which in turn is a colloquialism for prison."

Rastaman suddenly slapped the table. "Your lead, Kipper," he said. "Rastaman is rollin' high."

Later, as they waited for the Class Officer to round them up, Kipper Naughton said to Cassie, "Trouble with Burslake was, he got on the wrong side of the big boys."

"Inside *and* out," agreed Leslie.

"You got to watch out for the ones inside," said Kipper, "but the ones outside are even worse. They got all the clout in the world. They can pay someone to do someone over as easy as putting money on the 2.15 at Newmarket."

"Specially when it's drugs involved."

"But I thought Burslake wasn't involved," Cassie said.

"He was," said Haslam-Jones. "He just didn't realise it."

"That's what was burning the poor fucker up," said Ginge.

"See, none of us mind, miss," Taylor said earnestly, "if we get done fair and square. It goes with the territory."

A chorus of agreement greeted this.

"But that poor sod Burslake hadn't done nothing, and he didn't dare speak out, wouldn't let his brief say nothing. Made a mistake when he got here, didn't he? Said he was going to write to his MP."

"Silly plonker," said someone else. "He wouldn't have lasted a week in Durham."

"Don't forget that next week," Cassie said, hoping to change the subject, "we're going to look at pre-emptive bidding. You've all got information sheets, and I hope you'll find time to read through them at least once." She looked round at them, thinking how much lighter the atmosphere was without the threatening presence of Steve. "And I hope you all noticed how well Nigel played his four Hearts bid—I was really impressed."

Rastaman smirked, rolling his big eyes. He pointed a long finger at Haslam-Jones and said, "You got my drift, man? No honky lawman calls Rastaman a fool."

"Perish the thought, old boy," said Haslam-Jones.

If Rastaman could do it, why not Chilcott? The thought nagged at Cassie as she drove home. What had induced him to bid on so recklessly, despite the lack of any positive response from her? In the past, Cassie had known him to take occasional calculated risks, but given the stakes they were playing for, his bid of seven Spades had been little more than suicidal. Unless, of course, he was hoping to ingratiate himself with Darcy Wickham, or possibly attempting to show himself as less competent than he really was. But in that case, he would have told her when she asked whether they were to play well or not. She hoped that when she partnered Marling at the end of the week he wouldn't do the same thing, and then try to blame her when they went down.

Another question continued to niggle. Had she reached the gates of Halkam Court earlier, would she have been in time to save Portia Wickham, who must have been shot only minutes before Cassie showed up? She had relived that rainy walk so many times but still could not say that she had heard or seen anything that could help.

As she turned left at the end of the village, towards Back Lane and her cottage, she thought with a sudden lurch of the stomach, of Steve. One advantage of his threatening presence inside the nick was that it wasn't therefore being threatening outside it. For almost the first time, living alone in relative isolation seemed an undesirable state to be in. If Walsh were coming that evening, she would feel less vulnerable, but he hadn't said when he would be back, if at all.

But the problem of Steve could easily be a non-existent one. It was part of the man's character to enjoy frightening others, particularly if they were female. Inside, the only way Steve could frighten Cassie was by vague threats of coming to see her. Outside . . . well, there had been other inmates who had said they would look her up when they got out, but she had never heard from them again. Outside, Steve would realise, if he thought about her at all, that she would inform the police, who would immediately contact his probation officer, if she saw him anywhere near her home.

Back Lane was dark. Charlie Quartermain was right: she should have left lights on in the cottage. But—the realisation shook her—Steve would know that she taught at the nick on a Tuesday night. He would have had all evening to get into the house, if he wanted to.

She parked and got out. Yesterday Walsh had said that someone on a motorcycle had turned up and then raced away at the sight of a police car. Could that have been Steve, casing the joint? He had been released only yesterday: would he have had time to sort out transport and so on? Perhaps he already had a bike waiting in some garage somewhere, in the lock-up of a friend, in his parents' shed, whatever. Just because he had been put away did not mean that his previous life had been expunged. Homes waited, families waited, possessions waited.

The dark house gave no indication of anything amiss, no sign that anyone was there. Cassie told herself that this was ridiculous. She could not spend the rest of her life, or even the next few days, worrying about whether some psychopath was lying in wait in order to kill her. Marching round the corner of the house, she unlocked the back door, fumbled for the light-switch, filled a kettle and put it on the Aga to boil. Then, feeling both idiotic and nervous, with a knife in one hand and an unopened bottle of Perrier water in the other, she went round the house, switching on lights, checking window-catches, looking under beds and into the cupboards. Nothing. Just as ninety-nine per cent of her had expected. There was no message from Walsh on the answering machine, nor from anyone else. Locking and barring the doors, and making sure the windows on the ground floor were all securely fastened, she made some tea, drank it over a book and went to bed.

Cassie woke from a confusing dream full of guns and grand slams and Albert Finney as Hercule Poirot. It had made sense while she had been asleep, but none at all in retrospect. Beside the bed, the phone bleeped shrilly. Beside the phone, the clock told her it was three-thirty in the morning. When she lifted the receiver, a voice said, "Hello, Cass. How's it going?"

She said nothing. The hair on the back of her neck prickled with alarm. She knew instantly who it was.

"Aren't you going to speak to me, then?" the voice said.

Dumbly she shook her head.

"How's your dog George?" the mocking voice went on. It knew how her mouth had dried, how her heart drummed with terror inside her ribs, how the pulses throbbed under her skin. It was a voice which had frightened other women in other lonely bedrooms. "Didn't hear him barking earlier this evening. Not even when I walked right up to your front door—nice shade of green, that—and banged the knocker. Not a peep out of old George. Thought you said he was a terrific watchdog, Cass. Thought you said he barked at strangers. Didn't you say that, Cass? Didn't you tell me—"

Gently she replaced the receiver. There was no way she could prove that the person on the other end of the telephone had been Steve, nothing that could be used as evidence to prevent him—how?—from doing it again. Sitting up against the pillows, she tried to think of the best way to handle this. She could keep the answering machine on all the time. She could go and stay with Kathryn or the Sinclairs, or one of her cousins. She could ask Walsh to move in for a while. Or even Charlie Quartermain. But none of these ideas would solve the problem of Steve. Nor did she see why he should drive her from her home. She spent the rest of the night with the bedside lamp on, dozing off about five, as it began to get light.

In the morning, she rang the police station and asked for Walsh. This time, she got straight through. "It's me," she said, and when he did not react, added, "Cassandra Swann."

"Yes," he said.

"Look, I know how busy you are," Cassie said. "But there're two things I wanted to ask you. One is, are you free tonight, because if so, a friend of mine is having a birthday party and I wondered if you'd like to come."

"What's the other?"

Did he know how off-putting he sometimes sounded on the telephone? "The other . . . the other is . . ." Her voice crumbled with remembered terror, so that she could hardly get the words out.

"Yes?"

"There's this ex-prisoner I used to teach. He was released on Monday, and last night he . . ."

"He what?" This time his attention was caught. "What did he do, Cass?"

". . . he rang me in the middle of the night."

"Did he threaten you?"

"No. He asked how my dog George was."

"Are you sure it was him?"

"Absolutely certain."

There was a pause. "You haven't got a dog, have you?" Walsh asked carefully.

"No. But I pretended I had, last time I saw this man in the nick—the prison. But he knows perfectly well that I haven't.

He's obviously been to my house: he mentioned the colour of the front door, and said how he hadn't heard the dog bark."

"The dog you haven't got."

"Quite." She could feel herself on the verge of hysterical laughter.

"This party: what time tonight?" Walsh said.

"Eightish. It would be wonderful if you—"

"I'll try to be there." Walsh rang off before she could say anything more.

Ivy Cottage was packed. Kathryn seemed to have made a vast number of friends in the short time she had been here. Most of them were people Cassie had never seen before: a few were local. Everyone had brought something with them and the table in the tiny dining-room was laden with food and booze.

By ten o'clock, the smoke levels had risen to such a degree that Cassie needed to breathe fresh air if she was not to fall gasping to the floor. With so many people milling around, she might well be trampled into the carpet if she did that. She began pushing her way towards the long windows leading into the garden. On the other side of the room she could see Charlie Quartermain chatting with Mercy Laughton, Giles' mother. Even as she watched, he made an expansive gesture with the hand holding his wine glass, the contents of which slopped over the front of Mercy's blouse. Mercy didn't seem to notice. By the fireplace, Giles was scowling at something an aristocratic woman in a black velvet jacket and matching hood had just said to him.

Cassie walked through the windows on to a patch of lawn. It was peaceful out here: white garden furniture showed dimly in the dark and she sat down on a chair wet with night dew, wishing Walsh had made it. Before she left her cottage, she had rung the police station and left a message giving directions on where to come; she was beginning to realise that if the relationship was going to continue, she would have to learn to tolerate the uncertainty of his working hours.

There was the sound of a car on the road to Market Broughton, which ran past the end of the lane. Voices from the front of Kathryn's cottage. A screech-owl and the shriek of a fieldmouse. A motorcycle, its engine cutting out as it took the turn along the road from the village. A sudden trill of birdsong, each note as pure as water. Cassie listened entranced. Was that a nightingale? She could not recall ever having heard one before. Scraps of remembered poetry came into her head. Philomel with lullaby. So rudely forced, tereu.

Did she want the relationship to continue? There was no doubt at all about the answer. At her age, she was hesitant to talk of love. Just like Portia Wickham, she liked sex: that did not mean she slept with every man who asked her. Walsh had not asked: he had not needed to, nor, when she thought about him, was it only sex that set her heart beating. Was it possible to love someone you hardly knew?

A shape darkened the rectangle of light from the house.

Walsh said, "Cassandra."

"I'm here," she said, and stood to walk towards him.

He held her tightly. "God, I missed you," he said, at the same time as she said, "I'm *so* glad you got here."

"I can't stay long," he said softly.

"Oh," she sighed. She closed her eyes as his mouth touched her forehead, her eyelids, her hair, her mouth. Did she really hear the nightingale again as she leaned into his arms, or was it merely her sense of the fitness of things?

They stood there together oblivious of anything but themselves. Then from the house came the sound of glass smashing and a shriek of laughter. Cassie opened her eyes. Over Walsh's shoulder she could see, standing at the doors into the garden, the unmistakable silhouette of Charlie Quartermain. How long had he been watching them? Had he recognised her in the dark? She felt a sudden stab of pity for him. Poor Charlie.

Poor or not, Charlie had managed to break the mood. Walsh shifted restlessly, his back muscles moving under her hands. "When this blasted case is over . . ." he said.

"It's all right."

"It isn't. I want to be with you . . . I think about you . . . I'm burning for . . . can't think about anything . . . wish we were . . ." He murmured words of longing into her hair.

Cassie suddenly remembered: "I *still* don't know your—"

There was a buzzing sound close at hand, as though a giant bee was trapped somewhere among Walsh's clothes. He reached into his trouser pocket and pulled out a portable phone, and unfolded it. "Yes?"

He listened for a while, then said into the receiver, "I'm on my way." Holding Cassie tightly, he looked down at her. "I'm sorry. The bloody job."

"I understand."

"I promise you it won't always be like this."

"I believe you."

He kissed her passionately. "Oh, God, Cassie," he said. Then he was gone, running round the side of the cottage. She heard a car start up, and the sound winding away into the night as he drove to the end of the lane, turned right and took the long road towards Bellington. She could still hear him as he crested the hill, the noise of his engine growing ever fainter until the woods of Moreteyne Hall sponged up the sound and she was finally alone again.

"All right?" Charlie Quartermain loomed up out of the darkness.

"Yes, thank you."

"It can be hell sometimes," he said, and she heard the asthmatic catch of his breath as he lit a cigar and blew Havana-scented smoke into the air.

"What can?"

"Love."

She moved towards the open windows of the cottage. "I shall have one more glass of wine and then I'm going home."

"I'd better shift, too," he said. "I'm off to Rheims tomorrow afternoon."

"Are you working on anything local?" she asked politely.

"Couple of churches over towards Gloucester. And someone wants me to have a look at their private chapel about thirty miles from here."

"I didn't realise people still had such things."

"There's plenty of them," Charlie said. "Not all in use, of course. But still needing to be repaired and maintained."

"And what about the gardening thing: Mills & Runes?"

"Looks as if it's going to be a winner, girl." Charlie's laughter rumbled through the smoke of his cigar. "Marling's just gone to Germany for a week, to drum up custom. He's a good front man—the krauts are dead chuffed with him. Lots of public money over there; they're much more into art and museums and that than we are. They've got some interesting ideas about municipal landscaping, too. None of these poncy petunias and dead ugly clocks made of plants, like we have here."

"Today Germany: tomorrow the world," said Cassie.

"I wouldn't need the world if I had you," Charlie said.

"Well, you haven't," Cassie sounded tart. The moment of empathy she had shared with him evaporated.

"Not yet."

"Not *ever*, Charlie."

"Don't bank on it, girl." As they reached the long windows, a bearded man staggered out and made for the bushes, over which he was violently sick. Kathryn appeared and watched in a clinical way. Charlie went and stood behind the retching figure. "Need any help, mate?" The man groaned.

"You'd never believe he was a Professor of Jurisprudence, would you?" Kathryn said.

Cassie said quietly, "It's been a wonderful party, but I think I'll just slip away."

"What happened to your policeman?"

"He had to get back."

"I only met him briefly, when he arrived, but I like him."

"So do I."

"Poor Charlie," said Kathryn.

"Yeah."

The lane was dark as Cassie walked towards her cottage. Stars glittered above her head. From the fields on her left rose a pungent scent of wet grass, earth, cowpats and wild honeysuckle. And, oddly, smoke. She sniffed again. Perhaps one of the party-goers who had parked their vehicles along the grass verge was a smoker and the smell came through an open car window. Although she herself enjoyed the occasional cheroot, she still thought smoking was a disgusting habit, as well as a dangerous one.

The white cat was waiting beside the gateless wooden post that marked the boundary of Honeysuckle Cottage. It came to greet her, picking its way across the grassy patch leading up to the shed-cum-garage: in the light from the uncurtained cottage windows, its fur was the colour of clotted cream. She ran her hand along its fluid back, from ears to tail, and frowned. Something she had heard recently suddenly struck her as odd. Someone had mentioned that . . . that what? She knew that if she probed at it, the information would not come. Best leave it, like a splinter in the hand, to come to the surface at its own speed.

Even so, she kept trying to remember.

The cat followed her as she ducked to avoid the trails of ivy over the back door and fished the big old-fashioned key from her bag. Arching against her legs, it mewed, and she bent again to stroke it, the knobs of its spine hard against the palm of her hand. At the same time, there was sudden violent movement somewhere close at hand, a creak of leather, a rank whiff of sweat and stale tobacco. Still crouching, she whirled round, and felt pain in her side, like a flash of brilliant light, pain which was so excruciating that she fell against the wooden support of the little porch, shrieking as the pain came again and she saw, in the faint light from the windows upstairs, a metallic line slash through the dark. A momentary vision of Steve's last victim as she must have looked when he had finished with her crashed like a bullet through her brain. *Over a hundred stitches* . . . Instinctively she covered her own face, and felt the knife slice into her upper arm. Blood was trickling down inside her dress, warm and sinister. She tried to scream again, but terror had dried her throat so that only a squeak emerged. The knife-blade flashed once more, ready for another blow, and she followed the fiery line of it upwards into the dark where Steve stood above her, faceless, featureless, monstrous in the dark, like an alien from another planet. Even as she registered the fact that his head was encased in a black-visaged motorcycle helmet, his arm was stabbing down at her again.

She could feel herself weakening. Bleakly, she realised that she was going to die. Her nearest neighbour was Ivy Cottage, and the noise of the birthday party would drown any screams for help, supposing she were able to make them. She scrabbled away from him, out of the enclosed space of the porch into the garden. There was nothing wrong with her legs: if she could stand up before he struck her down again, she would have a chance to run for it, back to the light and safety of Kathryn's place. She felt him against her side as she crawled like a baby on to the grass and rolled fast away from him, at the same time kicking out, trying to get him off balance as he lunged after her. She caught one leather-clad leg and felt it buckle, as he swore viciously at her under his breath. Before he had straightened, she was on her feet, one arm hanging uselessly against her thigh, blood running down her leg and into her shoe.

Away from him, her throat opened. "Help!" she shrieked. "Help! Somebody help me!"

His feet were pounding the grass behind her as she made for the lane. "Bitch!" she heard, the word muffled inside the helmet. "Come back, bitch."

Was this what it had been like for Portia Wickham? Was the gun more merciful than the knife? Had it been quicker? Had she ever known her murderer was behind her before the bullet extinguished her life?

He caught up with her halfway down the lane. His hand grabbed at the thin material of her dress. She screamed again, knowing it was hopeless. Ivy Cottage was pulsing with music now: nobody would hear when he plunged the knife into her again, and she died there, on the ground, just like Portia.

And then, miraculously, a shadow leaped from the open door of a car and someone roared, jumping on to Steve, knocking him to the ground. Despite the blood thundering in her ears, she heard the ouf! of breath being knocked from the ex-inmate as he hit the roadway.

"Go and get help, Cassie." It was Quartermain. He spoke calmly. His voice steadied her. "I can take care of this bastard." She heard the sound of a fist slamming into Steve's kidneys and a shriek of pain, followed by a thud as of a foot making contact with flesh, and a distinct crack of bone.

She continued down the lane and staggered through the door of Ivy Cottage, like something from a particularly realistic version of *Macbeth*. Her appearance brought the party to an immediate halt.

A couple of women gasped. Someone laughed nervously.

"What is this?" demanded someone else. "*Nightmare on Elm Street?*"

Kathryn came running to Cassie's side. "My God!" she said. "What the hell *happened*?"

"Charlie's out there," Cassie managed to say. "He needs some help." Now that she was safe, her legs began to tremble so violently that she had to clutch at Kathryn's shoulder in order to stay upright. One of her hands was running with blood and there was more blood pooling on the floor from the knife-wounds in her side.

Giles took off at a run, with half a dozen of the men close behind. The other party-goers followed more slowly. Despite Kathryn's efforts to make her sit down, Cassie trailed after them, her entire body now shaking as though struck with the palsy.

Steve lay writhing on the ground. As she came limping up, Charlie called, over the heads of the onlookers, "Are you all right, Cassie?"

"I'll live," she said.

"Fucking bastard!" Charlie made as if to kick Steve again, then changed his mind and hauled him roughly to his feet. He wrenched off the motorcycle helmet and Cassie looked at the face of the man who stood in the middle of the lane, with a trickle of blood running down the side of his face.

It was all so familiar. The pitiless expression. The close-cropped brutal hair. The hard face, devoid of any vestige of human feeling. Only one thing had changed.

The young man who stared contemptuously back at the people surrounding him was not Steve.

She had never seen him before.

18

"He hasn't said anything yet," Walsh told her on the phone. "But he will."

"Isn't that what you said about Jamie?"

"I don't remember. How are you feeling?"

"Lousy." Cassie was lying in her own bed, having been fetched from the hospital the day before by Giles and Kathryn. She had needed stitches in two of her knife-wounds; the rest were relatively superficial.

"You'll survive," the cheerful young intern had told her, "but you're not going to feel like turning out for the Harlequins for the next week or two."

"Shame," said Cassie. "I've always fancied one of those rugby shirts."

"And try not to laugh too hard until those stitches under your ribcage are removed. I know your boyfriend's a bit of a comic, but it won't do you any good if they open."

"Which boyfriend are we talking about?" Cassie said, the

words coming out through teeth which had gritted themselves without any conscious action on her part. As if she needed to be told. Dammitall. She realised she owed her life to the fact that Charlie Quartermain had been helping the Professor of Jurisprudence into his car as she came screaming up the lane pursued by the man with the knife. Even so, he had no right to misrepresent himself like that.

"Big chap, with a—"

"I know exactly who you mean."

At the other end of the phone, Walsh cleared his throat. "I ought to be able to get over to see you later on today. Things are at a bit of a standstill at the moment."

"I know who killed Portia Wickham," said Cassie.

"What?"

"Or I'm ninety-nine per cent certain. I'll tell you when I see you."

"Cassie . . ."

"Yes?"

He laughed. "I'll tell you when I see you." He replaced the receiver.

It was anger, Cassie reflected, which had cleared her thought processes. Seeing that young man in the summer dark, the indifferent look on his face when his hard eyes met her, she had felt a rage which overcame all the pain he had inflicted. Why had he tried to kill her? What possible reason should he have? And having asked the question, all the answers suddenly became clear.

Reaching for the telephone again, she dialled Jamie's number. He answered himself, sounding much more assertive than previously "It's Cassandra Swann," she said.

"Hi."

"How are you, after your experiences?"

"Great."

"Were you worried when they arrested you?"

"Not really. I knew I was innocent. No, as a matter of fact, I found it rather interesting. I'm thinking about applying to join the Force myself."

"Before you do anything else, could you answer a couple of

questions for me. One: why did Lord Wickham change the venue for the bridge game?"

"You asked me that before. I don't know why, except that someone asked him to. One of the people playing. And since several of those playing were reasonably local, he didn't mind too much. The ones who weren't seemed happy to come from wherever they were, too."

"When you came back from taking Tamsin home, you didn't notice anything, did you?"

"Like what?"

"Another car turning in at the gates to Halkam Court. Someone on a motorcycle. Anything."

"I told the police a million times: I didn't see anything."

"And you drove round to the back of the house, parked and came in?"

"Yes."

"Was anybody around? Any of the guests?"

"No."

"They were all in the drawing-room?"

"Not all. You'd left, with your partner. The people driving back to London had gone. Roddy Symington had gone, though he came back later."

"The rest were in the drawing-room, were they?"

"One of them had been to the loo and was just going back in as I came into the hall."

"Who was it?"

The name he reluctantly gave her was the one she had been expecting. "Good luck with the police," she said.

"My mother will go spare," said Jamie. "She hates the pigs only one degree less than the House of Lords."

"That's her problem, not yours, Jamie."

It hurt, getting dressed. Putting a bra on was such torture that she left it off, pulling a big sweat-shirt over her head to hide the jostle of boobs, and tugging into a pair of leggings. She prayed that no one was being caring down in the kitchen and would try to stop her: she had to get this whole thing nailed.

She found a place to park about three streets away from her destination. Although the place had figured largely in *Great Expectations*, she bet it hadn't looked like this then, the brick scrubbed back to its original colour, the pointing like new, and artsy sort of window frames, the general air of smug Thatcherist prosperity. There would have been grey mud, waterlogged moorings, fog-slippery cobbles, and the great hulks lying alongside the shore, waiting for their contents to be shipped to Australia: a cargo of criminals. England's poor and desperate, chosen to populate their antipodean colonies. Deportation was no longer an option when you came up for sentencing, but, thinking of Steve, Cassie wondered whether it might not be a good thing if the rules were waived for Stanley-knife-wielders.

New Horizons Software announced its presence by a big brass plate beside a door. When she pressed the buzzer, she was let in without having to identify herself. The door opened into a small brick-lined lobby containing nothing but a large green plant in a weathered copper pot. Wooden stairs led upstairs: when she got to the first floor, she found herself in an enormous single room running the entire length of the converted warehouse. It was divided into areas by plants and long tables, on which there must have been at least a hundred VDUs of various sizes. Two giant video screens took up the whole of the narrower wall at the far end of the room, across which splashed a constant flow of multicoloured graphics: pie-charts, graphs, comparison tables. They unfolded like speeded-up film of flowers coming into bloom, rearranging themselves without pause, a never-ending stream of up-to-the-minute information.

Cassie took a step inside the room, and paused. She had expected a hive of industry, white-coated figures watching their screens, tapping in figures, perhaps the odd video game being tested, a Ninja Turtle or two.

Instead, there was nothing except the busy screens. Lines of green figures slid silently across the surfaces; there was no sound except a faint hum, so low-pitched that she heard it only because there was no other noise in the room. She realised it must be sound-proofed. At the same time, she realised she had made a bad mistake in coming here. At three o'clock in the afternoon she had not expected to find herself alone in the headquarters of the man she now knew had murdered Portia Wickham.

Even as she backed towards the tiny landing, meaning to turn and leave, she heard footsteps clattering down a flight of wooden stairs leading to the upper floor. Turning, she saw Jacko Dexter coming towards her with a file in his hand.

"I recognise you, but I don't remember your name," he said, seeing her. He took off his thick glasses and rubbed his eyes. Around his neck was slung a pair of headphones.

"Cassandra Swann."

"Ah, yes. You were playing with Roy, weren't you?"

"Yes." Cassie was astonished. "Do you know him?"

Jacko laughed. "Of course. I've been a consultant with Purves & Reed ever since I got back from the States."

Cassie's brain was behaving like one of the monitors, information gliding across it at a rate of knots, assessing and reassessing. "I didn't realise." What was Purves & Reed: Chilcott's company?

"No reason why you should. " Jacko came further into the room and Cassie backed away in front of him. She felt foolish and extremely vulnerable. She knew she was in danger. However mild this short-sighted boffin might look, he had already killed one woman—admittedly by default —and would probably have no compunction whatever in killing a second.

"The whole thing was a set-up, wasn't it?" she said. If she could get him into the middle of the room, she might have a chance to dodge round him and get to the door and into the street. Otherwise, it was the windows, though being both narrow and double-glazed, they offered little hope.

"What?"

"You were in it together, weren't you? You and Chilcott. That last game, he deliberately played like an idiot so that he could go down and then blame it on me. Thus giving him an excuse to kick me out of the car." Wasn't that what they did in detective novels: keep the villain talking, play for time in the hope that rescue would arrive in some form or another? There was a pretty remote chance of that here.

Nor was the villain playing his part. "What in the name of fortune are you talking about?" he said. He seemed genuinely puzzled.

She was halfway down the length of the room now. On either side, the banks of monitors pulsed and shimmered; behind her, the two big screens endlessly changed. Glancing over her shoulder, she saw that the end wall was in fact a fake, intended to create a more private space in the last ten feet or so of the huge area, that though it extended from floor to ceiling, it did not meet the walls on either side. If she could get that far, with Jacko following her, she might have a chance to dodge in at one side and out the other and then go hell for leather down the long room to the doors.

"It must have been a pretty nasty shock," she said scornfully, "when you woke up the next morning, thinking you'd disposed of the only person—or so you hoped—who could put the finger on you, and finding not only that she was still alive, but that Portia Wickham was dead."

Jacko stopped and stared intently at a screen for a moment. He touched a key on the keyboard below it, then pressed a switch attached to the wall beside the VDU. He looked at her. "Sorry? Portia Wickham? I don't know who you're talking about." He snapped his fingers. "Or is that the wife of the man whose house we were playing in?" Frowning, he added, "You're saying she's dead?"

"That's who you shot, Mr. Dexter," Cassie said. "You were there in your car, your black VW, and in through the gates, right on time, came what you thought was the woman you were waiting for. She probably didn't even notice you there, in the dark and the rain. As soon as she'd gone past, you drove up behind her, shot her, continued on up to the house, parked, and were back inside before anyone had realised you had gone." She moved closer to the brick screen. A few more steps, and she could get behind it and move rapidly to the other end, then make a break for it. If he had his gun handy, she was dead meat, but otherwise . . .

There was a wary look on his face now. "How did you find all this out?" he asked. He quickened his pace towards her and she moved correspondingly nearer the opening at one side of the end wall.

"It's a question of putting together the facts," she said. "Like Chilcott's bidding. There had to be a reason why he played like that, but I have to admit that what it was never occurred to me. It wasn't until you set that little punk on me, the day before yesterday, that I realised who you were really after."

"That little punk?" echoed Dexter.

"What's the going rate for taking out bridge teachers?" asked Cassie. The two wounds in her side were beginning to throb, whether with emotion or because at some time in the past couple of hours the stitches had opened, it was difficult to say. "Ten thousand? Twenty thousand? For someone prepared to pay out forty-two thousand or more on a hand of bridge, that can't be more than petty cash."

He nodded. "Petty cash."

She was there. She dashed between the side wall and the end of the fake one. As she had expected, the area was like a reception room, with soft couches against three of the walls, a huge Navajo rug in brilliant colours on the floor, three or four paintings and some more plants in verdigrised pots.

There was a man sitting on one of the couches. "Hello, Cassandra," he said.

Even in extreme terror, she noted the gun in his hand, small, black and deadly. Was this a Baby Browning .22? Was this the gun that had killed Portia?

"You're no Miss Marple," he said.

"You're not the first to say that," said Cassie. "But I never set out to be. I'm a bridge teacher—"

"If it's of any interest, the going rate for those is around fifteen thousand. We're prepared to pay substantially to protect our investment, and that includes buying silence."

Jacko Dexter came round the side of the wall. "What the hell is going on?" he demanded. "Is she nuts, or what?" Then he saw the gun. His eyes widened. "Hell, Roy, I don't think she's dangerous."

"Oh, she is," Chilcott said. "Extremely dangerous. She

could destroy everything I've set up over the past few years. That's why she's got to go?" He raised the gun.

"Roy, you can't be serious," gasped Dexter.

"I'm deadly serious, Jacko."

"He is," confirmed Cassie. "He thinks I know enough to break up his extremely successful drugs operation. He thinks that one of his pathetic donkeys has given me information which could set the police on his trail."

"Donkeys?" said Jacko. "I'm not following any of this."

"What you don't realise," Cassie said, "is that in fact I knew nothing. Only that you played bridge, and that you wore a particular kind of watch."

Chilcott smiled unpleasantly. "Not me, lady. That's the kind of shit my partner goes in for."

"It's hardly enough to identify either of you," said Cassie.

"That's a risk I'm not prepared to take," Chilcott said. "I take risks when I play bridge—partly for pleasure, partly because we aim to lose at least one per cent of our profits on gambling, in order to turn it into clean money—but otherwise I try to cover every eventuality which might arise."

"So it must have been a shock to discover that, by sheer coincidence, the person you had chosen as a bridge partner also knew John Burslake."

"Cassandra, please," Chilcott smiled wearily. "Think back. There was no coincidence involved. As soon as Burslake was moved to Bellington, we set up the same monitoring system we'd used at the other prisons he was sent to. Easy enough to ring up the Chaplain—men of the cloth are usually ready to believe the best about people—and express concern about the poor bloke, find out if he'd made any particular mates. 'Doesn't talk to a soul,' says the sky-pilot. 'Good,' I think, 'learned his lesson, then.' 'Except,' continues the good padre, 'this *teddibly* nice bridge teacher we have. I know poor John confides in *her*.'"

The expression on his face was terrifying. Contempt, dislike, above all complete ruthlessness, the same total lack of compassion she had last seen on Steve's face.

"So you came after me, made me an offer I couldn't refuse, found out what Burslake was telling me, and when it seemed that he'd told me too much, decided to eliminate me, is that it?"

"Money, Cassandra. At our different levels, that's what we're all after. You were happy to play for five hundred an evening. I was happy to be turning over hundreds of thousands in illegal importations, and that punk who made such a balls-up on Wednesday was happy to take fifteen thou for sticking a knife in you and keeping shtum about it afterwards."

Jacko was still staring at the gun. "I wish you'd put that away," he said nervously.

Chilcott pointed it at him. "Shuddup," he said viciously. "You've been bloody useful to us, but there're plenty who can provide the same kind of electronic information when we need it. I could do it myself, if I had that kind of brain, but it's easier to pay someone to do it for me."

"I didn't have the faintest notion that you were involved in drugs," said Jacko. "I'd never have worked for you, otherwise. I just like gambling. I've earned myself a big enough pot to do it at whatever level I want, I don't need be doing anything illegal, this whole thing is just not my scene at all . . ."

He was babbling, and Cassie wondered why. She had realised some time ago that she'd miscalculated. Although Chilcott had been working hand in hand with someone else at that fatal evening at Halkam Court, it was not, after all, Jacko Dexter. What was more, Jacko seemed appalled at having been dragged into Chilcott's drug ring, however peripherally. Which meant that there were two guys in white hats against one in a black hat. It was the worst kind of break that the black hat had the gun. As she saw it, she was not going to be given the chance to get away from Chilcott; the next best thing was to see if she could at least get the gun.

Jacko had backed up against a long table which stood against the back of the fake wall. On it were a number of keyboards, pieces of equipment fashioned from black plastic and matt grey steel, recorders and units and dials, a whole mess of controls presumably intended for the equipment in the big room behind them.

"How did you get Wickham to let us play at his house that evening?" Cassie said. She was trusting her instincts now, hoping that Jacko was going to spring some surprise on them. If she could deflect at least some of Chilcott's attention away from the other person, they might stand half a chance.

"Who was it said that the rich are different from the rest of us?" said Chilcott.

"Scott Fitzgerald," said Cassie.

"Well, they're not. Wickham's no different from you or me, Cassandra. He likes money. And when my partner rang him up and suggested we play at his place since he knew this Ozzie with the wine interests—" disconcertingly, Chilcott's accent changed from faintly cockney to full-fledged Australian—"who played bridge and would be tickled pink to be invited to the home of a real English lord, why, he didn't hesitate for a minute."

"I don't suppose he realised it was going to cost him his wife."

"No, well, if that dozy sheila had kept her brains somewhere else than between her legs, none of this would have happened."

"And if I hadn't wasted a lot of time looking for my shoe in the ditch by the road," said Cassie, "I'd have been there sooner. "

"Too right."

"And, of course, after that, you didn't dare get rid of me too quickly, because the police would have started wondering if there was some connection."

"Right. Believe me," Chilcott said, raising the gun, "that bunch of bloody roses cost me a lot more than money. Boy, I hated paying for them." He aimed at Cassie. "But, here you are. So, hello and goodbye, Miss Cass—"

There was suddenly the most appalling noise. A cross between several hundred sirens and a million souls in the uttermost physical agony, it ripped through the air, filling the brain with unbearable sound, devastating the entire space as surely as if it were a bomb. Cassie clapped her hands to her ears but it had little effect. She saw that Chilcott had instinctively done the same, but not before loosing off a single bullet, probably a reflex action as his finger tightened on the trigger with horror at the sudden row. The bullet had caught Dexter in the shoulder. He stood with one hand covering the entry hole, a look of total terror on his face. Somehow, he had managed to slip the headphones over his ears.

He was mouthing something at her. Bending under the weight of the intolerable noise, she tried to lip-read. "Run! Run!" is that what he was saying?

She hesitated. The gun lay on the rug where Chilcott had dropped it in his unthinking need to block out the terrible sound. She made a dive for it. The noise was so huge that she could not hear herself hit the floor. Her bones felt completely numb, her teeth literally rattled. She could see Chilcott's mouth open, and thought that, like Dexter, he was shouting something. Her fingers reached the gun, and she pulled it towards her at the same time as Chilcott's beefy hand clamped around her wrist.

The noise was intolerable. She knew she must be hurting, that yesterday's wounds would be bleeding, but the noise was an effective pain-killer. She held on to the gun. She too was screaming now, though she could not hear herself. All she wanted was to die; she could feel her body disintegrating under the relentless hammer of sound, she could feel insanity creeping around inside her skull. She kept her eyes on her hand and her hand on the gun.

Then Chilcott's fingers slackened. Through half-closed eyes she watched them peel away from her wrist one by one. Her jawbone seemed to be dropping off her face, she had no feeling in her lower limbs, she knew that the noise would kill her if it continued for a microsecond longer. Slowly she pulled the gun towards her, but did not have the strength left in her hand to pick it up.

And then, as abruptly as it had begun, the dreadful sound stopped. It was as though she had been tightly bound and had now been released. The effect was like being dropped from a mountain top to freefall into the valley, way, way below. With an effort, she raised her eyes and saw Chilcott sagging against the back of the couch on which he had been sitting. There was a trickle of blood coming from his mouth. She rolled over on her back and closed her eyes.

"Sorry about that," she heard someone say. Though she understood the words, they fell against her eardrums like so many flung stones, without shape or form. Her body cramped; the whole of her right side was wet with what she dimly perceived was blood. Her ears ached and tears burned her eyes. She turned over on to her side, exhausted. If she could sleep, perhaps someone would give her bruised brain back.

"Is she awake?" The voice was directly over her head.

She held out her hand, and someone took it. Her lips were dry and she felt enormously tired. "Um . . ." she tried.

"What?" A different voice spoke, nearer, as though its owner had bent closer to her. With an enormous effort, Cassie opened her eyes. Walsh was standing by her bed, holding her hand in both of his. Kathryn and Giles stood together on the other side, Kathryn's face very close to the pillows.

"Walsh," Cassie tried. Her voice boomed inside her head, unrecognisable. She had no idea whether she had spoken in a whisper or a shout.

"Cassie. Cassie," he said.

"Tell me . . ." She licked her dry lips again.

"Yes?"

"What's your first name?"

"Oh, God," Kathryn said. She bit her lip. "Her mind must have been . . ."

"You don't think she's been driven—you know—" said Giles "—mad, do you?"

Cassie's head ached abominably. "I'm not mad," she managed. "I just don't know his name."

"It's Paul," Walsh said. He seemed astonished. "I didn't realise you . . . I wondered why you never used it. I thought you didn't like it or something."

Cassie smiled and went back to sleep.

"I should have realised much sooner," she said. "It never occurred to me that the murder of Portia Wickham was a mistake."

"Nor us." Walsh lay beside her, his naked body warm where it touched her. The bedroom curtains were drawn, the lamps cosily lit. A nearby empty bottle of red wine stood on his side of the bed, next to his glass.

"What about Marling?" asked Cassie sleepily. She handed him her empty glass.

"He's been picked up in Bremen," said Walsh. "With any luck, with those two in custody we'll be able to break their entire organisation. We're only looking at the fringes, right now, but it's huge, multi-million stuff."

"I should have realised," Cassie said again. "When I told Marling, at that dinner-dance at the Randolph, that I taught at the local prison, he immediately started talking about Bellington, although if he knew nothing about me, the natural assumption would have been that I meant Oxford Gaol. And then when Charlie told me Marling had gone to Germany for a week, even though he had arranged to play bridge with me—having hired that punk to knife me, he obviously never expected me to still be alive." The cold-bloodedness of it made her feel literally sick. "It was after I'd told him about that psycho from the nick that he got the idea of using a knife instead of a gun."

"What a couple of con-men," said Walsh, almost admiringly. "Especially Marling. All that stuff about trust funds and inheritances and being on the stock exchange. It was all a front, to explain why he was obviously not short of a bob or two. And he had the public-school bit down to a T. I'm not saying they weren't clever. They salted the money away pretty carefully: nothing ostentatious, none of the kind of spending that would make anyone—particularly the Drug Squad—start asking awkward questions. Sailing, bridge, racing: nice occupations for a gentleman. Even nicer for laundering dirty money, or adding to the source of it. With a perfectly legitimate construction business as a cover."

"I don't know which is worse: Marling or Chilcott."

"Marling is a proven murderer."

"But Chilcott was going to kill me. And he'd have had to kill Jacko as well, after that?" She looked up at Walsh. "He's really nice, isn't he? And sexy, too."

"Who, Chilcott?"

"Jacko."

"I don't know about sexy. Nutty, perhaps. Driving that VW when he could buy six of any car he chose without even noticing."

"Not everybody's car-orientated," Cassie said. "Gosh, when I think of the risks Marling took that night." Since the police had come charging into the warehouse, called there by Dexter's summons on the wall-mounted bell half-way down the room, she had learned that the method of operation she had attributed to the innocent and bewildered Jacko had in fact been more or less how Marling had disposed of Portia, thinking her to be Cassie. The story of suspect *moules* was nothing more than a cover to explain long absences away from the drawing-room: it was only by pure chance that Jamie had seen Jacko Dexter in the hall after delivering Tamsin safely home, rather than Marling.

"Anything illegal is risky," said Walsh, "it's part of why they do it That adrenalin rush, that's what your gambler goes for. The knife-edge between success and ruin."

"Paul."

"Yes?"

"Kiss me," Cassie said. "Kiss me goodnight."

Walsh chuckled and put his arms round her. Within seconds she was asleep again.

When she woke the next morning, he was gone. There was a note on his pillow. *"The bloody job,"* it said. She guessed those three words were going to become an essential part of their shared vocabulary. Getting out of bed, she went over and drew the curtains. Outside the open window, the sun shone warmly, there was a fluff of cloud drifting across a blue sky, and there was no sound except the occasional semi-indignant exclamation from the sheep in the field at the front of the house. She leaned further out. Her pond gleamed in the sunshine and a bird of some kind was splashing about in it, while a heron looked on with the expression of an indulgent schoolmaster. She hoped the indulgent look didn't stem from a stomachful of expensive goldfish.

She slipped on a big T-shirt and went downstairs. For the first time for days, she felt relaxed, even though her ears and throat still ached from the massive onslaught of sound they had endured. With Marling and Chilcott banged up somewhere, she really had only one thing to worry about. She caught sight of herself in the glass-fronted cabinet that housed her Angelica Kauffmann plates. All right: two.

Her weight she could come to terms with. She wasn't fat, just big. Just gorgeous, if her ears had not deceived her last night when she and Walsh—Paul, that is—were in bed together.

It would be more difficult to try and forget about Steve. He was out there somewhere, on the prowl, looking for another victim. She knew that. She had to forget about him, had to assume that it would not be her. She wished there was some way of warning the women with whom he came into contact. S for Slasher tattooed on his forehead, perhaps. Or an exclamation mark. A skull-and-crossbones.

And there was another piece of unfinished business, too. Her father. The death of Handsome Harry Swann had never been satisfactorily resolved. Perhaps for very good reason. But until she had determined that for herself, she was not going to allow the events of that long-distant night be swept under the carpet any longer. Tomorrow, next week, next month, she would go back to Islington. She would talk to Old Ruby again, speak to the police, get the files reopened. She had a feeling that she might find it painful—it was, none the less, something she owed her father.

She opened the back door and stepped barefoot out on to the gravel, wincing slightly until she reached the grass. She walked quickly to the pond. The heron turned its head slightly in her direction, then flapped its broad wings a couple of times and took off. There were still goldfish, Cassie saw, their orange bodies gleaming under the lily-pads. She saw something else, too, which had definitely not been there before, reflected in the water.

A rough slab of dark slate. A chiselled heart with a carved C inside and, above it, a stylised swan, its fine curves beautiful against the stone. The elegance of slate and carving and sentiment, with a clump of spear-leaved water-iris near by and the whole repeated in the calm water, struck Cassie to the heart.

As did the emotion which had inspired that serendipitous grouping.

"Oh, Charlie," she said aloud. Her eyes filled with tears. Oh dear.

Poor Charlie.